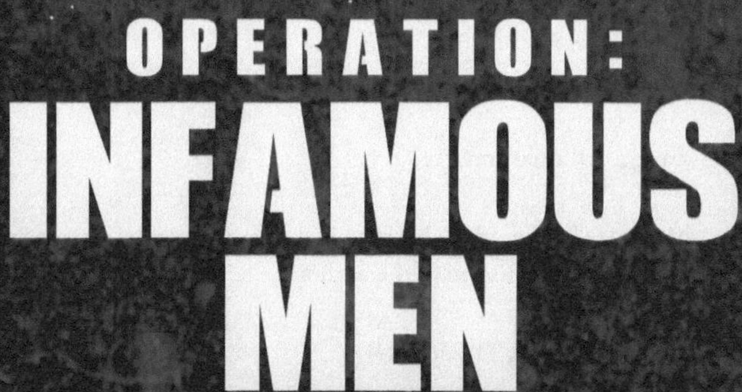

OPERATION:
INFAMOUS MEN

DOCUMENTED JOURNALS OF TIME SERVED

Kilo Company 3rd. Battalion 8th. Marines
2nd. Marine Division
1988-1992

XAVIER ZAVALA

Primix Publishing
East Brunswick Office Evolution
1 Tower Center Boulevard, Ste 1510
East Brunswick, NJ 08816
www.primixpublishing.com
Phone: 1-800-538-5788

Published by Primix Publishing: 11/25/2024

ISBN: 979-8-89194-273-8(sc)
ISBN: 979-8-89194-274-5(hc)
ISBN: 979-8-89194-275-2(e)

Library of Congress Control Number: 2024916448

CONTENTS

DEDICATION

This Book is dedicated to my sons who didn't make it into this world alive, and for those marines who also never made it home alive.

Entry Access List:

Zavala, X. M.

Spritz, L.

Whalen, M.

Perez, M.

Olivarez, L. III

Botello, Roger

Piver, R.

Knightengale, R.

Smith, Jimmy James (RIP)

Holy Mike (Mr. Unfinished Business)

Archie

Poff, Clayton

Green, R

Feldman, K

Lt. Brown, M.

Smith, G.

Rowland, T.

Prichard, M.

Calentoni, J.

Garcia, Martin

Law, Timothy (RIP)

Lt. Payton, D.

Bartenson, R.
Williams (The Sucka)
Colonel Mark Masterson
Sgt. O'Riley
Lt. Haley
Lt. Sheppard
Spears, K.
Voltz
Vega, F.
Frampton

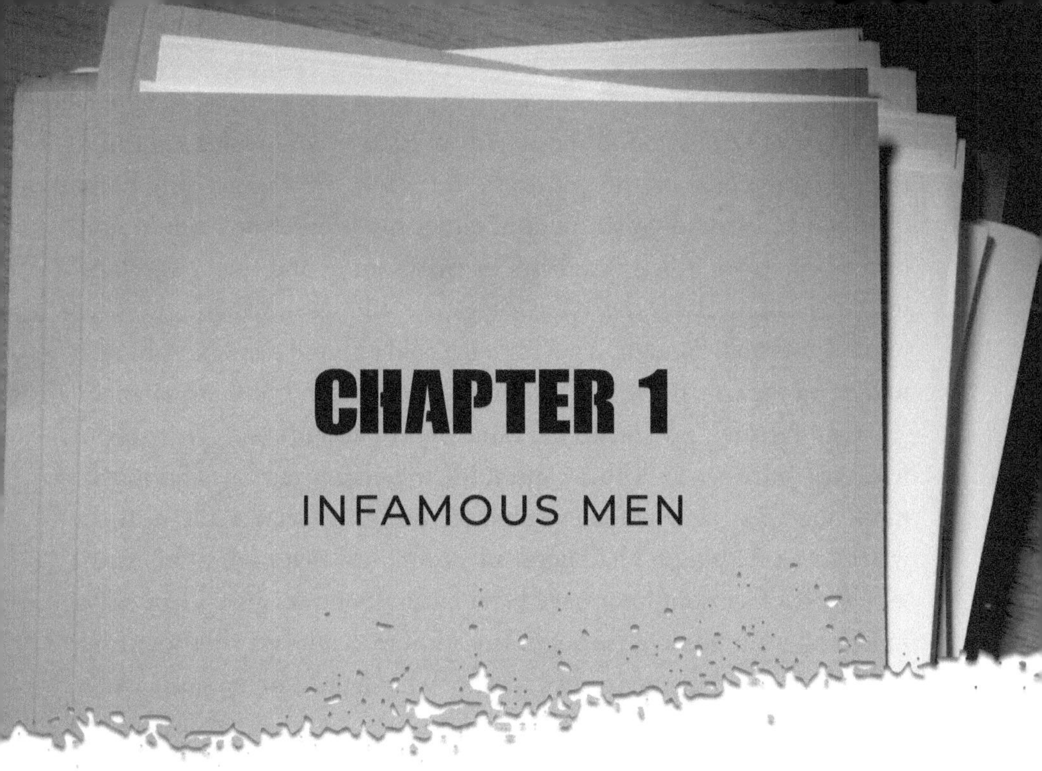

CHAPTER 1

INFAMOUS MEN

An Unborn Breed

I didn't know what the hell Vietnam was about; I didn't even know it was a country. In fact, I only understood Vietnam as a part of life, which was war. I remember seeing the newsmen Harry Reasoner and Walter Cronkite on the evening news as I watched footage from the war, and those were the only images I had to relate to Vietnam. It was my cousin Joe who initially inspired me to join the Marines. My cousin Joe joined the Marines in 1959, and his first tour to Vietnam wasn't until 1965–66, so I hadn't ever met the man before all this because I wasn't born until 1968. By the way, my name is Xavier.

I know now that war changes a person, and next to the thousand-yard stare—which could burn a hole through just about anything—I knew that Joe wouldn't harm me because we were family; we had no beef. But my perception of him was that he was a scary man. Something unusual must have happened in his life to make him face the world the way he did: somewhat cynical and disturbed by the way some people he once interacted with acted toward him now.

Every late afternoon, while playing outside or doing some kid thing, the signal to come in and get ready to eat was my dad arriving home from work. I would go sit by him; either my brother or I would grab him a beer, open it, sneak a drink or two from it, and then hand it off to the old man. After those few swigs, we'd be set for the night. One night, I was bold enough to get myself a cold one and drink it right next to him on the couch. He was too tired to notice, but I took my chances.

One evening, my cousin Joe came over to visit my dad. He had this fearsome stare—a look that caused me to become curious and maybe made me want to experience some of the things that made him the way he was. Although I had never met him until that night, I knew the look on his face could not have been natural, and for sure I had never imagined what he went through. But I knew that he was in something called the Marines, and to get a taste of what he had done, that's where I would have to begin as soon as I could.

Back in those days, kids my age didn't have role models—or at least, I didn't. I was too busy mastering being myself. I did have a favorite football team, and other than my two brothers, whom I spent most of my time with, there was no one to look up to.

I finally asked my dad why my cousin Joe was so scary-looking. My dad never broke anything down to my level; it was his way of saying, "If you don't understand what I'm saying, then it isn't time for you to know." The unknown was the forbidden topic of discussion for them: the Vietnam War.

My dad was a painter; he began his profession with the union in the fifties while he lived in Chicago. I guess he raised us the same way my grandpa raised him: tough and very stern. He was much more lenient on me than on my older brothers or my older sister.

My younger sister Margaret escaped his strict ways of governing, although she didn't press her luck too much because he was still our dad, and yet there were some issues that we as siblings could not discipline one another for having done.

Some of the things we did, though wrong, were okay. We could beat each other up as long as it was to discipline one another. At times, I would consider my dad too strict and thought if I could just make it through the Zavala Boot Camp, I would be alright. I realized that when my older brothers and sister Magdalena left the house, things became tougher for me with my dad. I think that was because my dad blamed my mom for being a little too soft on me, and he felt it was time to toughen me up for the real world.

Nowadays, my dad tells me stories about his younger years and how there were more than a few times that he did get on me for something that he did while growing up. I realized that tolerance comes with the changes of time; back in his day, it may not have been okay to do some things that are allowed to be done today.

Time progressed, and we, as a country, seemed to evolve. The hostage-taking situation in Iran under the Carter administration became my first real political conflict; then there was the Beirut campaign under Reagan. Every crisis that we underwent as a nation reminded me that I had to stay focused because there was something I needed to do after I graduated from high school. In the meantime, the networks continued showing scenes from the Viet Nam War—not many, but enough to help me piece together some of what happened over there. This was necessary for my personal understanding, and the stare on my cousin Joe's face finally had its very own meaning.

Church played a big factor in my life, since we lived just across the street from it. I came to believe that praying would help me get over situations rather than avoid them altogether. My mom always asked, "Did you say your prayers?" Before eating, going to sleep, before anything, even crossing the road. I prayed so much, I figured I had at least one crime-credit.

School years came and went, and the things I looked forward to the most were girls and football season. Every year, I would get stronger, better, and more experienced on the gridiron. Football was the closest thing to combat, aside from the occasional fights I had growing up.

Football and girls made those years more meaningful; it had become my pastime along with working out and partying. My oldest brother Gabriel, a four-year letterman in football, instilled in me the importance of working out and lifting weights. My other brother Paul showed me that it was OK to drink more than once in a while—or maybe I just selected the bad habits when it came to him—but in hindsight, they prioritized school and their studies. Both were smart and athletic, but I think my brother Gabriel was better in football.

We, as football players, had to be careful not to get busted drinking by the coaches or their peers; in a town that small, the word would get around. When a few of us did finally get busted as juniors in high school, we thought the end of the world was near. In order for us to maintain our eligibility to play football as seniors, we were faced with the consequences of having to run four miles every morning before school for two weeks. Most of us accepted. The first week of running was beginning to get to me; by the second week, I was out of it, and in order for me not to continue to be late for class, I began to spend the night at the field house.

After the first week of running, others were busted as well, and they joined us in the morning runs. Only a few of us were recognized as the "40 Mile-club" upon the successful completion of our punishment phase. I wasn't proud of it, but why not live up to what I could?

Before I knew it, it was time to graduate from high school. No one ever emphasized the importance of college to me; my brother Gabriel would beat around the bush with the idea, but by that time, it was a little too late. I figured that I was academically screwed.

It was 1987. I got a job and decided that since I was academically screwed, I was going to accept life's challenges without the tools needed for the journey. As the time continued to pass by, I found myself unchallenged, and fired from my prestigious job as a night stock person at the local grocery store. It was on Christmas Eve when I was fired. I didn't say a thing to anyone about it. My brother Gabriel caught wind of what had happened and became upset with me, so without any insight on what to do with life, I simply waited out the holidays.

On January 3, 1988, I made the desperate phone call to my recruiter and said, "Hey man, this is Zavala, come pick my ass up as soon as you can . . . bye." The recruiter had known who I was because I would toy with the idea of going to the Marine Corps; from that point on, I began to prepare myself for the things that I thought would change my life.

I started running, doing all sorts of exercises, and working out became my night job. The funny thing was, people who knew I had made the commitment to serve in the military, began to treat me differently; somehow they thought they were preparing me for boot camp, even though they had not been through it themselves. For example, my brother Gabriel would yell at me saying, "Get used to that! It's not going to be any different when you leave."

I thought to myself, "I don't see the point in going." He meant well, but no one thing could have come close to preparing me for Marine Corps boot camp.

I had a girlfriend, but we broke it off for our reasons, and life began to change from the way I was once used to living. My recruiter gave me the date of departure—when I would be leaving for Boot Camp. I trained more and more, and finally it became easier. The closest thing I could get to thinking about what boot camp would be like was two-a-day football practices, but just imagine practicing all day—that was only the easy part. Little did I know.

Sunday, April 24th, 1988, I got out of church nervous as hell, preparing my mind, and taking care of some last-minute details that I needed to do before leaving. I said goodbye to my true, close friends, and told them that I'd see them when I got back. One friend I thought that I would not see when I got back from boot camp was Lawrence Olivarez. He was going to boot camp two months after I left. We trained together when we could; we were into the movies that motivated us to push ourselves to workout even harder. We said our farewells.

I was out, definitely trying to score my last piece of ass—three months without it was hard to imagine. Also, I needed some time to myself. My time was up; the recruiter was there at my front door around 5 o'clock. I said goodbye to my parents, and I was on my way.

My recruiter drove me to the bus station, dropped me off, and wished me luck. Now it was time to put everything in perspective, get rid of unnecessary thoughts, feelings, emotions, and needs—all that—while feeling alone, but that was part of the deal.

As the bus made its way to San Antonio and we reached the terminal, I was taken to a hotel and given more instructions. "Sign in right here and we'll give you a wake-up call at 6 o'clock. From there, you'll go eat, then we're boarding a bus to take you to the MEPS Station for your physical."

What was about to unfold next was a good thing; it made boot camp much less difficult, mentally. My friend Lawrence caught a break; our recruiter was able to send him early because one of the guys scheduled to go the same day I was leaving had been arrested, and Lawrence was sent in his place. I didn't learn of that until Monday afternoon, when my name was never called to board the van that was going to the airport.

Lawrence is a friend from school; our dads grew up down the street from one another. His family had some of the same type of old-school values as mine. He enlisted in the Air Force but got into some trouble with the law and was taken off the waiting list. In fact, the Air Force did not let him join because of the small troubles with the law. Of course when I found out, I made fun of him. I remember telling him, "Come over and become one of the world's finest; I'm sure we won't tell you to get lost!" Days after his run-in with the law and the torment that I gave him for it, he called the recruiter and all the paperwork had been transferred.

The next day, I was wearing the same clothes as the day before, just waiting around. On Monday, I managed to meet a girl from La Feria, Texas, who was also there for her physical exam. She used the name Kathy, and she was one of the girls who would write me throughout the first two and a half years of my four-year duration. I enjoyed receiving mail from her, especially during boot camp. I called her in 1994, but I had since become a blur to her; she had forgotten me, I guess.

I met up with Lawrence that Monday night and told him that I was aware of what was going on. When he completed his physical the next day, our names were called to board the van. The flight to California was no joke; my ears were driving me crazy due to the cabin pressure. Upon our arrival at the San Diego Airport, we were greeted by several Marines, who directed us on where to go. Shortly thereafter, we found ourselves on the magic bus to Marine Corps Recruit Depot.

The bus stopped, its doors opened, and then all hell broke loose. Drill Instructors were in our faces and very much in control of our hell, a post of which they had become masters. Some of us were yelled at more than others, but it was so chaotic that it seemed like it happened in about three seconds, which in fact took closer to a minute.

First was accountability: medical and dental record verification, shots, haircuts, and, of course, the swearing in. This process took the better part of fourteen hours, continuing throughout the night. Before completing this process, we would first have to undergo the "Moment of Truth," which consisted of an interrogation by a Marine to see if there was something in our past that we may have purposely not mentioned—maybe the recruiters instructed us to say nothing that might have disqualified us from joining. Sounds easy?

Not if you have been put in a coma for eighteen days and fractured all kinds of bones in your body; technically, I don't think I should have been able to join the Marines.

The Coma

When I was about five years old, I was standing at the corner, waiting to cross the street. I was waiting for a truck that was pulling a trailer to pass. The trailer became disconnected from the truck—nothing had control of the trailer—and it struck me and continued until it ran into the church across the street, which was about 80 feet away.

My mom felt that something bad had happened as she came running out of the house to see the aftermath. Thank God that the driver was a doctor and had a sense of composure; he administered his lifesaving steps. I believe that his response is one of the reasons that I'm still alive today; he helped me start breathing again.

Eighteen days later, I awoke from a coma. The doctors said to my parents that if I were to survive, I might not be normal; they may need a miracle to get me back to the way I was before the accident. I was pretty bad off: massive head injury, a fractured skull in three places, a broken leg, collarbone and wrist; and I had slipped into a coma.

I don't remember many things on the day I came to, but as every day passed, I began to become more aware of my surroundings. Most of my cousins would stop by to be reintroduced to me and spend the day with me; some even stayed the night along with my dear old grandpa. Shortly after, I met my roommates: Ronnie, a three-year-old boy who had a brain tumor, and next to him, Kathy—she had leukemia. I'll never forget these two kids because they were my first best friends that I had, and our common denominator was to try and resume a normal life while running from death. By the time that I understood what death was, I didn't have the "Why me instead of them?" guilty feelings. Instead, when I thought of them later in life after I healed enough to do things on my own, I would try to do something extra just for them.

I progressed as the weeks went by, from slurring to actually saying a few words; my equilibrium was so out of whack that crutches were even a challenge. I became mobile by way of a wheelchair; both the speech and physical therapy sessions seemed not to be doing me any good. Frustration had become my worst enemy. I just wanted to be able to talk and not lose my balance at any given moment, and yet the terrible headaches had begun to fade. I remember my doctors smiling every time they dropped by.

As for Ronnie and Kathy, I couldn't tell that they were becoming sicker, but they were. I never understood why their parents were always so sad and sometimes crying. One morning Ronnie was gone; I didn't see anyone take him. When I asked where Ronnie was, they just said he'd gone. My last memory of Ronnie was him in his little red wheelchair and me in mine, cruising the fifth floor together.

I did remember that Kathy didn't look the same as when I first met her. Soon she left, covered by a blanket from head to toe, her parents weeping. My parents felt somewhat guilty or just lucky that it wasn't me; my mother cried on both those days. I'll never forget these little friends.

My dad had returned to work, and my mom was busy with my four siblings. Someone was assigned to assist me, and my cousins visited occasionally.

Before leaving the hospital, I underwent numerous tests to ensure I was well enough for discharge. Due to poor equilibrium, I never progressed to using crutches and remained dependent on others for mobility. After my cast was removed, I continued therapy. As my frustration gradually subsided and I began feeling normal, others still viewed me as "the kid who was in a coma" who needed gentle handling.

By March of the following year, I was back in school, already a survivor before stepping out the door. Though I didn't consciously think of myself that way then, subconsciously this identity was taking root. My mom, more than anyone, would coddle me. Rather than seeing my ongoing recovery, she'd insist, "Here, let me do this and get that for you." I understood her behavior stemmed from my near-death experience.

I disliked having the same teachers as my siblings, all of whom knew about my situation. Being treated as less capable than my peers frustrated me, so I worked to change their perceptions. I had to prove myself and match the abilities of other children both in class and on the playground.

By fourth grade, I began shedding the special treatment. Physical therapy had ended in first grade, leaving me to progress independently. In seventh grade, I was nearly fully recovered, though I accepted I would never reach 100 percent. By freshman year of high school, I felt I had achieved my maximum potential recovery.

After the moment of truth, I found a quiet moment to pray: "God, thank you for getting me this far. I know I'll need help through boot camp, but I promise to make the most of it. I don't care if I never live a normal life from here on. Thank you again, God."

Once past the Moment of Truth, we joined what was simply called "Receiving Platoon" after several hours. There, we learned what would be expected of us and received preliminary instruction on essential knowledge: who warranted a salute, enlisted and officer ranks, and similar information. We tried to absorb as much as possible during that week before joining our actual boot camp platoon.

CHAPTER 2

HELL

The day came when panic, chaos, and fear were not just words describing emotional states; each held its own distinct meaning that I could link to an actual time in my life. Additionally, we were now in the presence of a relentless source of involuntary motivation. Minutes before Hell officially opened for Platoon 2043, Hotel Company, we were formally introduced to our drill instructors—the Four Horsemen of the Apocalypse—who would break us down and rebuild us into the Greatest of Men.

First was Senior Drill Instructor Staff Sergeant Daniels, followed by Drill Instructors Staff Sergeant Dixon, Munger, and Van Cleave. The order was given: "DRILL INSTRUCTORS, TAKE CHARGE OF YOUR PLATOON AND CARRY OUT THE ORDER OF THE DAY!" From that instant forward, for thirteen weeks, I dreaded waking from my sleep to face another day of Hell, for that was when the nightmare began.

The first couple of days were spent learning the countless rules, the do's and don'ts of boot camp. "And one final thing," they said. "If you think you might take your life, here are some razors so you can do it tonight while no one's watching. You have a 0400 deadline—that's 30 minutes before reveille. Carry on. Carry on, ladies." We would respond loudly and with enthusiasm, "AY, AY, SIR! AY, AY, RECRUITS!" Afterward, we would return to what we were doing.

Each morning began with sessions of taunting and tormenting, best known to recruits as "GAMES," games we never had a chance of winning. We only believed we might win due to a brief drill instructor oversight. To me, it seemed that these drill instructors woke up every morning with one thought: "How can we break these nasty civilians down?" I didn't know any better then, but breaking us down was already part of their daily schedule. The opportunity to mess with us in a morning thrashing was always seized by them and dreaded by us. These thrashings occurred at any time of day or night, and the fear was ever-present. I was out of shape, and a thought crossed my mind: "What if I get thrashed so badly that I pass out?"

Yes, I was out of shape, but not so much that they put me in the PORKCHOP Platoon. These recruits in the PC Platoon—they were fat, and they did the same things we did, I think. The only food they got at a meal was maybe a piece of lettuce, a carrot stick, some milk, and all the water they wanted. PORKCHOP Platoon wasn't the real name; it was a derivative of the acronym PCP, which stood for something else. I felt for them, but it wasn't my fault. I was starving. Who knows what might have happened if anyone had been caught sneaking them extra grub?

Some mornings, I woke before the lights came on, stirred by the sound of cadence from other drill instructors marching their platoons to morning chow. Sometimes those few minutes or seconds were enough of a head start to stay on top of things.

This cadence had a rhythm that was almost too relaxing, and I haven't forgotten its tranquility; the cadence was sometimes interrupted by a drill instructor ordering a morning thrashing for one of the recruits. It was hard to hold back my laughter, but knowing I was in the same Hell kept it to a minimum.

The jet airplanes taking off and landing at the San Diego Airport became a part of life for us that no one could stop. The first few days were spent on initial tasks like the Physical Fitness Test (PFT), which consisted of however many pull-ups and sit-ups they could get out of our "disgusting bodies," and a timed three-mile run. Drilling commands were shouted repeatedly, followed by more commands; it seemed endless.

Classes, classes, and more classes—these took up a third of the day. The rest was spent running, thrashing in the pits, learning how to march, or cleaning our weapons.

The classes on the curriculum ranged from the Code of Conduct to Leave and Liberty, but the classes in between were the most vital for making it to the next level. Take Marine Corps History: from the beginning of its existence, through every battle fought, and each major player involved in these conflicts, to the significance of those individuals and the tactics used to win. It was interesting, but too much, too fast.

General orders and deadly force, life-saving steps, first aid, assembly and disassembly of our weapons, pay—everything about the Marine Corps that could be taught in a classroom was covered. It was mostly information designed to be picked up quickly, with the rest taught in the field or on the parade deck.

One might say, "They learned that in school last semester; that's nothing." The prestige came only after the journey was complete, when we marched on the parade deck for the last time, and a Colonel or General announced to the world that we had completed the training offered by the United States Marine Corps. Then they addressed us as Marines.

Routine start in boot camp

Every morning began the same for everyone in boot camp. Preparations were useless because no recruit could beat the system.

I would slip under my covers as carefully as possible, trying to make as little mess as I could out of my rack. In the morning, the rack would be easy to arrange, with just the right tucks and folds required. A wake-up call would sound, and we'd jump out and get "on line," which meant everyone standing in front of their beds. We would stand there and count off, making sure every recruit was accounted for. There was a history of recruits escaping during the night. Following the count, there was a step-by-step procedure to getting dressed: "Grab your left sock, put it on, do it now. Stop, you're done." If someone didn't have that left sock on their left foot, we'd start all over. Sometimes a recruit would put their left sock on their right foot. "Now grab your right sock and put it on your other foot; 3-2-1, stop; you're freakin' done." These instructions were always given by the drill instructor as they paced the floors, waiting to catch someone slipping.

We faced the same consequences: "Now grab your trousers and put them on!" Nothing seemed to change except for the article of clothing; we were always under the gun. Sometimes it was just a game, or our scheduled time for morning chow was still a ways off. We'd be almost fully dressed, and then someone would take a little too long tying their boot or something, and we'd have to start all over again. "Strip 'em down! Now get your left sock and put it on… you're freakin' done!" And so it would go on.

Everything was on a strict timetable, and games filled in the gaps when there was "nothing to do." Thrashings often took place in the morning hours before breakfast, and the guys who were borderline fat, as opposed to just overweight, would dress up, starting their day with a thrashing. After getting dressed, the racks were arranged, and everything was straightened up before we fell into formation.

The word "hat" was removed from our vocabulary and replaced with "cover." If we were caught outdoors without wearing our covers, we'd have to put our hands on our heads and walk around that way. This was done to embarrass us and to reinforce the importance of keeping track of our personal belongings.

"Thrashing" is the Marine Corps term for punishment, which simply means going to an assigned area and doing countless sit-ups, push-ups, leg lifts, mountain climbers, and an array of other calisthenics on the DI's command. When the drill instructors called someone's name, the response had to be immediate. We'd sprint to the location of the sound, only to be told, "TOO SLOW, GET BACK!" and we'd repeat it for the better part of ten times. What made it worse was when the drill instructors would yell, "GET AWAY FROM ME!" and look at us with utter disgust.

Causes of trashing

We were constantly drilled to help us retain what we were being taught; that was the main reason we were thrashed. Questions, ranging from Uniforms to History, General Orders, the Uniform Code of Military Justice, and even politics, were always being asked. If we gave the wrong answer, we could expect to be sent to the classroom.

The classroom was where we'd meet for instructions or to have our mail handed to us. It was an area just before the exit doors of the squad bay. It was called the classroom because that was where we'd learn many things, such as what was going on at home through the mail, answers to questions we hadn't known before our thrashing, new information, or just other general knowledge. We were also thrashed simply because there wasn't much else scheduled for that hour. The boot camp system was so meticulous, and the drill instructors were so knowledgeable, that anything going wrong was bound to be our fault. The system simply couldn't be beaten.

One day, Lawrence asked me, "Hey man, that fucker Van Cleave is giving me shit; how about you?" I answered, "Yeah, Dixon has it in for me. I don't know why." Later, we found out that was just the way it worked.

After four to five weeks, I could feel myself slowly transforming into a better man, both physically and mentally, affected by small things like hustling, thrashing, and marching. I never thought something could whip someone into shape so effectively. Above all, boot camp builds character, discipline, and attention to detail, which led me to become more and more of a perfectionist. This was the type of therapy I needed after I recovered from my coma, which I unofficially didn't experience as a kid. Physical, mental, and speech therapy—it was all part of the package.

Mail call was the most important morale booster for the recruits.

The type of news we might receive was a mystery, but at least we could write back. Some guys were lucky because their girlfriends sent nude photos. Not only were these photos sent in by the girls of a few fortunate ones, but others received cookies and care packages. The sweets were always given to other platoons because we weren't allowed to have them in our diets. Then there were other guys who received the greatest news they could ever have—they'd become new dads. Having a baby on the government's dime was priceless. Some received the unforgettable Dear John letter. I think the Dear John letter was why I was okay with not having a girlfriend while going through boot camp.

The good thing about boot camp was that we didn't have to do anything unless we were told. There, we were told what to do, how to do it, when to do it, and eventually, we learned why we did it. Everything had its purpose.

I found that the Ten Commandments were somewhat replaced by Eleven General Orders drilled into our heads every day. My vocabulary was becoming more and more vulgar; my sentence structure was violated with the word "fuck" almost every other word. I would catch myself saying it to people who deserved more respect, and all I could do was apologize, hope they understood, and move on.

10 Commandments vs. 11 General Orders

As the Ten Commandments are guidelines for life, so were the 11 General Orders. Without them, we would lack structure in the basic things we were told to do, which were to guard and protect. I wasn't sure how these 11 General Orders were used in other areas of the Marines, but everyone needed to know them. I'm pretty sure that every Marine in the Corps worldwide is required to perform a job where they'd need to know the 11 General Orders. At any given moment, I'm willing to bet there are over 2,500 Marines standing some type of post that requires them to know their General Orders, understand when to apply them, and maintain the safety of their assigned area.

Most importantly, the 11 General Orders, when deeply considered, could reveal the definitions of a true leader. The 11 General Orders demand bearing, courage, decisiveness, dependability, endurance, enthusiasm, judgment, initiative, integrity, justice, knowledge, tact, unselfishness, and loyalty. When one leads using these traits, they utilize their General Orders in the most powerful but still the most basic way of doing things. It takes teamwork to foster great leadership—from those who follow to the one who leads.

The first phase of boot camp was learning the basics, such as the wearing of our uniforms, the meaning of the Eagle, Globe, and Anchor, the history of the Corps, etc. In adapting to a new way of life, I needed to change my habits, body, and mind, and understand that I was only to do what I was told—no more, no less. This process was carried out in accordance with a tradition that's over two hundred years old, and if people before me had made it through the hell I encountered, then I had more than half a chance.

The parade deck was a classroom within itself, situated on a giant simulated parking lot—or so it seemed. We spent countless hours there falling into formation and having marching-drill commands instilled into our brains. Covertly, we were taught teamwork, team precision, unity, and discipline; but most of all, we learned how to accept victory or defeat as a team.

The second phase was mostly spent out in the field, learning the unchanging facts about combat and how to avoid becoming a statistic. We finally had the opportunity to fire our M-16 A-2 service rifles and qualify with them. In the series of recruits before us, one had lost his bearing and composure to the point of taking his own life with his rifle. We were never told how it happened; maybe it was an omen to the drill instructors, or maybe they didn't want to reveal how someone might go about ending their life. I believe the first couple of days any platoon spends on the rifle range are the most unpredictable.

To the instructors, this was no joke. Imagine how they must feel at the thought of losing a recruit that way—it's likely their worst fear about the job, above all the other stresses.

I'll never forget carrying my weapon into the restroom, which we called "the head." That was my worst day there. All four drill instructors dropped whatever they were doing, putting everything else on hold to thrash me and make an example out of me. In the middle of the squad bay, they stood over me, telling me how I'd messed up and taunting me with questions like, "Do you want to kill yourself, Zavala?" I had to convince them it was a mistake by raising my voice and moving as fast as I could. They were determined to make a lesson out of it. I remember Van Cleave saying, "Oh! Zavala just wants to interrupt my schedule by trying to kill himself... Everybody say, 'Thank you, Zavala.'" The message was clear: "This is what happens if you carry your weapon into the head"—something they'd already explained.

After 45 minutes of being thrashed by all four drill instructors, I was soaked in sweat; it felt like I'd lost weight. One of the instructors eventually ordered me to change into a dry uniform, but it felt pointless since we still had a five-and-a-half-mile hike ahead of us.

We made it through the rifle range without any fatalities and were qualified as Marksmen, Sharpshooters, or Experts. The remainder of the second phase focused mostly on physical training, night maneuvers, and patrols, all at a learning level.

One night, I was assigned fire watch while up on "Alpha-shelf," the side of a mountain. Dixon pretended to be a recruit, and I couldn't tell who I was talking to because it was nearly pitch dark. He struck up a conversation, asking me what I thought of the drill instructors.

I replied, "Man, I thought they were going to kill me the other day. I guess that's the stressful part of being a drill instructor. And that guy Dixon—he's constantly on my case, which is good in a way. I've lost 31 pounds already."

Around that time, we noticed a flashlight turning on in the drill instructors' hooch, so I said, "Man, I've got to go."

As I began to walk away, I felt a sharp pain in my lower back. Dixon had thrown his flashlight at me. At first, I thought it was McCory, the only Black recruit in our platoon, since I could tell the person I was talking to was Black. But I'd never spoken to McCory before, so I hadn't recognized Dixon's voice in the dark.

Dixon was furious. He said, "Zavala, you ever disrespect me like that again, boy, I'll have your mother-fucking ass. You got that, son?"

I thought for sure I was about to get a free ass-kicking when I saw him towering over me. From that night on, I was unofficially added to a list of recruits who had earned extra scrutiny.

In the second half of Second Phase, there was no mercy out in the field. The wake-up process remained the same: before dawn, in the biting 40-degree mountain cold. Those 14 mornings were the worst. Each one started like a bad day at the office and somehow managed to stay that way from the opening formation to the end of the training day.

"Grab one sock, put it on your left foot. No, not yet! You wait until I tell you to do so. Do not anticipate the command!" Our bodies were shocked from the warmth of the sleeping bags to the icy air of the high altitude, and you could hear everyone's teeth chattering.

"Do it now! Move! 3, 2, 1, you're done!" And God help you if you put your left sock on your right foot. The worst part was that we weren't allowed to move around to get our blood circulating; we just stood there, freezing, until we were fully dressed. I'd been in cold climates before, but never this cold, or maybe it was just that my mind hadn't yet adjusted to the conditions. Mind over matter was the only way we could tolerate things that would otherwise bring us to a breaking point. Sometimes I'd wonder just how much of this had been studied by psychiatrists or doctors in Human Behavioral Science.

When someone screwed up or gave a wrong answer, I'd often end up right beside him, paying for something I didn't do. Drill Instructor SSgt. Dixon made sure I paid my dues in sweat for that slip-up on Alpha-shelf.

One guy was so terrified that he wouldn't even ask to use the restroom. We were standing in formation one day, and he just wet his trousers. Even the DIs were baffled and a bit embarrassed, and they held a meeting with us to prevent something like that from ever happening again.

Some of these recruits had never seen or experienced much of what others had. One guy had never seen a Black man until boot camp, and the first one he met was a drill instructor. Another recruit, one of our squad leaders, had never seen a television set before boot camp. The ironic part was that while he finally saw one, he never actually watched it since it was never turned on.

As Marines, regardless of role—from cooks to administration—we all shared the same job description: "To locate, close with, and destroy the enemy by fire and maneuver, or repel the enemy's assault by fire and/or close combat." By this point in boot camp, if that description didn't motivate a recruit, he was in the wrong place.

"Agony Hill" was its old name; we knew it as *Mount Mother*. Reaching the peak brought only one thought to mind, besides death: "motherfucker." That word lingered in my head, and I knew that, eventually, we'd have to climb it. The mountain's incline was so steep that, with each step, I could place my hand right in front of me without even fully extending my arm. Thoughts of falling down the slope filled my mind, along with the punishment waiting at the top. The hell we'd been through already suddenly felt meaningless in comparison.

As I climbed, I avoided looking down, focusing intently on each step. Placing my foot was no longer automatic—it required full concentration. One slip could spell disaster for everyone behind. Gasping for air came more naturally than walking at that point.

The Climb up mount Mother

I remember when the recruiters in high school emphasized Mount Mother. They framed it as a turning point in boot camp. I was too excited about the climb to worry about the daunting aspects of the ascent. About 100 meters from the base of the mountain, I had the chance to reshape my perception of fear regarding this climb. It was either going to be too high, or I was going to reach the top. In that moment, I resolved that the mountain wasn't going to get any higher; it was simply a matter of climbing.

After climbing for some time, I didn't want to look down to gauge my progress; instead, I wanted to look up to see how much farther I needed to go. When I did, I noticed fewer recruits in front of me, which made me mentally ease off, thinking I was approaching my goal. Still, I had a long way to go, and getting back into the right mindset to finish the climb was one of the hardest things to do.

As we ascended, the fear of falling diminished, slowly giving way to a sense of accomplishment. At this point, maintaining fear would only increase the chances of falling.

Yet, with every step closer to the summit, my frustration grew; I just wanted it to be over. I had to remain calm; rushing could lead to a misstep and a fall, but I couldn't afford to be overconfident either since we were nearly there. The entire climb demanded respect for the mountain. No matter if we completed the ascent or not, the mountain would remain, unchanged—even if someone were to fall. Regardless of whether we reached the top or stayed at the bottom, that mountain was going to change us.

No one in our series fell. We reached the summit, rested, and drank water while the drill instructors plotted our next destination. My legs were spent from the climb, and the descent proved equally demanding. The challenge of reaching the top likely contributed to our underestimation of the climb down.

In the following days, we engaged in more weapons training while staying out in the field. For some of us, this would become a daily routine, while others wouldn't practice as often as needed. For all of us, it was our first experience with the tools and tactics of war. Third phase was upon us, and we acted as if we had seen and done it all. One thing was certain: we were better that day than we had been the day before. Back at MCRD in the barracks, we could taste graduation day—we couldn't wait for it. At this point, the drill instructors could do whatever they wanted as far as thrashing because I was in the best shape of my life, and there was nothing I couldn't handle. Physically, we had fully transformed; now, getting our minds to catch up was next on their list.

We didn't yet realize that transformation takes more than just good health; it required more than our physical endurance to get this far. It was the drill instructors' job to paint a clearer picture for us, uniting body and mind.

Our duties had been shifted to the chow hall, where we would help feed everyone on base for a week. This was a break from the usual boot camp routine, a time for our minds to catch up. We had access to just about anything we wanted to eat.

I made sure I was out of sight while indulging in ice cream, but I was eventually busted. One of those in charge threatened me, saying, "Who's your drill instructor? He'll be finding out what you're doing!" In that moment, I couldn't have cared less; I had ice cream in my hands, and I was loving life.

Graduation day was fast approaching, and something that once had been my hell had become my refuge. I felt as if I could do this forever. I recall thinking, "I don't know life as a Marine beyond these walls. I can't ask my mom, family, or friends—what was I to do?"

I knew Lawrence would soon be going his own way, and I wouldn't be able to ask him, but everything came together as a daily routine for me once I arrived where I was going.

Before graduation, all that was left to do was finalize everything: drill on the parade decks for competition, the physical fitness test, testing our book work, known to us as "Our Knowledge," getting fitted for our dress uniforms, updating our records, and handling other minor details.

The graduation ceremonies were held every Friday, and it was by far the most exciting day of the week for us. Families and friends, including women from the local area, attended to witness the final transformation from recruits to Marines.

On Friday, July 15, 1988, we were no longer recruits but officially United States Marines—the World's Finest, as some would say. As I made my way out, Drill Instructor SSgt. Dixon approached me to explain why he had created a hell within a hell for me. "Zavala, I'm a grunt (0311), and I know what it takes to be a good leader or just to survive in the bush," he said.

"Thank you, Sir," I responded, my eyes filling with tears of pride. At the time, I didn't fully understand what he meant, but I had a lifetime to make sense of his wisdom. I felt emotional because he did this to help me become a better person. I realized I had become a great follower and had even better leaders; if I held onto what Dixon told me, I would be on my way to becoming a good leader. That brief conversation with Drill Instructor SSgt. Dixon put everything into perspective for me.

Now I was anxious to get home; I just needed to find my way off the Depot by bus. In my attempts to leave the base, I encountered the Base Sergeant Major, who, by the end of my four-year stint, would become the Sergeant Major of the Marine Corps. He was a chiseled man, aged with pure toughness and a world of wisdom. While his uniform and rank were impressive, it was truly his character and presence that commanded respect and attention.

In 1996, I met Tom Landry at a gas station during my drive to Dallas from Austin. Aside from these two men, I have not encountered anyone else who possesses the characteristics I speak of.

CHAPTER 3

HOMEBOUND

A military flight brought me from San Diego to Lubbock, Texas. From there, I caught a commercial flight to Austin, and I was home. A special thanks to that dear old couple who picked me up, took me to their home, fed me, and safely returned me to the airport during my three-hour delay. When I disembarked the plane in Austin, Gabriel and a friend of ours were there to greet me. They were shocked at how much weight I had managed to lose, and for once in my life, I felt great.

My mother was so happy to see me, now a new man. As soon as I could, I wanted to try to get me a piece of ass, but first, my friend picked me up, and we had a few beers and talked about what went on and how mind-boggling boot camp really was. Then I was delivered to my ex-girlfriend's house, where my needs were fulfilled.

The first few days home were okay, but they quickly became boring. I had to stay fit and do my thing; it wasn't about being home anymore; it was about making the most of life and living it up. I wasn't worried about what was waiting for me beyond the walls of MCRD anymore; I was ready to take on the world. One doesn't go through training like this to come home and hang; I definitely felt out of place.

In California, the School of Infantry was physically demanding; we were driven to push harder. There, if you jacked around, you were left behind, and that was your ass. I knew some of the Marines at Camp San Onofre from boot camp, and I had seen some familiar faces, but I wouldn't see most of them anymore after this training. Piver and Knightengale I remember seeing in my platoon during training, but I didn't really pay them any mind; I figured I'd wait to get acquainted with a few guys until my next move, which I thought was going to be my duty station.

Before going on to a training platoon for our Military Occupational School (MOS), it was mandatory that we do a couple of weeks of guard duty, where I met Botello, who was from San Antonio. Both Holliway and Sadler were from other states. I wouldn't see Sadler after this training, but Botello and Holliway we'd be in the same unit later on. Botello was as crazy as I was and didn't give a shit; my problem was that I cared. Both Holliway and Sadler were a bit on the crazy side as well.

The E-club was a forbidden place for those on guard duty. Suppose something went down and someone tried to overthrow the armory or anything; the Reactionary Forces wouldn't be able to do their duties if they were smashed.

The last evening before ending our two weeks of guard duty and being transferred to our training platoons was when it happened at the E-club: I put away about three pitchers of beer. I got so hammered that when I lay down to sleep, I didn't get up for anything, which got us busted. No one was ratted out or anything; a headcount was done, and some individuals were not at their appointed place. The staff sergeant in charge told us the next morning, "It being such a short time for you being Marines, I'm going to let you men slide because I don't want to tarnish your service record book." Disobeying a direct order would have provoked an Article 15; besides, the Infantry already gets the shortcomings that the Corps has to give.

Earlier, I mentioned an MOS; it was our job, which had a number attached to it along with a nickname. My job was the Infantry (a.k.a. ground-pounder, the first to go in, dead-men, or grunts). The list is longer, but that's what I'll give you for now. The numbers were 0300 and up, mainly using 0311 for small arms and 0331 for machine gunners, mostly crew-served.

Each individual within that crew needed to be able to take care of business if his crew happened to be taken down; the same applies to the mortarmen, 0351. Finally, training was two days away, belonging to Alfa Company, School of Infantry—a place we called home for the next eight weeks. Training was just part of the system and the toughest way to get to where we were going. Following SOI training, some of us would go to the Fleet in Jacksonville, North Carolina, or California. The Fleet was a place that never had good stories told about it; it seemed as if they wanted to instill fear into our minds about the Fleet, and they made it sound like the Fleet could make a grown man cry, which I could believe. Some Marines were sent overseas, and still others would go to do more training. I had no idea where I was going to end up.

I was familiar with this area since this was where the field training for boot camp was done. We did a lot of the same drills and training, but many times more intense. Mostly everything was live fire, so the possibility of someone being killed never slipped our minds. We had to carry all of our equipment with us on our backs everywhere we went— places like Alfa Shelf, where Drill Instructor SSgt. Dixon fucked me up with that flashlight, Mount Mother, and the grenade range. This site, that site; we just got out to train. Everywhere we went was mostly done on foot.

Reaching deep down into our innermost selves to pull out that little extra just to make it a few more feet became an everyday task for us. Our feet would throb with pain after humping out eight to twelve miles within two hours. Some of us, when changing to a fresh pair of socks, would find our feet soaked in blood, and whoever had the most blood in their boot after removing it would have the bragging rights. It was just our way of having a positive outlook on life. Times like these worried me a little because I didn't want to believe that my daily work routine wasn't going to be any different. One of the highlights of SOI was a fifteen-mile hump fully packed and with our weapons. I understood then why the Fleet never had any good stories.

SOI forced me and everyone around me to grow mentally and

increase our threshold for pain. Assuring our canteens were topped off was always the first thing on our list; always reminding one another to keep hydrated was equally important because no one wanted the burden of carrying someone back. It was also for one's own good not to become dehydrated.   We were told that once it happened, it would be easier and easier to become dehydrated with every incident.

Altogether, we carried about an extra 75 pounds of gear: helmet (4 pounds), web harness (13 pounds), topped-off canteens and flak jacket (9 pounds), M-16-A2 service rifle (8 pounds), and a backpack weighing at least 40 more pounds.

It was a lot about endurance and teamwork, but there was always that 10 percent who didn't care about teamwork; soon, they learned one way or another, and in time, the platoon was like a fine-tuned machine trained to cause death to those who threatened our country's freedom.

SSgt. Angstrom was the main source of my motivation; he made us laugh but did his job well. He was the oldest of the instructors and seemed like he may have caught the last few legs of Vietnam. His classes would begin with either: "Good morning, men . . . good afternoon, men. How was chow? . . . My name is SSgt. Angstrom; when I was in Vietnam, I . . ."

The way he would hit on the topic of study was always in good character, and at times, he would go 100 percent as we trained, just like one of us.

During a class on the Marine Corps K-bar, which is the glorified knife developed for the Marines, he stated, for motivational purposes, "And when the fighting's done, you take out the trusty K-bar, put the enemy's eye out, and skull fuck him."

He was a hard charger; at best, he knew how to keep us focused because that was what the Infantry was all about—fucking, fighting, and drinking, and the way history tells it.

Nighttime maneuvers were much more intense, and it took discipline of every form to be done correctly, but it served its purpose. We also had the opportunity to familiarize ourselves with pyrotechnics, explosives, hastily made guns, booby traps, and landmines.

During the weekends, we were allowed to go out and explore the great state of California, but the only places we really went were to the nearby off-base dance clubs, bars, and the beach. Most Marines in training would go to the mall during the daytime.

On this particular Saturday afternoon, I ran into Robert Martinez, a friend from back home; I'd known him since the first grade. We said hello and told one another where we could be found, hoping that someday I'd have time to go visit. Things were always hurried in the Corps, especially when there wasn't any place I could really call home except for only a few months. I never made time to pay Robert a visit, but I'm sure he understood.

A Physical Fitness Test was usually administered before going to another duty station. My personal best time for a 3-mile PFT run was 18:16. After doing so, we would take care of a few minor details— paperwork, turning in gear, and exchanging addresses, depending on where the Corps was sending us. Next, plans were being developed accordingly, and then we were off to our next stop.

Those who stood 5'11" or taller had the option to go to 8th and I, the White House, to march for the President at ceremonies. I didn't want any part of it; I couldn't care less. I still remember this staff sergeant freaking out and saying to me, "Man, what are you, fucking crazy? Do you realize what these California mountains can do to your knees?" I replied, "Who knows? I may get lucky and not have to stay in California."

Walking a straight line was okay and kept me out of trouble, but as I entered my next phase of training, it became almost impossible. I had to become daring, edgy, and take risks that I otherwise wouldn't take.

At that young age, it was also difficult to leave the daring, edgy part back in the barracks with our uniforms. The daring, edgy, risky part of us was a lifestyle; we wore it proudly and paid heavily when it wasn't controlled.

We had plenty of downtime in SOI; our Platoon Leaders always gave us tips and techniques on how to get things done easier, better, and faster. One guy taught us how to make a hasty gun using things found in a garage. But one of the most helpful techniques taught to us was how to move from point A to point B in a fast and tactical manner;

one of our fastest times covering three and a half miles was just under twenty-three minutes. Most people can't run that fast. Other topics covered included booby traps and the radio; more importantly, we learned the things not to do during the cover of darkness.

There was one thing many of us didn't like about SOI: in my days, the only way to be a reservist was to go through our training, which separated us from the others. I didn't talk shit to them because my older brother was a reservist in the Army, and at the same time, I made it clear never to mistake my kindness for weakness.

One tension-filled evening, we had just returned from the field, and tempers were flaring; most of us were broken down. One of the reservists made a comment like, "Fuck this shit hole, at least I'm not stuck here like the rest of you fuckers."

The next thing I remember, one guy got up out of his rack and began to beat the hell out of this reservist.

The next morning, we faced an interrogation; questions were asked in private rooms, but no one spoke, not even the other reservist. They understood not to disrespect our choices. For some unknown reason, the guy who was beaten the night before continued to press on about his situation and wanted something done. For about a week, one of us would wake up just to kick this dude's ass. We policed our own problems, which was one of the unwritten rules for an Infantry Unit.

One thing I found myself doing in the Corps was breaking the barrier; that meant going the extra step to reach my next level of mental capabilities. Physically, there was almost nothing I could not do. I guess "breaking the barrier" was a survival technique for me. I think, mostly, it was a way of transforming a certain fear into some type of motivation that couldn't keep me from performing the task at hand. Also, everything was subject to change, and I needed to become versatile. Adaptation to change was a must.

CHAPTER 4

MORE TRAINING

Up in the air, was it a bird? No, it was just a plane with a few Marines being sent off to yet another training facility in Virginia. This time it was to train to be part of the Security Forces guarding a nuclear weapons station or something else just as vital to national security. There, I teamed up with a few guys I knew from San Diego, a dear friend, Ron Piver, and Robert Knightengale. We became the best of friends there and did some advanced training. We were right there with Navy SEALs Team 4; their training facility was down the road a distance of a few blocks. 9-mm qualification, shotguns, handcuffing, the several different types of handcuffs, clearing rooms, urban terrain combat—training that was more advanced than before.

We were constantly asked, "What if?" followed by a scenario, unknowingly being prepared to think, sleep, and breathe antiterrorism 24/7. The reason behind this thinking was that the Marines who would further advance and choose to go on to the next level of antiterrorism training would be halfway ready and into the thinking mode where they needed to be. Those who went on to their duty stations following this training would be ready for that type of work environment, and their way of thinking would soon fall back to regular day-to-day thinking, not "what if," followed by a terrorist situation.

By the time we went through weapons training, our way of thinking had been altered. Piver, Knightengale, and I always asked each other, "Hey man, what if we wanted to take these guys out? Where would you position yourself, and who would you take out first?" We were referring to our own training company while we had fully loaded magazines of 9-mm Berettas and access to many more guns and ammo.

The thought was indeed freaky, but it would have been easy because we knew each of the troops' potential and who would and would not fight. We would think of these types of situations just to set up our strategic rescue situations and how we would go about accomplishing them with minimal casualties. I learned to read faces to a certain degree by this time; I could tell if someone was lying or guilty, especially if I'd known that person for some time. We would also try to see who would be the first to most likely snap, the subjects of the worst-case scenarios. We even made our own dream team from the guys there, including ourselves.

We didn't have any idea what type of training this would consist of, but when we were being oriented, we thought for sure it was going to be great. We saw these four other men doing something different as far as training went; maybe a spotter and a sniper would train, developing an eye to find the enemy and tracking techniques, hand-to-hand combat, and an assortment of tactics. We were blown away. I knew someday it would be us going through the same type of training that these more advanced Marines were going through, and to me, that's what it was all about.

The entire time in Norfolk, we trained in accordance with Navy, Army, and Marine Corps regulations such as OPNAVINST, SECNAVINST, and NAVFEC-DM. To name a few classes: Hostage Incident-5500.29A, Bomb Incident—3440.15, Unarmed Self-Defense-FM-21.150, Physical Control of Apprehended Personnel-5580.1, Nuclear Accident/Incident Response and Assistance, and Security of Classification Information. We had Civil Disturbance, Locking Systems, MCSF Duties, Enclave/Special Weapons Security, Logbooks, and the list went on. Most importantly, (SERE/TC) stands for Survival, Escape, Resistance, and Evasion, Terrorist Counteraction—a skill or tolerance many more should develop due to the possible captivity of American men and/or women, because does the government expect you to die and/or leave capture to chance?

The Mossberg shotgun was one weapon that was hardly ever thought of as being phased out; the handgun was the 9-mm Beretta, which just replaced the .45 caliber within the same year. The assault weapon used was the MP-5, which I thought just kicked ass. It fires the same rounds as our handguns and disassembles almost like the M-16 A-2 Service Rifles, which added just the right amount of confidence to our capabilities and wouldn't slow us down. We also test-fired as we went over and studied AK weapons; it looked just like an AK-47, but this one had a folding stock and had a lot less trigger pull pressure than our American weapons.

Every morning, we would be bussed over to an undisclosed location, crossing into North Carolina for our live-fire training. Most everyone slept on the way there; those who didn't sleep listened to headphones or mentally prepared themselves for the long day.

Batons and handcuffs were more of the basic tools of the force that we became familiar with as our training progressed. Volunteers were asked to be the "bad guy," and two of the instructors told these volunteers to resist by every means capable. As they did, it just got worse for them. These two instructors knew their stuff, and it fell into place as teamwork was being demonstrated to us.

When it came down to it, fist for fist, it became paramount to know and understand the importance of pressure points; knowing these points would give us an advantage over the average John Doe.

Most would agree all of the training was equally important, but it was almost useless without knowing what to look for, where to look, and how to categorize and pre-assess a situation. This made everything we learned complete.

Being one of the most senior Marines at this particular training facility, I was made squad leader. I made sure the other troops didn't think I was placed as a leader under those certain circumstances, so I needed to be stronger, smarter, faster, more daring, and more over the edge than the Marines under me to show them I did, in fact, earn the position. Soon enough, having seniority there didn't matter because they knew I had what it took to be their leader.

The training focused on how to recognize the development of many terrorist activities, how they were carried out, how to fight them if necessary, clearing buildings in a tactical manner, and locating snipers—lots of those types of situations. There was always a worst-case scenario.

The first couple of weeks was an introductory period, with practical knowledge from handouts and our morning runs while there was still time. During one of our morning runs on the beach, we were in a state of misery; it was about twenty-six degrees, and we were dressed in shorts and T-shirts. I found myself leading a fearsome pack of Devil Dogs into a deeper part of their minds—and into the ocean. To alter the state of mind, I charged into the ocean and swam about fifty meters or so inward. When I saw the rest of that pack following me, I knew I had truly become one of their alpha leaders. We were all freezing at this point; someone said to me, "You're crazy, man." I was looking for that type of response to feed off. One guy asked, "What the hell was all that for? Why did you do that?" My response was, "I know why I did it. Why did you follow me?" What else could he say?

Thanksgiving was upon us, and it was the only time that I felt homesick. I didn't like it and told myself, "I am never going to feel homesick again." The only way not to be homesick was to accept the Marine Corps as my real home. If I'm at home, how could I get homesick? Sure, I missed my family; I would call them, and that was the quickest solution, but not everyone functioned the way I did. I wanted to be home eating turkey. We always made the best of it; I figured if we couldn't be home eating turkey, then we could at least be there in Virginia drinking Wild Turkey. Soon, we were cured of our homesickness, talking shop while drinking and relaxing—anything to make the feeling of wanting to be home with family go away. We were by the strip in Virginia Beach, so we didn't lack much; the streets provided the rest, and we always had women there with us. If we wanted drugs, they could be acquired there too, but none of us did drugs, and that was the best thing about the whole experience.

While on leave at home, I hooked up with my old girlfriend. During these tough and fun times, I needed to maintain a little sanity. It doesn't matter who you are; everyone needs that security and someone from home to share with about the changes we went through.

The day came to decide whether to go or stay. We were screened by a staff panel of Marines, but these guys were from an elite force called FAST Company. I made the list; the East Coast and West Coast commands were both there. FAST, which stood for Fleet Anti-terrorist Special Teams, was a group that I had never heard of. When they asked me to be a part of it, I knew I had achieved the ultimate goal for the first phase of my four-year tenure. I turned them down, and for some time, I laid in bed at night, hoping not to regret my decision. My choice to stay behind was based on the bonded brotherhood; I knew that these few friends would put their lives on the line for me, as I would for them. I understood that being there for each other on a day-to-day basis would outweigh the chances of helping one another in the heat of battle. If and when we were to go to battle, we'd be more than prepared to kill for one another. Maybe the most important reason was that all of our training had become synchronized. I knew how Piver was thinking; Piver knew how Knightengale was thinking; and "The Night" knew how I was thinking. I couldn't forget about Vega from Denver—he was always thinking, as were Rat, Mayer, Scarno, Wilson, and the rest of the guys. Together, we could confidently tell someone to leave the dirty work to the professionals.

Turning down FAST was a decision that I will always wish I had a second chance to make, if only to see what adventure and excitement it had to offer; most of all, how often it would be offered. I didn't think anything else could ever top the feeling of being a part of FAST. As I see it, those who don't work their way up to that degree of excellence won't have time to mature; like karate, you can't start as a black belt.

Maybe if I had had a career counselor to prep me for that and to tell me what FAST consisted of on a day-to-day basis, because a lot of what we heard was mostly rumor control. Maybe my life would have been different, better, worse, or over—who knows? A quick decision had to be made, and that's the lifestyle that the guys in FAST lived. I just wanted to be in the Marines and have a regular Marine Corps lifestyle, and I wanted to see what it was like before I made any hasty decisions and joined an elite team like FAST.

Nine months passed, and the fun had not even begun. In the friendly skies once again, but this time it was to an actual duty station in Charleston, SC. It was around this time that I had been promoted to Lance Corporal, and with that came maturity—and that's what they got. We were taken in and told that this is the real thing now, and that the games were over. Background checks were being administered for Secret Security Clearances; we endured yet another indoctrination that took about three to four weeks. Of all places, the South! Why the hell couldn't I have been placed somewhere else? Maybe in a third-world country; anywhere else would have been better than South Carolina.

I never imagined being stationed in South Carolina when joining the Marines. I was still in middle school and even high school when my take on the Marines was that they were working in the field and the jungles all the time—mission after mission in faraway lands, gathering intelligence and then going amongst the foreign nationals to gather more intelligence. A Marine's job was a never-ending task of maintaining our edge over our world enemies on every level of security.

Our duties in Charleston were to guard special weapons, transporting them from one location to another, maybe onto a ship, a submarine, or just to another area. There, the Marines were responsible for watching over more than just one site; everything seemed to be scrambled together until we got situated. We learned about the different platoons and what their responsibilities were.

Other than the information I just provided, I'm not sure that I can disclose any more without compromising the duties of other Marines around the world. I'm also sure that the foreign nationals already know what goes on in their own parts of the world.

I've always known that racism existed within the Corps, but thank God I never experienced it too badly. Most guys I ran into always told me, after knowing them for a few weeks, "Man, you're fucking crazy."

I'll admit that I kind of was way out there; I didn't think, when it came to giving 110 percent, that there was any way someone could be racist against my efforts. I have reason to believe that when I put myself out there like that, people wouldn't see me as belonging to a certain race or maybe even think of me as one of their own. After all, we wore green and were fighting for the same cause. So if I made myself a valued asset, people just needed me with them. That's my opinion on the whole thing of racism, and yet that opinion was also subject to change.

After all the training we endured, it was time to go on post. The one to show me the ropes was a short-timer who was timid and always careful; I guess he had his reasons. He familiarized me with the ground rules and kept talking as if he wanted to say, "This is how I did it, and if you want to make it out of here intact, do exactly what I'm showing you and you'll survive."

What he was doing was giving me the impression that the Marine Corps was all about doing the bare minimum just to get by, and I didn't like it because I knew that there was more to it than the bare minimum. I don't know when, but at some point, I decided that I was not going to be like the next guy who just goes through the motions.

The first few times on post, I was excited about it because I didn't know if or what I would see out there. The excitement of being on patrol neither elevated to the next level nor diminished itself. I knew something was wrong; I never thought about how I would react to the idea of seeing some unauthorized person in the area. The thought kind of scared me, so I had to figure out a way to deal with it.

Every day wasn't always the same; at times, we were off and could sleep in, while another platoon was on their training cycle and another was on duty doing working parties. On our days off, we slept as late as we wanted, or of course, if we had personal things to do, we'd get them done. If you chose to sleep in, chow wasn't going to wait; we'd just have to wait for it the next time around. Our other option was going off-base to eat or going over to the E-club.

Maybe we didn't make it back the night before, and then we'd eat wherever possible. Some bars stayed open until 7 or 8 the next morning anyway, and for sure we'd go eat someplace after leaving the bars.

On training days, reveille would sound about 0530 or maybe 0600. Then we'd get dressed and either tidy up everything before going to eat, or go eat and then come back to our rooms and straighten up. Time efficiency was very important to beat the system here; unlike boot camp, this system was somewhat different and beatable. It was easy to differentiate between those who lived like pigs and were always late getting to where they were supposed to be because they had to clean up beforehand. Those who had their act together were able to sleep in more and take their time doing things.

This is how it went: I woke up, showered, got dressed, and went to chow; then I came back to my room and slept until 0745 because there was no organizing to be done. We had days when working parties were needed to take care of things around the barracks; we were kind of a self-sustained group, except for the Navy cooks at the chow hall. Otherwise, there were only Marines at the barracks. A working party was mostly needed for groundskeeping and cleaning up the area, along with other details. Other times, we just did the same stupid tasks to stay busy.

Noon chow was two hours most days, so again we were able to eat if we were hungry and work out or do anything else, just as long as we were back in formation at 1300. The day ended for most around 1630 or 1700. It was then that we did whatever we wanted, as long as we were back in the morning to do it again. At times, we were selected or volunteered to go on a patrol.

Patrols were live, meaning we went out hunting for people. Just how real it became was up to those who were not supposed to be in our area. The potential for anything was always present. If they shot at us, we'd shoot back; if they ran, we'd chase them, and they never made it too far. We would apprehend them and take them to the authorities, who would then have to deal with the problem. The people we'd be looking for out there in the woods were almost always poachers and never anything worse.

I was never the type of guy to hit the books every night, like those who were trying to get promoted the next day. I would go on a thousand patrols before I would study that hard. They came across as impatient and a bit selfish. The Marine Corps allowed me the opportunity to know and understand what it was to hunt another man or to be hunted by another man; you couldn't study for that, you just had to live it. I'd study later. Many mental deviations occurred in order to want to do this. When on duty, things were done in a highly organized fashion and in a ceremonial manner. First, we'd draw our weapons from the armory, then a Change of Command between the two platoons would take place, along with a pass-down of instructions and other formalities, culminating in a march from point A to point B. Upon arriving at point B, post assignments were issued. Then, a slow and time-consuming formal changeover of every post was performed until complete. The off-going platoon was more than ready to be relieved, yet they had to account for and turn in all their weapons and ammunition to the armory.

It was very important that everything was accounted for. If a single round (bullet) was missing from anyone's count, we were told, "If you're missing a round, then bring me a dead body. If you're missing those two items, then get ready to go see the Colonel."

If we somehow didn't produce either of the two items, the Colonel would demote us for destruction of government property. The more senior Marines had it figured out and would purchase rounds of the same caliber, stashing them away to replace any rounds we might happen to lose. We always had someone who needed to lose rank or be disciplined for previous issues; something other than an ass-kicking was needed to do the trick, and this individual was left to fend for himself. It was a dog-eat-dog life.

Patrols

A patrol had its preparatory stage, and it seemed to take the longest. It was hard for me to deal with the anxieties and anticipation; maybe I was just overly excited. First, I had to get psyched, ground myself for a moment, and complete my gear checklist. Then, I would meet with everyone going on the patrol and return to that state of mind, maintaining it for the next few hours. The first time I went on a live patrol didn't seem too real because I hadn't reached a certain level of my psyche; I realized this only during the second time.

That second time, I seemed more scared, but I was actually more in sync with my instincts. My alert level had skyrocketed, my second nature had taken over, and I felt an altered form of concentration.

The command normally gave out the order for a patrol around 1500, which was enough time. Volunteers would join if there were not enough people, then the mandates were issued. For those Marines who were ordered to come along, their best option was to postpone anything going on and hope the other person would understand.

We ate evening chow, conducted another gear check, and a departure time would be given. Knives, water, dummy-cord, first-aid kits, live rounds, and anything else we thought might be needed had to fit snugly to our bodies without being too bulky, as that would slow us down. "Travel light" was part of the concept of a patrol because we needed to move quickly and with stealth; our gear had to fit snug against our bodies, and water canteens had to be topped off; otherwise, they would make noise. When we stopped to drink water, we couldn't leave a canteen half empty. Either drink it all or pour it out. The next few times I went on patrol, I had already bought separate equipment solely for these missions. I put it together to allow me to be more stealthy and agile; without stealth and agility, we might as well just make a campfire and drop leaflets warning anyone that we were on our way.

Rules of engagement applied to us every time we carried our weapons. Many of us in the Marine Corps thought the rules were unjust: shoot only if we fear for our lives or if we feel that we are about to die; don't fire any warning shots; don't shoot to injure if at all possible. The next rule was the craziest one, especially in foreign countries for political reasons, I'm sure: don't fire the first round.

In addition to the hand and arm signals in the Marine Corps training manual, everyone had their own signals, each with its own meaning. There was even a signal for "get your head out of your ass" and one for "cover me, I'm fucked."

I was continually assigned to post with individuals who would do the bare minimum to get through the two or three days we were on duty. Their lackadaisical attitudes pushed me to do more, or I would end up being someone I despised. Soon after I began to feel emotional about being on post, my job took on more meaning, and my excitement elevated to the next level. Finally, a sense of maturity washed over me, and I allowed those who didn't care to remain indifferent, as long as they didn't get in my way.

There were two guys who had been at the weapons station for quite some time, waiting to be discharged. They were good-to-go and very professional; their names were Clever and White. They lived in the same room, and only a few of us knew that they were running a scam involving more than just a few women. I asked Clever, "Hey man, who's going to run your bitches when you leave?"

He gave me a stare as if I had disrespected him and said, "'Cause you're new, Zee, I'm gonna let you slide. But next time, please refer to them as my ladies. Plus, don't go thinking too far ahead of me, 'cause that tends to make things a little more complicated for me.

I wanted to volunteer, but my knowledge of their line of work (running bitches) was minimal, so I left things as they were. In the end, I think he took his ladies with him.

CHAPTER 5

BOOTS

Every eight weeks, the Command received new Marines from Security Forces schools that trained us for these duties. The whole nine yards had been administered to them. The newer Marines were referred to as "BOOTS," not just at this duty station but worldwide; it is the term "BOOTS" used, though not everyone chooses to use it for their own reasons. I never liked using the word because it gave me a sense of false power over them without giving the new guys the benefit of the doubt. "Salty-dog" was the word referring to those Marines who had put in some time (blood, sweat, and tears). This may not be the exact definition behind the term, but I'll leave it as is for now.

From the new group of Marines who came in, I met Spritz from PA. He was as crazy as they come, the life of the party; he had a way with the ladies. It became no task for him; there was no strategy on how to approach them. At any given time or place, he just reached for one of the nicer-looking ladies, and they would follow. Women were always around, now even more. Everyone started to get to know each other, old and new; after a while, we were just like brothers.

Every weekend, I would call my girlfriend and talk for a while.

She told me how things were going back home and everything else. A lot of what was told to me didn't always pan out, but I couldn't worry about her too much because I knew that soon one of us would break.

I needed to be able to come and go more freely and decided to purchase a car; there was no stopping me. Different girls, state to state, serving my country to the letter. Spritz, Piver, Knightengale, and others loaded up the vehicles, and off we'd go to almost anywhere up and down the East Coast, spending the weekend partying with lines of ladies—clubbing, swimming, boating, cruising the streets, and drinking.

We were driving back to the barracks from a weekend at the beach, and the EMS Team was at the chow hall; we knew nothing of what went on. Later, the word was: "This guy shot himself because of a Dear John letter from back home." I was worried that it may have been one of my Marines. As hammered as I was that evening, I went around and conducted a headcount to see if it was any of the guys from my training class. This wouldn't have made a difference, but at the time, it seemed like it did. Overall, it was a distressed brother who cried out in need of help.

The day came when I was so tired of this long-distance love that it had to stop. As I was up to no good, I gave her an ultimatum: Come live with me, or it's over. She said she was staying, and so it was over. I kind of knew her answer before I asked; it was just my way of getting results.

This was sometime in early June of 1989. On that day, I began to write a journal. An entry was made almost daily, drunk or sober. If I wasn't able to make an entry before going to sleep or passing out, I'd make a note mentally or physically to do it later. If this meant staying in and writing it over a few beers or twelve, it just didn't matter.

CHAPTER 6

THE JOURNALS

JUNE 14, 1989: This day is when it really started. A few guys who had become very good friends helped me. We took the idea from the process of the daily events of our job: changing of the guard, taking over our command post. A LOG was opened and established; everything that went on or was worth recording was recorded in our daily lives.

I began to LOG events that occurred out of the ordinary soon after we all referred to it as a Journal. Of course, our backgrounds had been learned through our friendships. I don't think anyone on the base had ever done this, so I gave it a try. Whalen was from Queens, NY. His favorite foods were heroes and White Castle burgers; his favorite sport was lacrosse, and because it wasn't as popular, he enjoyed football, but not as much. His dad worked on Wall Street. Among other ways to describe him, he was the most articulate guy I've ever known at this point in my life, especially when he freaked out or lost his temper. For example, when I would ask him a "yes or no" question, his answers would require him to tilt his head, shrug his shoulders, and bend his arms at the elbows at a 90-degree angle, with the palms of his hands open as if he was about to be handed a bundle of firewood.

The gestures on his face were just as detailed, and the same held true if his answer was yes or no; what made the difference in the type of expression was whether it was beneficial for him or not. If it didn't benefit him, he would cringe from the nose down, then close his eyes with a very slow blink, and finally give you his answer. Yet he gave me a briefing on the matter. If his answer was more positive for him, he'd give me a positive expression and plan his immediate future accordingly.

Spritz, from PA, had a twin sister. He was spontaneous and somewhat edgy. Spritz and Whalen were doing their own journals, but they seemed to have dropped the idea within weeks, and we just kept one: mine. I was in charge of it, and at times, they would make detailed entries on what may have occurred.

We had also established an EAL, which was an acronym, as most things were in the military. EAL stood for Entry Access List. On the inside of the cover was a list of names of those who had written access to this book. This idea was taken from the classified, secret, or top-secret documents that would pass through our post, carried by DOD, scientists, or government employees. Other duties included ensuring that anything unauthorized wouldn't make it in or out of the gates, from personnel to vehicles to documentation. The critical area was where only a few were allowed, such as the US Marines, naval officials, scientists, and highly trained personnel who worked on nukes and anything else within the compound.

The first night we went out barhopping, hoping not to be bothered with ID carding, Whalen and I were of age, but Spritz was not. Everything was fine until we got to this bar in historic downtown Charleston. They carded all of us, thinking we had the situation covered. This guy by the name of G-11, who was well over 21, had forgotten that Spritz was carrying his ID card the day before. What Spritz did was tape the two IDs together so that G-11's age would correspond to Spritz's ID, putting Spritz over the age of 21. G-11 was this guy who was kind of goofy looking but very cool. His code name was given to him by the command because his name was somewhat difficult to pronounce. It began with G and had 11 letters. G-11 had one rule: "Don't Piss ME Off; otherwise, we're OK."

We were firm believers that if you're old enough to defend your country, you should be able to party without any hassle from anyone. Our luck seemed to be running out before we even got started on our mischievous adventures. The bar management had confiscated the altered United States Government document, and the question was asked, "Shit, now what?" Lucky for us, another Marine from the Citadel was present, and he stepped in to help us out by claiming that he was our commanding officer, and yes, he was a captain. He told the manager of the club that he could not hold the IDs and must return them to Spritz; by law, that much was true. So it all turned out for the best.

While I was in the bar waiting for Whalen and Spritz to get in, an older woman came up to me and fixed me up with a few drinks; she had been seducing me. I had forgotten for a bit that I was waiting for the other guys. This woman was maybe twice my age and possibly a freak. I'll never know; at this point, I had more important things to take care of.

We had a feeling that we were not wanted there, so we took off to another bar called the Night Life. There was no ID problem this time. There was no one we knew from the barracks, so the coast was clear. In time, the Night Life would become like our home away from home. ["Maybe I should name this book 'What Other Bullshit Can We Get Into Next.'"] We were in the bar drinking, and after a few beers, I said to Whalen, "Hey, I'm stepping out to get some fresh air."

I got outside only to see this one long-haired dude beating the shit out of his 'ole lady. As I staggered, I said to him, "Hey, leave her alone, man; there's no call for that!"

He turned around and yelled at me, "Hey, Squid, you need to turn around and mind your own business."

I would have, but he made one small mistake by calling me a Squid, so I yelled back at him, "Hey, man! I ain't no damn Squid; I'm a United States Marine!"

Then he asked, "What, you want some?"

I was standing there mentally preparing myself for battle. After about 1.33 seconds, the switch was flicked. I said, "I'm right here, big man, and I don't see you making a move."

This all happened while Whalen and Spritz were inside the bar trying to hook up with two girls. There I was, with the steps of deadly force going through my mind. Seconds later, we finally engaged. I delivered the first five, six, or seven blows, and then he began to get the better of me. When I hit him that many times, I think I knocked him out of his dope high. I remember thinking to myself, I need to put an end to this quickly. I started to set him up for a deadly point of contact because I was sure he planned to kill me. Everyone from inside came out to break us apart just in time. One thing we could not forget was that we were trained killers, and this was our disadvantage when we were out with civilians. I understood that if I hurt this man really badly, it could be detrimental to myself and to the Corps. As soon as somebody from the military hurts or kills a civilian, even in the service member's own self-defense, it's going to make the news and maybe even go worldwide. I couldn't afford that, so I then had to control my defeat.

No battle cry sounded; it happened so fast, in about thirty seconds, and the skirmish was over. Weapons weren't drawn; it was purely man-to-man. Spritz took the honors of performing the victory dance only minutes later. The glory ended for me before it even started, but I lived to fight another day. I took that as my victory.

You might ask, "How the hell did I get that many punches off at one time?" In the brotherhood of badasses, there are all kinds of people who know karate, judo, boxing, wrestling, whatever. You may have the opportunity to gain some of that knowledge, and there may come a time to test your skills, which in this case I did.

It ended right there, at least the fighting part of it; they sent us to separate restrooms to get cleaned off. On my way there, someone handed me a Bud Light. The owner went in and sort of interviewed us about the fight because the one with the least acceptable reason was facing banishment from the bar. I told him my story. I don't think he really had a choice because we were patrons of our country as well as of the bar; this other guy had nothing to offer but drugs or even caused the place to get shut down. The code name "The Birdbath" did, in fact, become a place of refuge for us three, and we were well accepted.

The next morning, the day began with a driving class and physical training. I was totally out of it and decided to go back to sleep, knowing that later there would be consequences to pay. Lo and behold, there I was, going up for office hours, Article 15, for not going to my place of appointment. I'm being charged with an unauthorized absence, which may have cost me money, rank, and time. I had the feeling that I would be made an example of to the newer Marines who came in since January of '89.

While I was there facing the colonel, he asked me if there was anything I had to say before he made a decision. I thought about saying something, not knowing what might happen. I said, "Sir, I had an alcohol incident last night." With this certain information that I told the colonel, all the charges were dropped, and there I was in another interview, but this time they were going to send me to some classes on awareness and all that stuff. At best, I kept my rank and money and didn't do any time for the incident. The fight and the ID all happened during this particular weekend, so I still had to answer to the LT for what happened downtown.

The command knew about the ID because when the man at the club wouldn't give back the ID cards, we called in and asked the Sergeant of the Guard for advice. Whalen, Spritz, and I were in front of Lt. Sheppard explaining what went on there. He asked me, "Now, Zavala, since you've been here, it's twice that you've been in a fight. Does drinking make you violent?"

I replied, "No, Sir, but in my short Marine Corps career, I've become more prone to a lot of things that I would, in other cases, not go through or turn away from. And, Sir, how can you live a good life turning away all the time? And, Sir, it has only been one fight."

He looked at me and then said, "Oh, that must be someone else." Well, the day went as scheduled, and we were finally released for liberty into the wild.

The chow hall food had become stale, so I went off base to eat. On my way out, Whalen and Spritz stopped me and jumped in the car. Off we went. What was about to happen, nobody knew. Those were my thoughts every time I went out with these two guys, but that's what was crazy about it. Soon after, it became a necessity to go and create some drama. On our way back that evening, we saw some ladies while driving and asked if they wanted to meet at the next exit. They pulled over, and we met and set up a date for the following Saturday.

We decided not to drink, just cruise, and found more bars to hang out at; I could foresee trouble at these establishments, and some places I would only visit once. We became curious about the locations of these other bars and the type of women patrons they might have to offer us for our pleasures.

I'm going to get back to the more important things, and that was safeguarding the nation. There was this one fire team leader who was a short-timer; he didn't really care about doing things at full force. I took it upon myself to let him know at that moment that I didn't want him as my fire team leader because he was lazy about his duties and responsibilities. He said to me, "Man, be for real, man; this is just a big game." I thought to myself, OK, you and I will have time to straighten up and adjust a few things.

While on duty, someone said they had seen some people in the wood line. Routinely, Marines are sent to check it out. The chosen ones were my trusty fire team leader, the short-timer, and me.

We got the location of the sighting to investigate; he allowed protocol to get away from him and put me in danger by doing everything wrong. Not being tactical or anything, I was madder than I was scared, but as duty was calling, I did take an oath.

I was saying to myself that if and when I made it out of here, I was going to kick his ass. However, I figured this guy had way more seniority over me, so they wouldn't budge on my complaints or any accusations of his negligence. I just let things slide and pressed on. I did tell him that even I could see he was not being tactical enough and that if he put me in danger like that again, he'd have some explaining to do.

"You know you're probably one of the luckiest men I've come across in my short months of being in the Marines because I haven't whipped your ass for putting me in danger, and since you're a short-timer, you might get out of here unscathed." Some of the things I said were somewhat stupid, but at least I said something.

I was too bold for him to try anything; he understood after he found out that I had a reputation. Still, the reputation that followed me needed to be adjusted to where it would do me more good than bad.

Sgt. O'Riley was another person who tried to break me. I think he thought things were going smoothly and did not want a change in his routine. He took it upon himself to see if he could change me instead. He started by placing me on the sorriest post. He told me, "Zavala, I don't know what you expect from being a Devil Dog, but I have had several complaints that you threaten Lance Corporal Askew, and I don't want to hear that again."

I told him, "Askew is a short-timer and doesn't give a shit about his responsibilities, so if you're going to put me on his team, expect there to be some differences between Askew and me."

He said, "Don't try me, Zavala. I'm not kidding." I didn't care; I took that with a grain of salt and wasn't bothered by it at all.

Deep in my mind, I knew that through the coma, I had reached certain depths of the mind that no one there had. I thought, "If I could get this far in life, I didn't see why anyone would half-ass their way through anything." Of course, I wasn't going to tell anyone about my situation; I might have been kicked out. I picked up a few skills from other fellow Marines and thought it would be better for me to learn how to handle a knife. I learned what I could to have an advantage over anyone who knew nothing about the weapon. One doesn't just stab and jab with a knife; it helps if it's held properly, and if you know the basics, then you're that much better. I've read a few things about knives and felt comfortable with them. A Marine at the barracks knew a little more than the average Joe; he took me under his wing and taught me a few additional techniques with the knife. I consider the knife to be the last line of defense, as it can be carried almost anywhere. Because it's one of the most primitive weapons, everyone should reasonably know the basics of handling one.

The deal that took place between Askew and me was considered by Sgt. O'Riley to be an act of insubordination. I felt Sgt. O'Riley was digging deep for any reason to set me straight or to boast his authority. My punishment for the insubordination towards my Fire-team Leader was to serve at the vehicle inspection check station, which was really okay. "How could I get over on these guys?" was a definite thought. I decided to just do my job and not let them break me down mentally as time went on.

One day, while on the same post, an engineer came by, drunk as hell and not very aware of what was going on. I had a job to do: to inspect every incoming vehicle for explosives or weapons. After I saw that he wasn't complying with my request, I was forced to put him on his face and call it in as a security violation.

When the Reaction Team arrived on the scene, they freaked out because they thought I had taken it too far by putting him on his face while I had my weapon drawn. The leader of the Reaction Team went up to help the poor man to his feet, but he jumped back at the surprising reek of stale alcohol. I made up a little story in case they might question me later.

Before I knew it, Sgt. O'Riley was making an example of my performance. Finally, I asked him, "Sgt. O'Riley, would you please not use me as an example due to our differences and a lack of support from you?" A remark like that landed me back on the same post—the same old sorry post. I knew that as long as I stood my ground, I would continue on the shitbird post, so I did. "That which didn't kill me would kill them for not killing me." Ultimately, they would break down and move me to a different post, and maybe then it wouldn't be so bad.

Sweet revenge was on its way. Like before a rainstorm, the way it smells of moisture, I can't describe the smell of revenge, but I knew it was on its way—maybe it was just a foresight. For some reason, I was taken off the shittier post and placed onto a slightly better one. At least I was out of the sun and the harsh elements, sweating my ass off, usually dehydrated, but it was much worse during the winter. What made my situation even worse was that the only water available to drink was past warm and closer to hot. It didn't seem fair at all because I had more seniority and rank than many of the guys at the barracks, and they were in air-conditioned rooms or trucks while I was stuck with the fucking elements.

By this time, the barriers had been broken, and I had developed enough character to deal with the elements. The rest were only games played by the not-so-high-ups. I was on the vehicle inspection post for a month, trying to find some advantage to keep myself out of their games. Because even when misery is your friend, everyone is considered a non-friendly. The games became old, but I found myself on truck patrol and was making the very most of it.

CHAPTER 7

PAYBACK

I spent some time on another post after being moved about a week prior, and while on my night-shift patrol of my assigned area, I encountered a brother from the South called Volts. A radio check was done, and everything was okay. Around 10:00 p.m., Volts and I noticed a light that would move from one place to another every 10 seconds or so. As we drove up to investigate, it began to look less and less like just a light; the sounds of rotors were becoming louder and louder. To both of us, it seemed strange to hear an aircraft hovering in the distance because we were in a restricted airspace zone.

At first, we thought it was far from our location, but we realized that it was just over the wood line, out of the immediate area. The road was near the outermost fence line, about 20 meters away, and the wood line was another 5 meters beyond that. We proceeded toward the area; I called it in as a security violation, and Sgt. O'Riley, over the radio, called me to his location, which was at the command post. When Volts and I arrived on scene, he proceeded to tell me in a loud tone of voice, "Zavala, I put you on a better post, and look, you fuck it all up by making a reintroduction like this! You really need to stop, or next time we're out here, I'm sticking you back on the Vehicle Inspection Post!"

We argued like fools; no one wanted to give in, and he looked at Volts as if he were asking, "Do you really expect me to believe this shit?" Volts even told him, "Sgt. O'Riley, he's not lying to you; we did see something that called for a security violation." Sgt. O'Riley said, "Okay, guys, just get back on post and do your jobs better."

Meanwhile, the aircraft was still hovering in the same location. The command post was about a half mile from the wood line, and the light of the helicopter looked just like a star from that distance, so we could not point it out from the command post. Volts and I went back to doing our jobs. We were parked in the middle of the street, staring this helicopter down. To make it more official, I called in the Roving Vehicle to cover our area. After a few minutes, I began to feel nauseous; the hairs on the back of my neck began to rise. I think I was ready for battle. Suddenly, we were lit up with a very high beam of light, so with our Mag-lights, I ordered Volts to do the same. These Mag-lights were about the size of a mailbox and pretty bright. At this point, the nauseous feeling was gone, and the adrenaline set in. Volts, being a Third Degree Black Belt in Karate, was surely in his own combat-ready state of mind.

I got on the radio and called a security violation while Volts maintained the beam of light on the aircraft. He rolled under the truck for cover, exposing himself just barely, still able to fire only if fired upon. Sgt. O'Riley again instructed me toward his location, giving us a bigger ass chewing. He went on for not even a minute; as soon as he paused, I started to call the Colonel, then Sgt. O'Riley stopped me, and just about that time, the helicopter flew overhead in the restricted area. A look of fear and disbelief came over Sgt. O'Riley's face, as if he wanted to say, "Please don't kick my ass after I lose my rank." Other Marines had him on the same shit list, and he feared that I was in power at this point. When he was yelling at us, there were other Marines who witnessed the aircraft do a flyby at the exact time that Sgt. O'Riley was preoccupied with his thoughts. Other Marines were freaking out over how Sgt. O'Riley was reacting.

I was pissed and said, "You see all these guys freaking out about what might have happened here? You put all of us in grave danger, and that's why I was going to beat the shit out of Askew. When I get off duty, I'm going straight to the Captain and then to the Colonel, and that's going to do it for you." The pleasure of seeing him tremble in fear of losing his rank—especially due to me, on behalf of his fuck-up—was the best thing that happened for me there. I also explained to Sgt. O'Riley what was going on during the time I called a security violation, and he was even more surprised by what he was hearing.

I threatened to turn in both my weapon and ammo cards and go to the Colonel to be relieved of my duties, out of harm's way. O'Riley understood that if I did, it would be followed by a big investigation. He said, "Look, Zavala, if you want to go on post seven, I'll put you there or on any post you want; just don't bother the Colonel on this." O'Riley had several wild cards, and he was trying to get me to accept one of them, but I remembered it was a big game, and I just kept playing.

I played along as if I was still upset (in fact, I was still upset), but knowing that I was calling the shots felt much better, and having other people meet my demands was great. I told Sgt. O'Riley, "When do you have time to meet with the Colonel, or should he just pull your rank from your collar whenever he sees you? Let me know, and I'll tell him what's more convenient for you. If you think I'm going out like that and not firing or having a chance to return fire, you're not very smart."

Don't get me wrong; I was ready for anything, and we were always in harm's way; that was our lifestyle. But when someone can prevent a situation, it feels trusting when everyone does his part. After our week of duty, I slept off some of my anger. Things were cool, but I was somewhat calling my own shots. Soon, I agreed to his peace offerings, and I would have reneged if things would not get better for me under his command.

Post 07 was where everyone wanted to be because ladies would come and visit, and we didn't feel so cooped up. Post 07 was the main gate to the base. Spritz duties were in the less critical area during this tour and were not where this incident took place. (I can't give any further information in detail at this time.) Whalen had been bragging to Spritz,

"Man, you should have been there; Zavala had Sgt. O'Riley pinned up against the wall, chewing his ass out after Sgt. O'Riley fucked up."

It never failed: when something of this magnitude went down, the words that came from Spritz's mouth were, "Well, guys, who's buying? If no one wants to, I'll get the first round or two." We headed out to this place just outside the gate, a few miles away. I didn't know what was wrong with us because, at the E-club on base, there was one of the most beautiful strawberry redheads I had ever seen, but we had to get away. There, we discovered the oldest trick in the book: the hustle. The bar owner would have some fine-looking girls asking to sit and talk as if they were interested, then ask us for drinks just to get up and leave for the next table, just to give the bar their business. I saw this move applied on the sailors next to us. This chick tried that shit on me, and I played her for the fool she thought I was. She ended up buying us a few rounds after finding out that we were from the Weapons Station.

So far, I had been on just about every post there; I pretty much had a handle on everything that went on, and I'd held every position there was for the reaction team. I would guess this part was one of the secrets I swore never to reveal about the positions on the Reaction Teams and posts because it could and would be detrimental to national security. I hadn't written too much, if anything, about these other posts because not much went on there, so it was cool.

Out on the town, we had women as our entourage every time we let them know we were going out. Piver and Knightengale were still around; in fact, they had these ladies out in their apartments at their beck and call. Either they got stuck in another platoon, or I got stuck in the wrong platoon. We still saw one another about once a week.

Earlier that day, Lou and I met these girls just a few miles outside the gate and set up a date with them. The next evening, as we were waiting for these girls to give us that important call, Whalen and Spritz hated the fact that we were going out with these girls, and one of the two said, "Man, just give up and get ready to go out to the bath."

Spritz could have had either one, but he wouldn't do us that way. These girls called a little later, and our hope was regained; they apologized for not calling earlier, saying they had been somewhere, I think at their grandparents'.

This was the first time Lou and I had taken some girls out together, and our signs had not yet been established. There we were: I was in the back seat with this girl's friend while Lou and his girl were in the front seat. We were all talking as a group, but when it broke down to two on two, I was lost for words. The pressure was on because I had never been briefed on the matter. Lou had just asked me to go with him because the girl didn't want to go alone, and that's why she took her friend.

As soon as I felt stuck or at a loss for words, I tried to make my move. She said to me, "Let's slow down, Big John," then just pecked me on the cheek, and then she had to ask, "Aren't you going to ask me a few questions first?" I said, "No, that's too cliché; I like originality." Then she played it off by laughing it off.

I asked Lou to pull over at the next lit area on the shoulder of the road. Of course, he asked why as he was pulling over. I pulled the girl out of the car and said to her, "You're very pretty, and I'm attracted to you. Now what's wrong with that?"

She said, "Nothing."

"Well, that's plenty to work with. But whatever happens tonight, if you don't see me for another four, five, or six weeks, don't take it personally. It's because I work for the government. I can almost bet you and I would win that I would be thinking about you the whole time I was without you." It seemed to have broken the ice between the two of us; I didn't exactly know how that would work for me, so I waited to find out.

Afterward, the pressure was gone, and conversation was flowing. Then she asked me the loaded question: "Do you date much?"

"Not at this time," I said, leaving it open for her to back up or proceed, but she didn't believe me. Lou tried to convince her since he was almost fully aware of my situation and how the politics of our work were getting the best of us, but she apparently just came to browse because she wasn't buying my story. That was the only time I'd seen her.

Lou said to me later that she thought I was too much of a freak because of the lines I used. "Man, I didn't hit her with any lines. I was stuck for the first time since I've been here because she's so hot. I didn't know what to say, so I just played with what I had at the moment, and sometimes it just pays to say what you feel."

His reply was, "She told me to tell you that she's sorry; she doesn't want to get hurt."

I asked, "Hey Lou, are you still going to see that girl?"

He said, "Yes." There was still a little hope, but as I tried, she still refused. I came to the conclusion that I wasn't going to wait around for women all my life, or at least while I was in the Marines. After that, what could I do except move on?

Prior to meeting these girls, we told Whalen and Spritz that we'd meet them afterward at the "Bird Bath." The owner remembered me, and by this time, he and Whalen had been shooting the breeze a while, kind of exploiting us. We walked in, and Whalen was the first person I saw; then everyone else was just carrying on. I thought, oh shit, that's it for us here.

On the contrary, he told me while kind of laughing, "Thank you for the other night because that guy who was kicking your ass—we were looking for a reason to get him banned from here." As he was thanking me, he beckoned this girl toward our position and said to me, "Just for that, I give you my favorite girl." She got closer and closer and flashed me her tits, and I thought to myself, "It's on now." I knew it was VIP time for us, and I was on good terms with the owner.

We spent a few minutes talking, and I noticed the necklace she wore; it belonged to me. I had to gather my thoughts so I could get back what was rightfully mine. During the fight I had the other night, I lost the necklace my girlfriend had given me for Christmas. I asked this girl if she didn't mind waiting one second while I went to change plans with my buddies. But I really went to ask Whalen and Spritz to verify if that was my necklace. I knew that it was my necklace, but before undertaking such a task, I needed to verify the evidence. Spritz and Whalen walked over to our location and played along. Either Whalen or Spritz jokingly asked, "Take care of this man, okay? You may not know it, but he's vital to National Security."

I introduced them to the girl; they said hi and confirmed that the necklace was, in fact, mine by using a duress signal we had established moments before.

It was really on this time; the plan went as scheduled. I asked her if she wanted to go to this other club. She said yes, and on the way there, we were making out. As one thing led to another, I was pounding that shit as if I had a conjugal visit in jail. Shortly thereafter, I got my necklace back, got rid of the chick, and was back at the party immediately after I accomplished my mission.

Sometimes we just had to get away from it all. Since we'd been going to this bar, we had yet to see another Marine from the barracks, which meant to us that no one knew of its existence. The stress level from our duties was high; we were always trying to save our own asses from nothing. The military governs itself mostly by the Commanding Officer; they made up shit to burn us. "Burn" was the term used instead of getting in trouble or going up for Office Hours; they would take our rank for the slightest occurrence, and because of that, many troops didn't like it there.

Back on duty, Sgt. O'Riley and I finally had a mature conversation. It began when I asked him about a book on the Marine Corps, where I had seen a group photo of him in one of his old platoons while they were training in some jungle.

He turned to me in a proud way and said, "Zavala, that was in my earlier days when it was a lot different."

"What do you mean different?" I asked.

"Were things new to you? Were you excited?" he nodded as I kept asking questions.

"Well, can't you let me be excited? Because things are new to me. The only difference I think there is that you now have a little more rank, seniority, and more responsibilities. How do I get to there," I pointed to his rank, "from here without doing what I'm doing now? Someday I'll be in the field just like you were, and I'll get a good taste of the Fleet."

We talked a bit longer about other things, then shook hands and carried on with our immediate responsibilities. From that moment on, we had an understanding.

A Marine named Bresso was on Post-07 during this tour of duty.

He surprised most of us when a civilian began talking smack to him. Bresso was too clean-cut of a guy; he didn't ever piss people off. Rarely does someone seem to think that by talking shit to us, they can change our protocol in handling situations.

If anyone tried to enter and proceed beyond Post-07 without proper authority or the necessary updated badges, they would be intercepted by a group of pissed-off Marines who were always ready to react to minor situations. Some guy gave Bresso some shit about his badge.

"Sorry, sir, your badge has expired. Please proceed to the blue building across the street to have another one made for entry."

Bresso knew his procedures and had a way of doing his job that was different from mine, but he got things done. This guy responded, "What if I don't want to?"

Bresso was very professional, always in compliance with the rules and using the proper military gestures. At Post-07, it was very important to be squared away; it demanded the utmost discipline and required knowing how to deal with the public.

Bresso calmly and smoothly told this man, "Well, sir, then my friend and I might have to take some serious action to prevent you from getting past me." I guess the man still felt a little jumpy and asked, "Yeah, what friend?"

"Oh! I have this friend named Beretta." He glanced down at his 9mm. "And just a few months ago, I qualified as an expert shooter. If you would like to take your chances, then by all means, take them." At the same time, Bresso stepped back, placed his right hand on his 9mm, and stared the man down. The driver knew what he was up against.

I don't know whether it was intimidation or respect that backed off people like this, but No meant No. You will comply because we weren't there for anyone to just do what he or she wanted with us. Most of us wanted something to break the monotony, and we had a plan just in case we were tested.

Post-duty formations were held around 0800, and simultaneously, we planned our off-duty activities: haircuts, going to the cleaners, and getting things done so we could relax for a few days. Although we were instructed not to do things in a routine fashion, some guys did; they took the whole thing for granted, thinking terrorists wouldn't catch them, but other forms of trouble would.

Later that night, I walked into the bar and ordered my beer. I went to the bathroom, and on my way back, this chubby guy said, "Hey, man."

I stopped and said hi. We had a short conversation, and I bought him a beer. During our talks, he told me his story about going to boot camp at Parris Island and how the DI broke this guy's leg or maybe caused him to break it. I told him, "Man, I wish you could have come on this ride of life with us; I think you would've enjoyed it."

I bought him another beer and went back to the bar. A few beers later, I found myself back at the restroom. But before I could make it there, this same guy stopped me and said to a chick, "Hey, I want you to meet my friend; he's a US Marine." That was all he said, and instantly that girl was all over me.

I include this to remember that being a United States Marine had countless benefits. If I had not joined, there are countless things I would not have done or had the opportunity to do. Best of all, I will never wake in the morning wishing I should have joined the Marines when I was younger.

Tommy's Sports Bar was a sports bar on the backside of a shopping plaza. There was this Marine who taught me a little bit of karate before he left the service. He introduced me to the people he knew, and for the most part, I blended in with the guys at TN's. I don't remember its real name; we talked in codes when we went out, and I don't think the actual name of the bar was ever mentioned.

I visited another bar a few nights after my fight at the Birdbath, drawn by the news that someone had been shot and killed there. I wanted to see that kind of chaos up close. I think we were on post the night of that killing.

Two guys who clicked with us were Pugh, code-named "Smallpox," and Williams, code-named "The Sucka." There was no specific reason for the code names; we just got accustomed to changing things up like that.

Whenever we went on post, we'd chat about our weekend adventures until we suddenly found "Smallpox" and "The Sucka" rolling with us. Both Whalen and I figured that if something went down, these guys needed to be briefed and warned because things could always go sideways.

Whalen mentioned that Williams, "The Sucka," was on post with him during this tour of duty and was interested in coming along. I don't think he believed all the stories Whalen told. The bystanders who went out with us hadn't established the necessary duress signals, nor did they have a secondary means of egress. In the end, I didn't want to find myself saying, "We should've had a plan."

Whenever they joined us, we had to revise our exit strategy for those two. Briefings took place right before unloading the vehicles. They were instructed to head to a specific area and wait for our calls for further instructions. Everyone carried a copy of the keys to the car we'd drive that night. We figured, why tarnish their records, especially since "The Sucka" was on the waiting list for Jump School, which was his main focus, aside from body-building competitions. We always joked with him, saying, "Man, with those chicken legs, you ain't gonna win anything." He started working them out and was consistent.

I'd like to think he returned to California when it was all said and done at the Naval Weapons Station, as that was home for him.

CHAPTER 8

JUMP-SCHOOL

Sunday night was soon upon us. I had beer in hand, my drinking buddies came into my room, and we went out to another club; we got kind of tore up. The next morning, we had to go PT (physical training), and for some of us, it was time for the Jump School qualification test, which consisted of 20 push-ups, 12 pull-ups, 80 sit-ups in two minutes, and a two-mile run. No, not "The Sucka"; he had secured a spot for himself on the qualification exam before this one. I aced them all, but I don't remember most of the qualification test. I snapped out of my drunken state of mind at the last part of my run.

I recall one of the pacers saying, "Come on, Zavala, you're almost there, about four hundred meters to go." I was tired, dehydrated, and about to quit. At times, we would stay out all night or until a few minutes before formation, living life like there was no tomorrow. The pacer was yelling at me to just keep running. I finished fourth out of 19 other runners, and it went down in the books.

Lt. Sheppard was surprised to see me so soon. After all, I reeked of booze, as did others, but these guys had not reached the finish line.

During our training days, we would fire weapons, rappel from the rappel towers, or go over some hostage-taking procedures; exciting things. Other times, it was just for the not-so-high-ups who were in charge to come up with their head games for us to play. Many days, the stress level was so intense, what was there left for us to do? I didn't know. I tried working out, running, taking walks, going to church, and many other things. I needed answers immediately; I couldn't wait for an act of God, and I couldn't wait for the higher-ups to stop playing God.

There was one time when this other marine was charged for being absent for formation: UNAUTHORIZED ABSENCE. He burned, but his excuse was, "I was doing something for the Colonel." Even though he was, they gave no mercy. The colonel himself took that man's rank and morale. Again, Lt. Sheppard called for me and ordered me to surrender my weapons and rounds card. He really thought I needed help controlling my drinking.

I was then ordered to Captain Usherson's office, and he said to me immediately after reporting that he had read a report on me and that it was outstanding except for a minor discrepancy. "Zavala, you enjoy drinking a bit too much." He was sending me to a psychiatrist to have me evaluated.

I knew for sure I wouldn't be doing the normal everyday activity. What's more, I may not be doing anything at all, and that kind of worried me. The following day, I was told to report to Sgt. Tidwell's office to receive more instructions. "Zavala, you're coming to my platoon now, and we'll keep you busy." He was in charge of one more able person, and for him, it was less work for him to do, fat lazy bastard.

Prior to leaving the platoon, I spoke to Sgt. O'Riley. He said, "Zavala, I didn't know you made the list for FAST and you didn't accept the invite. You've made the Jump School list, and who knows if you'll go there? But if I can help, I will. I'll get you back if it's OK with you." I told him, "Sgt. O'Riley, sometimes you only get one chance. You should've read my record book earlier, but how did you get the other information?" Not everything about me was in my Service Record Book. "Zavala, you love this shit, don't you? Someone told me." He never said who, but I kind of knew it was either Piver or Knightengale;

those were the only two guys I ever mentioned it to, and maybe Vega. I remember Knightengale said that I was stupid for not accepting FAST.

I mentioned earlier that in an Infantry unit, we police our own. I'm sure it's true in different units. What I meant by this was if there is a problem, we try to handle it among ourselves. If all else fails, we take it up through the ranks and let the higher-ups handle it.

Other than great friends and a very well-established sense of camaraderie, one can say that we see one another as an insurance policy. With some, you feel more protected and know they provide better coverage, while others will do only what it takes to get by, careful they don't get into any trouble and mastering the skills of befriending you only when they need good short-term coverage.

Suppose that you're in a situation and you get shot. The only one to help you is another marine, but he's overweight, and he can't handle both of you. He ends up getting both of you killed; that's as good as him cheating your mother, father, brother, sister—the entire family. Let's say that the roles are reversed, and the fat marine is down while the fit marine is carrying him out of danger. On the way out, they get shot. You can't help but wonder, if only he was lighter, could they have made it further out of harm's way? The man next to you might become your insurance policy, so you better discipline each other.

Sgt. Tidwell didn't really want to do anything, only what was relayed down to him from the higher-ups; he wasn't much of a thinker, just a doer. He was a nice guy and treated others like he would want to be treated. He followed every rule to the letter; most of all, he cared for the most important thing in his life, which was his family. That's the way an ideal American man should be, but leadership traits are paramount, and physical fitness wasn't too far behind.

That day at 1300, I was scheduled for an appointment to see a Naval doctor for a psych evaluation. I was waiting and talking to Spears, the driver. We talked for a little while about what his plans were when he got out of the Corps; higher education was his thing.

I heard my name over the intercom; it was the doctor. He introduced himself to me as I walked into his office and proceeded to interrogate me. "Do you know where you're at? What date and day is it?"

I said to him, as I sniffed around a bit, "Wow! What stinks, Doc?" He lost his concentration momentarily and said to me that he didn't smell anything. I understood that my meeting here allowed me a certain degree of amnesty, so I told him, "Well, let's cut the crap because you know I have the answers to all your minor questions." Then he asked if I had done any drugs. "Are you insane, Doc?" I answered. "I'm sure you know I'll burn if I do drugs."

So much for a good start; he then informed me that Capt. Usherson thought I had been hallucinating. "Sir, I may be the one terminating this evaluation. If these bogus questions continue, and Capt. Usherson is blowing this all out of proportion, you're on the same path and getting there fast."

He backed off and asked, "What about this imaginary friend of yours? Tell me about him."

"Sir, we all had them while growing up, and if you say no, I'll have to call you on that one."

He asked more questions, and I answered. He then concluded with, "Zavala, you're not crazy." He talked some more and repeated himself. "Zavala, you're not crazy." I replied, "Sir, I'm not deaf either."

"OK, Zavala, you're not crazy. In your Marine Corps career, where would you like to be?"

"In the FLEET," I said proudly. "You don't know what you want. The Fleet is tough; it's hard. You don't want that. I've been there, and I've seen some of the toughest become humble." I thought this guy was out of line; first of all, who the fuck was he to tell me what I wanted? God, I think it's safe to say he thought his rank was so mighty that it led him to think he was above those subordinates to him in every way—not this time.

I felt compelled to say something, and I did, "Sir, in the ads they have for the Navy, they don't include swabbing the decks as part of the great adventure, do they? I was sold on being out in the field, cammied up. I didn't know that places like this existed as duty stations for Marines. In boot camp, the DI's make better men from the civilians they receive, then for the Department of the Navy to send us to places like this to make us soft again. It's not for me, Sir."

He was pissed, maybe because I badmouthed the Navy; deep inside, I was cracking up. He asked me if that's what I wanted. "I'll get you shipped, son."

I replied with a simple, "Thank you, Sir, that's all I want. Give me the chance, and I'll do the rest." On the way out, I mumbled, "Tell Mom I said hi, OK? Bye, Dad."

I left there happy; down deep inside, I think it had become a learning experience for him, and he probably thought that I was crazy after all.

On the way back, Spears asked me why I was yelling at the officer. I explained. Spears then mumbled, "Man, you're a crazy motherfucker." I wasn't allowed to return to duty until I took care of some issues, as they might have put it; I simply called them things.

Weeks had gone by, and seclusion was taking its toll on me; the long weekends especially. I couldn't go out while the rest of my platoon was on duty. Spritz was thrown to the wolves with another platoon, but that was positive for him because he always enjoyed doing new things. He'd come pay me a visit from time to time; we'd play a few hands of cards over his enthusiastic discussion about his new duties.

The days were easy to make it through, but the nights were more difficult. I would find things to keep me mentally occupied. For example, some Marines who didn't have the time to press their uniforms paid me to do it; spit-shining boots was another moneymaker for me. Soon that became tiresome and boring; the sit-ups became so easy for me—500, 600, one night I even did 1,000—and after that, there wasn't much to work for.

I became so restless one night that the idea of going on patrol around the Critical Area came over me. I cammied up and got my personal weapons out and put them on. I had a Mac-10 in my locker, and I had to be very careful; if someone were to hear shots fired, I knew they would have some kind of reactionary force go out to investigate and maybe even take a head count at the barracks. Two daggers, a throwing knife, and a bayonet was all I had. I'd rather be caught by some crazy fucker and die trying to escape instead of being busted and suffering the consequences imposed upon me by the command. It was around 11:35 p.m. when I headed out.

Breaking the barrier was one reason for this patrol; the other was just to do it and get away with it. Before leaving, I wrote a note stating, "If I didn't report to duty, go look for my body out in the outer perimeter of the Critical Area. I had gone on a night patrol alone to see what I could find on my own, and y'all can kiss my ass."

In the morning, or as soon as I returned, I would get rid of the note. If I didn't return, they would eventually read it and act on it, but I wouldn't be around to reap the penalties of my wrongdoings.

The first rule was broken: never go alone. But I had to meet the challenge. To actually see some unauthorized people, get a "Situation Report," and then return to tell a few trusted friends would be great. I hoped they might look in the vicinity the next time they went on duty. Life had indeed become a worst-case scenario for me, and that is what kept me expecting the unexpected.

I was scared and paranoid about being out there alone; it was different. The feeling was eerie, and the fog had begun to settle into the teeth-chattering coldness; luckily, I had my mouthpiece. By this time in the Corps, stories had been told to us by instructors or other more senior Marines, which taught me to be better prepared for times like these. "A Marine lost his finger when his ring was caught in something while training. I highly advise you gents to remove your jewelry or anything of value that may hinder your well-being."

My senses heightened as if my nervous system were on steroids; I waited about twenty to thirty minutes for my night vision to kick in. It was amazing how the slightest sounds could be heard, or the way my eyesight adjusted to any movement while in this particular state of mind. For some reason, I believed this state of mind comes to one when premeditating a death. I felt like a savage, an animal with no soul. I understood that going out there could change, if not end, my life. Mentally, I was ready; spiritually, there was no spirit—it was all character. This was a decision I made to go the extra mile and test myself. It was about survival, and I found myself asking, "What would my cousin Joe do?" He survived Vietnam.

My cousin Joe never spoke to me about his time in Vietnam, and I never asked. To this day, I have never heard him say anything to anyone about it. I let my imagination do its thing. Drill Instructor Staff Sergeant Dixon's conversation about becoming a good leader came to mind, and I thought, "This was one of those things that needed to be done to understand part of what he meant."

The very first time I played hide-and-seek, I couldn't tell how fun it was, but I knew that I liked it, and when we had time, we played over and over again.

Here's the line-edited version of your text, maintaining your style while enhancing clarity and grammatical structure:

That's how exciting this was, but at a much larger scale—slower, at night, and with much more to lose. The word "extreme" came to mind. My gear checklist included my weapon, the three knives, and some dummy cord. I drank enough water before leaving. Three hours later, I returned to the barracks, but not without setting off the Intrusion Detection System sensors, which triggered alarms in the critical area, causing a react team to investigate the perimeter and find nothing. As I evaluated this operation, I found it had more pros than cons.

I was known to everyone on base; some people would say, "Aww man, that dude ain't all there." I heard one guy who trained in Virginia with me say to someone, "But you know him well enough; no one ever fucks with this guy, so there must be something crazy about him. The only people that fuck with him are those who outrank him or people who don't know him, and besides, he was a squad leader at Security Forces School."

Time went by, and things seemed to be going okay, when suddenly they threw me another curveball. I was transferred from 3rd Platoon to MPS, which was totally different from what we did in 3rd with Sgt. O'Riley. At the time, I knew nothing about MPS Platoon except what Spritz had been saying to me. Soon that all changed; I was quickly made aware of how it was structured and how things worked there, collaborating with Department of Defense personnel and Explosive Ordnance Specialists.

I found that people would get bored with this duty station quickly because they failed to keep their minds occupied. I was more than halfway out of Naval Weapons Station; at least I was headed out to the field on other assignments. I didn't realize I would be going to the same platoon Spritz was sent to until I arrived for formation. One would think that trouble was left far behind at this point and wouldn't even interrupt a raw deal such as this MPS transition. The weapons station was about 16 miles away; if anything went down, we were left to defend ourselves by any and every means necessary. The command wanted us to play by the same rules as if assistance was 1,000 meters away; not me—I was always ready for the worst, as I had been at the Critical Area.

At this present duty station, the only people I could really trust were Whalen, Spritz, Piver, Knightengale, Lou, and maybe a few of the newer Marines who were not very experienced. Implementing ideas was okay and all, but when the higher-ups knew of them, they would frown upon it because their system was purely bureaucratic. The way I did things was to get results and not just to keep people happy.

Captain Usherson, other than being ranked as a Captain in the Marines, was nothing more than an administrative bully and carried himself as such. Lt. Sheppard, on the other hand, was more tactful and methodical, but not in a brainwashed way. He seemed more intelligent than the other lieutenants—a hell of an officer—but the Corps has yet to harden him up. When that happens, his presence would speak as loud as his words.

Lcpl. Pender was all mouth for a black dude. "I did this, I did that, and I know this girl and that girl." I found this out when he asked me, "Zavala, why are you always in trouble? It seems like someone is out to get you." I said to him, "Pender, you're always saying you this, that, and the other thing; why don't you give me some advice?"

He bashfully informed me, "Look man, between you and me, I just talk shit so motherfuckers won't mess with me." From then on, he didn't talk shit to me like he normally did whenever I was around, and that said plenty to me.

Pender lived right across the hall from me, and he was wise about what he did know, but didn't know too much beyond those parameters. He seemed to have been a loyal person with a sense of integrity, so I returned it by never repeating his little confession to anyone. It was safe with me as long as he maintained his reputation; I wasn't going to fuck it up for him.

There were two Staff Sergeants: Sanchez, a Cuban, and Diablo, a Puerto Rican. Sanchez was a grunt, fresh out of the Drill Field, and not too far on the overweight side. It would have done him some good to shed a few pounds. I don't think it really mattered what you've accomplished in the Corps; if someone was overweight, their accomplishments seemed to be overshadowed by that factor. But SSgt. Sanchez knew how to deal with subordinates and put his rank aside to help steer us down the right path if needed. SSgt. Diablo was totally different from SSgt. Sanchez—self-centered and a liar. Lcpl. Brewster was tough but afraid to show it; he picked a few friends and only ran with those guys, as if he really didn't want to trust others, but he came through in the end. Sgt. O'Riley was cool off stage and really did care about us, in my opinion. If he stood a few inches taller, it would've been just enough to boost his confidence level to where it needed to be. Although he had done everything to earn most people's respect, being short got the best of him. My way of telling if someone had the right amount of confidence was to get an ass-chewing from them, and after, if it was powerful and impactful, then good; otherwise, there was a lack of confidence. I won't say that I didn't have respect for the man, because I did, but the way he did things didn't simply agree with me. All the ass-chewings and yelling I'd received by this point had some effect on me; only a few others didn't.

Robine, another guy from NY—Jewish, I think—talked a lot of shit. Maybe he could back it up, standing over six feet tall, but I've yet to see him in any action: fighting, lifting, or sports. He lacked the competitive edge that most of these guys had and was a neat freak too.

Here's a guy we needed to watch out for: sneaky backstabbing. I say he was about 5'3", and those were the only ways he knew to get by. Lcpl. Perez was sly with the ladies, also from NY, and not too much more to say about him.

Robledo was from the Valley in Texas; a good friend until he set me up with his sister. It was then that he decided not to be cool with me.

When I took his sister out, I couldn't have been more of a gentleman out of respect for him, but he crossed me afterwards.

Then there was Holy, from Largo, Florida. Out of all the individuals I've described, I would say that Holy and I were most alike in character. I noticed this almost immediately and didn't look further into his character. We would take turns doing daring things just to improve our inner selves and to destroy his good-guy status. I knew if there was any unfinished business to take care of, he would be the one to handle it. I called him (Holy Mike) since his first name was Michael.

Bartonsen and Archie, partners in crime, didn't give a rat's ass; they loved to stay drunk or high and have a good time. Completely different from one another, Bartonsen was from NYC somewhere, while Archie was straight out of the hood in Los Angeles, Pacoima, California—worlds apart.

Ratliff was just enjoying the ride. He did what he had to and moved on—a real well-brought-up guy. Wellerton tried; he really did. He was pretentious and talked a good game, but when it came down to it, he would always end up kicking himself in the ass. I realized this when I put him to the test. I asked him to do something stupid and daring that required some thought. Without any hesitation, he got started on the task right away. Less than halfway through, I warned him to think it out, but he wouldn't listen; I had to interfere. We began to grapple, and he was already winded from the task. It didn't last long before I put him in a wrestling leg lock just to add insult to injury, but mostly to ensure he wouldn't attempt to complete the task. It wasn't in my job description to test people the way I did, but if they were going to hang with the big boys, I had to know if they were true.

People got mad at me because I would test those who dared, but if I hadn't, I don't think anyone else would have. I tried anyone who appeared arrogant to see if they had what it took mentally because, in the heat of battle, I didn't want to be deserted by the ones I trusted.

Lou was Mafia-related, about 5'6" and a bodybuilder. Very cool, calm, and collected—or maybe it was because he had stopped using steroids? Lou was his code name because he mostly resembled a famous bodybuilder; his real name was Poole.

Then there was the Colonel. He wasn't a full bird Colonel yet, but he was the highest-ranking person there. It seemed he wasn't out to burn people after a while. There's one more guy I failed to mention: Cpl. Smith. He was someone I thought had it all together when I first saw him—well, he did until the end. Cpl. Smith was a perfectionist, coming from 2nd Battalion Reconnaissance, and pretty tough, I would guess.

I met this guy in a convenience store parking lot. He yelled out, "Hey Marine, come here! My name is Cpl. Smith. I'm going through the indoctrination classes over at the base. Man, can you set me up with that chick in there? There aren't many girls that turn my head like she did. I saw you kind of made her laugh and spoke to her as if you knew each other, right?"

I played along and did my best to hook him up because I knew he could be my leverage with some of these higher-ups, whom I simply could not reach. Maybe I foresaw Smith as my mentor at one time or another. Now, he owed me one.

CHAPTER 9

DEBRIEFING

Being briefed on the MPS site happened on our drive out to the site in the middle of nowhere. Spritz and I went on post together once again. I had to question, why do I always get stuck with Spritz to go on post? Not that I had anything against it.

The NCO on duty said, "Zavala, I know very little about you, but the other troops have spoken and don't want to go on post with you, so we'll leave it at that, OK?"

I sat back and tried to make good sense of that small bit of intelligence, and I had to be positive about it so that I wouldn't be preoccupied while on duty.

At the entrance of MPS Site III, there was a big tree. During the briefing, we were told, "At times you may see an apparition of some sort; others thought they were slaves who had been lynched and hanged to their death from that tree." I worried for a while; soon it grew on me, and I finally accepted it as part of MPS.

My call sign was given to me as we drove beyond that big old tree. The radio was handed to me, and I conducted a radio check as 93-Foxtrot. An inventory of the post changeover had been taken, and all the ammunition and gear were accounted for: 3 grenades, 1 M-60 machine gun with a round count of 1,000, 2 Beretta 9mms with a round count of 90, and 1 mag-light. A function check was performed to assure that all weapons functioned properly, only after everything had been counted piece by piece by both teams. Still, we had to make sure at the end of our shift that we had our personal weapons and ammo.

After a few days to a week, things began to run smoothly for me; we would go on post just like normal folks for about a month. We began to think that a routine was finally forming for us, no one messing with us, and we thought, "Being placed on this post was the best thing to happen to us."

I went on duty during the late hours, and again we found ourselves with another problem. I freaked out because it was the first power outage I had ever experienced there at MPS Site III. The power of the mind is what I learned that night; someone had been watching us and used the power outage to move in closer, and in fact, I came right up to him. My mind had blocked out the several seconds leading up to this moment to focus every fragment of my attention on the present. It took about a tenth of a second to register, and then my training or second nature took over. My weapon was drawn, aimed straight at his chest.

Uncertainty was about ten feet in front of me. Maybe he saw me as his uncertainty, dressed in dark-colored clothing, his face concealed. I noticed as I drew my weapon that he paused; he looked to his left, then his right, then focused on me for a second or two before he turned about-face and took off running. I started after him but aborted. I called out to Spritz and told him what had happened; he seemed to be in denial. He kept saying, "No way, no fucking way, man." But at the same time, I was showing him the boot tracks. I explained and proved to him that those tracks didn't match his boots, nor did they match the pair I was wearing.

This guy didn't expect to be compromised, and I don't think he had a backup plan. He was there to either gather information or cause us some damage. He stopped dead in his tracks and tried to figure out his next move. He couldn't go right because eventually he would find himself against Spritz, and I think Spritz would have taken him down.

He couldn't go left because he would have run into a small structure. His two alternatives were back the way he came from or to deal with a 9mm Beretta and me. I think we both understood our odds, and his were much greater. If he was to progress from this stalemate, he risked getting himself shot and/or arrogantly moving toward me, hoping for a misfire. This would have led to the next level, which was close-quarters combat; we would have ended up either hurt or dead. If my theories were correct, then he avoided action due to the knowledge of a Marine's combat readiness or as an order.

I couldn't bring myself to believe that someone had gotten that close to us while standing post. The time Volts and I were confronted by the helicopter, the feelings I had were similar but intensified many times over; nothing compared to this. A sense of confusion, chaos, and fear transformed from the adrenaline that came over me during the near possibilities of combat, but I quickly had to regain composure and evaluate the situation. Still, I had to rid myself of the savage-like feeling and withdraw from that character to think better and more rationally. We decided not to call it in and to go into CODE RED on the alert level. Afterwards, I only mentioned this on two other occasions to Whalen and now as I write this. We didn't tell Whalen until the situation presented itself, and if it hadn't, then Whalen was not going to find out.

Deadly force is that force which is used for the purpose of causing, or should be reasonably known to cause, the likelihood of death or serious injury or bodily harm. That definition is straight out of the USMC SecForcBatt, Naval Base, Norfolk, Virginia 23511-5697 Student Outline, and I never took this definition any more seriously; which meant to me if I feared for my life or if I had been fired upon, then I could have used deadly force; otherwise, it would have been a simple routine. If he had progressed, then the game would have had different rules; the rules change with every situation. Cpl. Rhae, usually our NCO on duty, arrived on scene with our relief. We closed the log for our tour of duty with one entry that stated:

Post Log for MPS SITE III

TIME 23:50: MPS SITE III is secure, and Lcpl. Zavala, along

with PFC Spritz, have taken charge of this post and are relieving the outgoing sentries.

. . . Time Unknown: MPS Site III experiences a power failure and has informed D.O.D. dispatch.

. . . Time 0545: Sentries Lcpl. Zavala and PFC Spritz have nothing further to report at this time and are being relieved by PFC Stevance and Lcpl. Winn.

Close page.

End of duty Lcpl. Zavala . . .

Cpl. Rhae was very punctual; the other sentries relieved Spritz and me around 0545. I could set my watch to Cpl. Rhae's punctuality more than half the time. He was an alright person; he lacked style, but I guess he was okay with that. He brought his own game to the card table. There were times he could have written us up, but he turned away as if he saw nothing. Who knew? Maybe by that time he had spoken to Sgt. O'Riley and decided to work with us instead of against us.

I think about it now, and maybe he thought there might come a day when he'd need a wild card and would hold us to all the "let goes" he'd done for me. I think we all had a little dirt that shouldn't have been noticed. The reason for our presence was to protect the nation from harm by beings, foreign or domestic. Who knows? He may still be in the Corps, and I wouldn't want to jeopardize any positive goings-on with him in his career, although he always talked of leaving the Corps.

A few days went by, and we ended up going to the Birdbath. While we were having a few cold ones, a man I had never seen before asked me, "Hey, Zavala, want to sell me some arms?"

I tripped out and kind of stalled, slowly piecing it together. I thought to myself, "The guy out on post the other night, maybe it was him." It was a thinking man's game, and I had to be fast, so I responded to him, "What exactly are you looking for?" He said, "What can you get me?" I became a little aggressive at this point and said to him, "When someone approaches me, either they know what they want, or they don't want anything." I don't think he was ready for me to respond like that, and now the thinking was pressuring him. He mentioned some small arms, and automatically, I recited all of the weapons at the

MPS bunker. "Man, you can get most of that shit at a gun store." I wasn't promising anything; I played to his move to see if he'd let up and back away.

I pointed at Whalen and pulled him aside, asking him, "Hey man, did you get that shit?" He was in disbelief and said, "Dude, man, we've got to do something about that." Not wanting to blow our cover, we agreed to meet that individual the next day.

Whalen wanted to fuck him up, and I told him, "If we do that, we might have to kill him, or worse, he might kill us, so don't do any stupid shit." As I was telling Whalen this, I could imagine where this killing would happen—over towards the end of the building on the grass before the wood line. I know that Spritz was there with us, but he wasn't in our immediate area.

We decided to meet at the mall because we had to make arrangements. On the way back to the barracks, we were freaking out.

We remembered in our initial brief to base that we were instructed to report any such activity. "Because chances are very likely that you will be approached by someone, and they will ask you to make them a deal."

The next morning, we went to Captain Usherson's office, and that motherfucker said to us, "Are you sure that's what happened, or is this some kind of a joke? Better yet, don't worry about it."

We walked out of his office totally discouraged. I don't know what normally would happen, but we both knew that it was very serious and deserved a serious reaction.

I, for one, took the Corps seriously and felt that I owed it back, but for once I felt anger toward it. This incident helped me come to grips with the fact that I did not understand the Corps and how the politics became very twisted for everyone, especially the higher-ups; it was a wicked game.

Why would one come do this and not be serious? We agreed to stay on base for the next few nights; there was always the bar across the barracks, one that we could stumble into whenever we felt like it. We canceled any plans, dates, or other activities we had scheduled off base to reflect on the events that had unfolded.

Whalen and I told Spritz about the dude who wanted to buy the arms. Spritz and I agreed that now was the time to inform Whalen of what took place on MPS SITE III to see if he had heard anything, in order for us to draw a more reasonable conclusion.

We pieced it together and concluded it was all for me and Spritz; the Navy wanted to test our integrity for the remainder of our time there. Now, looking back, my final theory is that this guy was with one of the four parts of the government.

First, it may have been the DOD; after all, we were on their turf, or it may have been the FBI, or by order of Naval Operations, or even some private firm. He wasn't a terrorist; he didn't fall into any of the categories well enough to indicate so. His plan failed; he didn't attack and wasn't ready to die for his cause. He had no weapons on his person, and it seemed that he was alone. Lastly, he ran. My training had paid off. (At some point, there will be things that I cannot disclose and may cause the reader to be somewhat lost in the story.) We were taught what to look for and recognize.

I felt I had become one to reckon with, and I didn't care if anyone knew it; I was content with what I had become. Now, the reality of the coma I had experienced as a kid felt more like a dream because there was no way I could go from that condition to what I have become. Piver, Knightengale, Spritz, Whalen, Vega, or Holy didn't even know about my coma episode, and they were the ones I could confide in the most.

Spritz and I figured we needed to look out for ourselves, disregarding protocol not just because, but for our safety. In classifying the intruder from the past event, Spritz decided to configure a sign in accordance with National Defense Area (NDA) stating: "Anyone caught trespassing is in violation of DOD and Navy regulations and codes thereof; if capture results, it may escalate to a DULL SWORD incident." We were in an untouchable situation because we only posted them during our time there, and at the end of our four- or six-hour shift, we would take them with us. If not all of the postings were recovered, it would indicate the presence of an outsider. If our speculations were correct, then the postings couldn't be turned in to the command. They didn't fear us, but I'm sure they wouldn't want to be compromised either. At some point, I wanted to ask Spritz if anything unusual or out of the ordinary had happened to him or if he had even witnessed anything. I'm pretty sure there may have been; I wasn't ruling anything out, and I guess I didn't ask him because he became like my little brother, and since I never had a little brother, I wouldn't know how to react if something happened to him.

First, the psychiatric evaluation, my drinking, then my overkill response to certain situations—despite it all, I love the Corps, but I wanted out. I thought the games were all too twisted and wanted no part of it anymore. I hung in there at first, just going with the flow of things. Being the type of person I had become wouldn't allow me to just go through the motions, so there I was, between a rock and a hard place. To fight or fold were the choices I had; I decided to go down fighting. That called for a round at the bar, and we were at it once again.

That evening, while writing my entries, it dawned on me that the journal was becoming a part of everyone involved with us or even those who had anything to do around us. I didn't want it to be announced to very many people because the higher-ups might catch wind of it, but it was too late. During a conversation I had with "The Sir" (Lt. Sheppard), he asked me, "How is your journal coming along?"

I had to think fast, but I couldn't lie to him, so I just told him what he wanted to know. "What did you write about me?" was his last question.

"Sir, I would tell you, but that's classified information, and you're not on the EAL."

He laughed with amazement and said, "Oh! You still remember all that stuff? I would think that was all forgettable information for you guys." I did mention a few things to him that were not written.

It was late August, and it had been a while since I had called my parents at home. I referenced the journal in my conversation because life in the Corps was going by fast, and it became a better way for me to recall some of my experiences. Somewhere in what I thought my dad would ask, I imagined it was just to see if I was as crazy and wild as he had been as a young man. I told my mom about the easier things, mostly just giving her yes or no answers to her questions; I didn't want her worrying too much. I think I didn't call home because I knew that at the other end of the line, I would be talking to someone who loved me and wouldn't want me to put myself in harm's way, and at the same time, they wouldn't have understood my situation.

The atmosphere became so untrusting that Spritz, Whalen, and I didn't speak for a couple of weeks about anything involving our duties. For some time, we wrote letters and mailed them to one another while taking care of things off base, and we destroyed them immediately after reading them. Nothing was left to chance; it even came down to where Spritz had developed an encryption system for us to communicate about work and other things. It seemed like overkill, but we didn't have any privacy.

CHAPTER 10

LOCK AND LOAD

After a few weeks and as many tours of duty, things were going okay at MPS, and it felt as if there was nothing to worry about anymore. I was a little upset because if that was the end of everything, I wasn't sure we proved anything to anyone, and I wanted to go out on a positive note. Trouble was never too far from us; it would look at us from around the corner, and at times like this was when trouble would reach out, grabbing at us and not letting go.

On September 3rd, Spritz and I went on duty, ready as ever to see what strategic communication plans we could devise. After a few hours at MPS, around 2 a.m., we received word that "the MOOD was on his way to our site to standby." All that meant was to watch out and be careful that we were not doing something to get in trouble because the Marine Officer of the Day was on his way to visit. The MOOD for that night was SSgt. Diablo.

A vehicle approached, and we followed protocol for when a Uniform Victor arrives on scene (Uniform Victor = Unidentified Vehicle). I challenged the driver, and he failed to comply not once or twice, but three times. The third time that I challenged him, he started toward my bunker as if he was going to ram his truck into my position. That was when I locked and loaded a round into the chamber of my M-16 A-2 service rifle, like always, being in total control of my post and the situation. He slammed on the brakes and jumped out, then began to follow my instructions. I had that motherfucker on his face, and I thought he was pretty shaken up. After he properly identified himself and I recognized him, I authorized him to be on my post.

In the Marines, we tend to remember things a little better when they're humorously revised. There's an unwritten Twelfth General Order, which states: "I will walk my post from flank to flank and take no shit from any rank." We've been taught that twelfth means only one thing, so whoever is on post, grab your pair and take command of that post because it is yours, and if someone takes it from you, die because you don't deserve to live.

I said to him, "Hello, Staff Sergeant. Are you aware that I could have killed you?"

"Well, I wanted to see how you'd react," he said.

"No, SSgt. Really, I could have killed you; here, eject any rounds from my weapon." I figured, why don't I let him see the round that could have killed him and hold it in his hands? Someone needs to teach him a lesson, and who better than Zavala?

He seemed to not be bothered by my actions; he didn't yell, nor did he freak out. He just unloaded my weapon and told us that we were doing a great job and to keep it up. I still think back on that night many times and wonder what he could have been thinking on his drive back to Post-7, or maybe it didn't sink in until later that he could have lost his life.

I was the authority at MPS-Sight Post, but Spritz always did his own thing anyway; the chain of command didn't really come into play unless someone of a higher rank was on site. We received word that the MOOD was on his way over. I positioned Spritz in a strategic location in case shit hit the fan, so he would do what was necessary; too many close calls—I was taking nothing for granted. Spritz and I always had our plan A and B if protocol failed. The night went on with no further action or incident, and it was a stretch before we would be relieved. I thought since I had done the right thing, it would be left alone. I was very wrong; we were relieved that morning on a regular basis. The LOG had only a few entries, and among the entries was the prodigious occurrence:

Post Log for MPS SITE III

TIME 0200: Uniform Victor approaches MPS SITE III. The driver was challenged three times before he began to comply with the sentry's instructions. The driver aggressively rushed the C.P. I, Lcpl. Zavala, then proceeded to LOCK and LOAD one round into the chamber of my M-16 A-2 service rifle, and at that time, the driver seemed to have become cooperative with the sentries on post.

TIME 0224: After protocol is met, the driver was identified as MOOD SSgt. Diablo. The MOOD looks around the area and then proceeds to drive off from MPS SITE III.

TIME 0545: Sentries Lcpl. Zavala and PFC Spritz have nothing further to report at this time and are being relieved by: XXX and XXX.

Close page.

End of duty, Lcpl. Zavala...

I don't quite remember who relieved us from post that morning. I hit the rack around 7:30 a.m. after my weapon and ammo had been turned into the armory. My eyes closed, and I was out like a light. Almost an hour went by, then Winn came by knocking on my door.

"Hey, Zavala, Lt. Hailey wants to see you in his office. Come on, wake up, or at least answer to know that you're in!"

I answered the door and said, "This better be important, and don't fuck around."

Lt. Hailey was a very wise man; he was a Black dude from Harlem. I reported as ordered, and he proceeded. "Zavala, tell me you didn't lock and load on SSgt. Diablo."

I said to the lieutenant, "Sir, you're asking me as if I did something wrong. Yes, I did."

"Tell me what happened," Hailey insisted.

"Well, Sir, we heard a vehicle approaching us and took our positions . . ."

"Who was on post with you?" he interrupted. "Spritz was," I replied.

"And what do you mean your positions? MPS doesn't have any set standard on taking your positions."

"Sir, in football, you don't just hike the ball; you run plays, even in sandlot ball."

He instructed me to continue.

"The vehicle approached, and I challenged it, meaning the driver. The driver failed to comply, and I challenged him a second time. Again, he failed to comply, and he had his high beams on. At this time, he was backing up his vehicle, then came forward with it aggressively. I challenged him a third time and thought he wasn't going to stop the vehicle, and then I locked and loaded."

"You didn't know it was SSgt. Diablo?"

"I recognized the vehicle, but I didn't know that it was him. Who knows, he or anyone could be overtaken at the gate on the gravel road; that's what I was thinking."

"That's very true, Zavala. And Spritz, where was he?"

"I positioned him at one of these trailers on this side," I said, pointing to the map, "and told him to stay covered."

"Winn!" I guessed was just outside the door.

"Yes, Lt. Hailey, Sir," Winn answered.

"Go and get Spritz. Tell him to get down here A-S-A-P!"

"Yes, Sir!"

Winn was a fake suck-up; he knew it, admitted it, and played a good role. He did that to stay clean and out of trouble; he tried to be gung-ho about the Marines. I don't doubt that Winn's still serving right now, and he's probably a Staff Sergeant or maybe even a Gunny. His dream was to be a Drill Instructor, and so was almost every other Marine for the first few months or even a year. Winn went through that phase and stayed in that phase, whereas most others had the idea vanish from their minds.

"Are you done?" Hailey asked.

"No, Sir. After the third challenge, SSgt. Diablo jumped out of his vehicle. I thought that he reacted to the locking and loading of my weapon, but I continued with my procedure and asked him for the proper information too. I even put him down on his face and told him to place his 9mm pistol on the ground in front of him. Spritz, at this time, ran up to our location to assist. I finally authorized SSgt. Diablo to be on the premises and asked him what the hell he did that shit for. That he could get killed. He looked at me with uncertainty on his face as I interrupted him with, "Here, can you clear my weapon?"

Lt. Hailey cross-examined my testimony with that of Spritz. It went well, and he asked me just to be sure.

"Zavala, now are you ready to go tell the Guard Chief and the Guard Commander?"

"Yes, Sir!" Of course, I polished it up, and I was on my way to see the man.

Captain McGowen, the Guard Commander, was the man who was going to try this, and Gunny Cook, the Guard Chief, was the jury. That sorry, pathetic, fat bastard—poor excuse for a man—SSgt. Diablo was the one who wanted to see me hang after I could have killed him. I told them exactly what I told Lt. Hailey, and Spritz verified it. This time, I illustrated better because they had a model of the site we were on right in front of them.

Capt. McGowen asked me after we told our story, "Zavala, do you know that you could have killed this man?"

"Sir, yes, I realized that the moment I locked and loaded on him, and I was ready to kill the man who drove there like some crazy fool."

"What would you have told his family, Zavala?"

"Sir, after I got out of boot camp, I realized what I had signed up for—not just getting drunk and chasing pussy everywhere I went. There was one thing I needed to do before my leave was over, and that was to tell my mother something. Mom, I said, one of these days, I may end up getting killed or not even come back because that is what goes on in the Marine Corps sometimes, and you can't stop that from happening. So just pray." She began to cry.

"If SSgt. Diablo has not broken it down to his family, then I think he should. Something else, Sir: you know when you come home, every time you tell your wife that you're going to be home. She needs to be reminded once in a while what your life is about because that's what happens in our line of work. We die if we have to, but before we realize that one day we may die, we're trained to think that we're invincible, and I think that's what makes us who we are."

They looked at one another—the Captain and the Gunny—then the Guard Commander asked us to leave. The door behind us was slammed shut, and the next thing my great ears beheld was, "God damn it, SSgt. Diablo, you could have got yourself killed. You owe him your life, and you need to go thank him the next time you see him!" I don't know if it was the rude awakening that I gave them or the wrong done by SSgt. Diablo that made them yell that way at that man, but it worked. After that, we got the hell out of there. Captain McGowen was maybe the fairest captain I ever worked with. I think it was because he was an enlisted Marine before he became an officer, and maybe he knew that some Marines were dishonest and did things out of spite. Gunny Cook was a hard man, but I think the Captain said to the Gunny, "This is my show, and this is the way it's going to be. No more rank-taking or money-taking; we need to be fair to these guys."

The Marines who had arrived here with me from Virginia had been assigned to different platoons, and all four platoons were being represented to ask a few questions. It was rumor control, and everyone wanted to get the facts straight. I took this opportunity to reinvent myself in their eyes. I answered a few major questions, then asked everybody to leave the room because I had been up all night long. This incident kind of took everything to another level, not within me but throughout the entire Security Forces Unit.

I still think most authority figures in uniform become so overwhelmed with themselves that they seem to forget to respect other people and other people's boundaries; they seem to forget they too can become the number one man on someone's shit list.

We partied not long, but just enough to enjoy the victory because winning over the staff was a big thing. Not like a lawsuit settlement against the tobacco industry, but it was big. I finally got some sleep and went on as if nothing happened, but not everyone else put the incident behind us. The next time I ran into SSgt. Diablo, he was singing a friendlier song. He got around to apologizing, but it took a while because first, he had to swallow his pride.

I saw him at the E-club/bar across from the barracks. While I was getting a burger, he approached me and said, "Zavala, thank you for not shooting me. I know I could have prevented the incident, but next time just unload the weapon yourself."

I said to him, "Staff Sergeant, next time I think I'll shoot, but I know it won't be you because we both learned something out there." He looked at me strangely, then I offered him a beer, trying to make him understand that it wasn't personal.

SSgt. Diablo was my immediate out source to the higher-ups, so if I kept my cool about the incident, then things may turn out a lot better for me. When it was all said and done, I wanted to be remembered as being extreme instead of unstable.

During the course of events, Whalen had been screened for alcoholism. He was all excited and said, "As long as I've been here, I've yet to see anyone do what you've done and succeed. I gotta give it to you, Zavala; it may not go down in the books here, but it's certainly going down in my book."

Short-lived, suddenly reality hit home for him, and he seemed to have gotten bent out of shape about something. "Hey, man," I said. "Hold on. What the hell is the matter with you?" Everyone that hung out with us was either from the East Coast or from California, and I had lost my Texas accent; I think I sounded more like a yank than anyone else.

"Man, you know that screening we were supposed to do? Well, I did it the other day, and they said I needed Level-3 classes."

I said to him that it was best that he go through with it and try to avoid any bullshit. He agreed, but not before Whalen became more hopeless about the entire process. Spritz and I underwent the same exact screening (on separate occasions), and we were told that all we were required to undergo was Level-2 classes, even though Spritz and I were far worse than he was.

The SSgt. Diablo incident worked out well for me among my fellow

Marines, and I started to see a change in them toward me. Respect was soon deemed appropriate, and they started coming to me for advice. I began to enjoy feasting on the fringe benefits of not only having seniority here but also from my rare and infamous achievements.

CHAPTER 11

MY LOST BROTHER

Time passes, and a few of the guys are shuffled around. Duty keeps calling, and we're back at the MPS Site III. It seems that the day shift went well, but on that night shift, things were becoming scary for Cpl. Smith. We heard on the two-way radios that DoD was looking for a suspect who fit Cpl. Smith's description. It was a given after they gave out the description of his bike. These stupid allegations a lady had made against him claimed that he pulled his one-eyed snake out and showed it to her at the counter of the store. As soon as we heard, we began brainstorming on what we could do or buy him some more time, at least until we got back.

We'd hate to see him go down for something like that or for any reason. We had access to a landline to the duty officer at the barracks; luckily enough, it was a Marine who would go clubbing with us from time to time who was on post. I told him to go warn Cpl. Smith, but by then, DoD was in the building and had taken him in for questioning.

We didn't want him to burn because he was allied with more rank than the rest of us, which could have benefited us a great deal more. I was feeling totally helpless because, first and foremost, he was one of my best friends, and in the Infantry, it's hard to get promoted back to his rank. Most of the time, if someone loses their rank in the first four years in the military, it is very unlikely that they will reenlist. Others just get out because the coast is clear and for a job that pays more, but mostly to enjoy the freedom, which they themselves helped provide.

I couldn't be there to help him out because we were on post. They actually arrested him and returned him to the military the next afternoon. Upon his return, I saw him and said, "Hey man, I'm glad you're all right; I hope things turn out okay."

I remembered him telling me, "Fuck man, I don't want to burn, Zavala. I didn't do that shit, man."

"Hey man, things are going to be all right, man. Don't worry about it." I thought he needed some time to himself. He had a spiral notebook with him; I left him alone because that's how he was, and Cpl. Smith sorted out his own problems.

The next night, he went to another NCO's house, where many of the other Marines would go on their off days to play cards and drink. Smith knew this guy had guns he kept loaded throughout the house. First, he made a scene outside of the apartment; then he took his life because of that woman's accusations. It was a life experience knowing Jesse James Smith, Cpl., United States Marine Corps.

When they told me how it took place, I pictured something I had seen on TV, and I felt I might have been there in spirit. I'll miss you, my Brother in Arms. I had never seen Cpl. Smith out of control; he was always calm and collected. I think he was at a point of desperation and didn't know what to do or how to ask for help without belittling his dignity.

Cpl. Rhae escorted the body to Massachusetts, and the family was taking it hard, but what could they do? Cpl. Rhae said that he spoke with the father for a little while, and then he handed over an envelope; we assumed it was a check for $100,000. There was a church service held for him by the command. The colonel was at a loss for words, and of course, we paid our respects. But at the same time, he wanted us to get a message from Cpl. Smith's death.

I tried to cry, but it wouldn't come out, especially after the colonel, by his own tears, gave approval for crying. The message became clear to me, and I had to take inventory and reevaluate myself; I was in search of a new mentor. I never believed that Cpl. Smith was dead. He had such a powerful impact on me, or it might have been that I just thought highly of him, being from 2nd Battalion Recon. Many times, we met up at places and just hung out like two friends; I moved aside the rank, but still, I showed enough respect to keep things cool between us.

For some time following his death, I felt that I was going to run into him out in the streets. I went to the store where the girl was working at the time Cpl. Smith asked me to introduce him to her. I said to her as I handed her a flower, "Here you go; James would have wanted you to have this." She asked why he wasn't giving it to her. "He's not with us anymore. All I can say is that he was killed by hostile fire during a convoy. Sorry, Ma'am." I waited for something, but I didn't know what it was. I comforted her and asked if everything was going to be alright with her. She indicated yes with a nod, and I left when the timing felt right.

There was another Marine who died in an auto accident. He and I didn't speak to one another much; he was quiet and had a few friends—no more than he really needed—but enough to keep him company while on post. It never dawned on me why he and I were never on post together. I think he was married because he didn't live on base, and that's how our system worked there; only if you were married or an NCO and above did you have the choice of living off base.

There were two guys with the same last name; one was killed, and it was kind of strange. Most of us really didn't know which one was the real victim until they reported back to duty. It wouldn't have mattered because both men had served their country in a sound and humble way. Some Marines seem to be trouble-free and live a routine life, but I'd rather deal with my troubles than retire early. Sound the trumpets and salute while TAPS is being played. We've lost another good man.

Article 15

A few days go by, but the show must go on. A rumor was floating around that my I.D. card was making its way around and that other Marines were using it to buy beer. I questioned it, but no one fessed up. I tried keeping it on the down low, but they surprised us with a walk-through room inspection; I guess the rumor had made its way to the office. It was found in the possession of that fucker, Perez. I went before the Colonel and got burned for it; my rank, time, and money were all taken from me because of that son of a bitch. He got burned too for using it, but Perez, on the other hand, received more time restriction for it than I did.

At this point, everyone was expecting me to whip his ass, but I knew Perez was somewhat undisciplined, and I could smell payback. After fifteen days of restriction, stripped back down a rank, my time was served for the offense, and I was out 500 fat ones.

My squad leader, Platoon Sergeant, the Platoon Commander, and other Marines who may or may not have wanted to see me burn were present. I stood there, locked and cocked, before the colonel. During my summary, he ordered me to hand over my rank and sentenced me to pay a five-hundred-dollar fine and 15 days of restriction. Monetary damages were to be deducted from my pay, and the restriction meant that I couldn't leave the base for anything other than military business.

As I was dismissed, I couldn't help but snicker while I mumbled, "I can't win them all." The Colonel called me back into his office and asked what I meant by that. I thought of spilling my guts, but some of the not-so-higher-ups didn't fuck with me as it stood, and I definitely had less to lose. I wouldn't have the dirt on them anymore, and besides, the damage had been done; I would be risking way too much.

I told the Colonel, "Sir, I've been in worse situations than this, and I've been somewhat resilient to it all. I'll recover."

"Zavala, you're like one of my gators out there in the creeks, but that's good; I know I can count on you," he replied.

I felt like saying, "Well then, give me my shit back, Sir."

The 15 days of restriction had finally ended, and I was going out to have some beers with the guys to celebrate my release from captivity. Perez showed up even though he was still on restriction. I got on the phone and made an anonymous call to the Duty NCO at the Barracks. "Could I please speak to PFC Perez? There has been an emergency at home in the Bronx," I said in a Puerto Rican accent.

Perez wasn't in his room; therefore, he was in violation of his restriction. A report was made, turned into the command, and he was sentenced to the Brig for 15 days and reduced to private in the United States Marine Corps.

I think it was Sgt. O'Riley who said to me, "Man, Zavala, I thought you were going to fuck him up pretty bad."

"Sgt. O'Riley, what else do you want me to do to this man? Haven't I done enough?"

"Sgt. O'Riley, sometimes one must do his fighting with the pen rather than the sword; there are times it might bring you sweeter revenge." I was quoting him from once before. I didn't like it when it was used toward me, but when I felt and understood the power of its meaning, how sweet it was.

CHAPTER 12

OUT WITH THE OLD

In early September, the more senior Marines had completed their time at that duty station or had finished their time in the Corps. The same Marines who had arrived at the Naval Weapons Station at the same time I did, or a short time before us, were now in charge of things over in the Critical Area. Before Colonel Mark Masterson, there existed a colonel who loved to take one's money, rank, and time. Of course, I had only heard of him, but the stories I heard were messed up. The more senior Marines would say things like, "If Col. Hood were here, you would have burned." This colonel was out of line, I think, and I say this because of the stories told.

Speaking of another old-school guy, it was time for Lt. Hailey's discharge; he had resigned. The story I heard was that he had an accidental discharge of his service .45 pistol. His best choice was to get out. Spritz and I were on post this particular time when he was MOOD for the last time ever. The following day, processing out of the Corps would commence, and he would no longer have to answer to anyone. Besides, he had his own business back home in Harlem, NY; it was in the communications field—beepers or cell phones.

He visited Spritz and me, and we talked for about an hour and 45 minutes about life after the Marines for him and what my goals were. During our conversation, he debriefed me and said, "Zavala, you may not think so, but you opened their eyes up in the office when that thing with SSgt. Diablo went down. They thought you were a lost cause before that, but you showed them. Even though you lost your rank, that was just to bring you back off your high horse with the rest of the command. I'm sure that soon you'll hear it straight from them, so good luck in whatever you do. If you keep doing things with such enthusiasm, you'll succeed. So far, you've shown an entire staff of officers and me that you can beat the odds. I think it was what you told the Captain and the Gunny that put you straight with them, and you're right: we need to constantly evaluate ourselves. Oh! One more thing: we know you're serious and all, but stop smiling so damn much all the time."

Before our little conversation that night, I didn't know how or what my status was with the other brass. I knew Lt. Hailey and I were eye to eye. "I thought I was just doing my job," I said to him.

"Yeah, Zavala, you were just doing your job, but now they see that you do it well and take it seriously. . . Spritz, you don't have anything to worry about; they placed you right next to him."

Small talk soon followed. We shook hands and wished each other the very best of luck. That night, Lt. Hailey became a memory. To me, Lt. Hailey leaving was a personal loss because I know he's probably the only officer I knew who went through more of a dilemma than I did, to lose his rank and have to give up his commission. I could tell it was painful for him to see other Marines go through hard times.

Hugo

On September 23, 1989, we would see more destruction—not within our ranks, but rather in the better part of the East Coast due to a tropical storm that upgraded to Hurricane Hugo. It would leave us in ruins; with no water to drink, the city was declared by the government to be under martial law, and the National Guard took over. I was relieved from post the morning before its arrival and began preparations for the great event. I couldn't sleep; everyone was ordered to help out. I was ordered to replace the Marines at the main gate from their post so they could make personal preparations.

Someone fabricated a big story about when the hurricane hit. I was at the main gate entrance to the base, taking charge of it. Once again, people thought of me as that gung-ho and dedicated individual. They believed I'd actually go to such extremes to do something like that. The storm was not too far from land when I was relieved from post 07; they secured it by order of the Operations Officer on the Navy side, so that must have been a Navy Captain or an Admiral.

I made it to the barracks on time to buy a twelve-pack; little did I know some other Marines had stocked up by the cases. It's not every year that the opportunity comes along to find ourselves in a hurricane of this size, so partaking in a post-hurricane celebration was necessary. During the storm, the NCO on duty ordered us to establish a fire watch for the entire barracks, all three wings. I took the first watch in our wing so that I would be done with it in two hours instead of the standard four. We could hear tornadoes touching down right beyond the exit door. I wanted to open the door to see what it looked like up close, and mostly so that I could say that I was "this close to a tornado."

I couldn't have imagined how much damage was done until I looked out the door, but I still didn't think too much of it as I worked it open from the debris that was blocking it. It was sobering to look at the devastation left behind. I wasn't able to fix my sights on any one particular mass of debris; instead, I looked for an area that was clear, then started to make my way around to assess the area. Most of the trees had been ripped down where the tornadoes had touched down. The road was blocked by broken trees, logs, and branches, so no one could come on or leave the station. I cracked open a beer and went to see if my car was intact.

Secret Security Clearance wasn't something constantly on my mind, despite the fact that the clearance was the reason I had these duties. On the flip side, I didn't dishonor it in any way, and still today I'll tell you the stories of a few infamous men while attempting to stay within the boundaries of the law. After ten years, it is said to be permitted to open a few files, and with the more advanced technical weaponry, the likelihood of most everything here being obsolete is high. But since Marines still hold these positions today, I'd rather not write about what I learned while stationed here. Just because something is declassified doesn't mean it is your need-to-know responsibility.

In the time I've been stationed here, other things have occurred that I've yet to mention, such as going to the rifle range in Georgia. There, we managed to get into a big fight with some Army guys from Victory Division. It was an Army-versus-Marine bar fight; no one won or lost, but the brass sure had a field day with it. We were not allowed back on that base again.

Robledo's wife was having an affair with his so-called best friend, and then Robledo was arrested for looting some places of business immediately after the hurricane around his house off base. I think he spent the rest of his four years in the brig.

There were some guys who just got water, and I didn't blame them. Water had more value than most other things. The storm ruined the entire water supply, but I don't know for how many cities. This one guy said they got caught taking water, but since it was only water, the National Guardsman said to go ahead, and if they needed more, to go back and get more. Man, times like those were the worst; the food cooked using the tap water tasted like crap, and the water tasted like richer crap. It tasted as if we were pulling it right out of the creek and drinking it with an added dash of sewer taste and smell. Showering was useless; it would leave us smelling like sewer. It was close to a month before the water returned to its normal state, and honestly, I had enough beer for some time.

We weren't limited to the types of training we could do; anti-terrorist training was my favorite course, followed by hand-to-hand combat training. This was all done to maintain our knowledge and develop our skills and techniques. We went on hikes fully geared and ran when nothing was scheduled; we did physical training.

Ninety-nine percent of the Marines at Naval Weapons Station were in the 0300 field, which meant we were infantry Marines, and war was the farthest thing from my mind. Still, we needed to refresh our knowledge for field combat. Convoys were basically secretive movements of special weapons from their housing facilities to a ship or submarine, or the other way around. They were conducted, and we'd go over every little detail and the possible mistakes within those details. Many different scenarios led up to the real thing.

In anticipation of the storm, the DoD removed the containers from MPS SITE III for 48 hours, and for that short time, our platoon was the detail platoon. Our duties included clearing the railroad tracks for the train's access to the different sites. We also helped the other groups clean off the road to regain access to the city. When MPS SITE III became reoccupied with its arsenal of containers, it had still been raining due to the aftereffects of the hurricane. We stood our post in a small shack—maybe 3 feet by 3 feet. It was small and located at one end; the other sentry had no cover over the guard shack at the other end of our watch area. We alternated every shift; we became miserable, but time passed, and so did the rain. The next time Spritz and I went on post, we were pretty much fed up, being out here like sitting ducks. Our sense of discipline was lost due to the storm's damages, and during that time, we allowed the fact that we were being watched at one point to start affecting us. The alcohol was breaking us down. After a few weeks, stores began to open, but everything went fast. Soon, we had our chance to buy a few necessary items, like more drinkable water. Slowly, it was back to normal, especially when we had drinkable water again. We commenced an undertaking to help us regain what we had lost.

The time came when a tranquil discomfort was upon us, and we were a bit more relaxed. We knew life at Security Forces Charleston, S.C., was back to normal. Things were bad but slowly getting better; there wasn't much that could make our situation worse. We had to believe our situation could get worse to be prepared for anything in case it did. Although there were times when we didn't keep our minds occupied, it would get the best of us.

MPS

Spritz told me one day, after our many ordeals had taken place, that some Marines from the 1st, 2nd, 3rd, and even Convoy Platoons had heard of the type of crazy event that occurred at MPS, and it seemed as if curiosity had gotten the best of them. Many requests had been made to be moved to MPS; we didn't really know what to think, and maybe the monotony was getting to these guys.

All of the guys who were in the Maritime Pre-Positioned Station Site-III just wanted to do the opposite: have a predictable couple of weeks of duty and come back to the barracks. They wanted to sit and joke about how someone screwed up or fell and busted their ass while we turned in our gear, weapons, and ammunition, and called it a day. I will even go as far as to say that we envied each other's professional lifestyles; we needed time to decompress, and they needed a change of pace.

Being on both sides of the fence, I knew for a fact that things did become boring in the Critical Area, but I didn't think the other platoons knew just how our duties at MPS really were and how dirty (politically) they could get. I wasn't going to criticize them, and I didn't complain about them either for having it easy because they helped mold me into the man I am today. Even recently, as I mentioned to Spritz, I would be writing a book on my four years in the Marines. I'm sure he'll read these stories from a different perspective, but this part of the process is what formed him into what he is today.

Out at the locations we patrolled, there was no reason for anyone to be out there, and at times I would go and check the perimeter just to verify. Fresh footprints would excite me because no one should have been out there without checking with DoD or the Navy. The LOG should indicate if there had been any visitors, and the word should be passed down to us, but nothing had come down from any of the sources. While I was out checking the perimeter, I moved things around to come back out at night. Like I said, catching someone would be something, and since the footprints I found were fresh, I had a reason to do what I did.

Later that evening, it was time for me to test myself, so I asked

Spritz, "Hey man, in a bit, can you flick the power switch to off so I can make it into the wood line?" He asked me why, and I said, "Man, if you just do me this one favor, I won't ask you for another favor for a week." He finally agreed with an "OK," and it was on. I had with me my 9mm Beretta and my M16. For the first 15 to 20 minutes, I had not seen anything but a few small alligators from the nearby creeks. I conducted a few radio checks while I was out doing my thing. More than an hour had passed when I noticed some more footprints that went back and forth for some distance; they'd disappear at the higher grounds and then reappear at the low grounds.

The night wasn't too dark; I was back in the area of the footprints I had seen earlier that day, just thinking, "What if?" A bit later, I heard someone running through the woods from the area of MPS. At first, I thought of calling out, "Hey, man, over here," thinking it was Spritz. At the same time, I lowered down to hide. I guess that was a reactionary habit that I had developed. I had unsnapped my dagger and prepared for anything minor. This person running was breathing too heavily; I could hear him from a distance. I knew it wasn't Spritz because Spritz wouldn't just abandon his post. He passed me, and I got up and ran behind him for a few steps. I'm guessing he felt someone behind him; I hit him in the ear with a closed fist—the part furthest from my thumb—and he fell. He shook it off, and then he came to. By that time, I was able to maneuver my knife against his throat while jamming my knee into the middle of his shoulder blades.

I carried a little extra gear with me at all times; in fact, we all did. It's what we call dummy-cord. I immediately put it around his neck for control and to cut off his breathing if necessary; his gasping told me what he valued most. I yanked at the cord and held it long enough to give him an idea, and I said to him that if he moved, I would choke him until he passed out, and if he understood me clearly, his hands were tied behind his back as well.

The questioning began. "Who's with you? Where are you going? Why are you running? How long have you been watching us out here?" I asked the questions all at once so they would cause him to stress and bend a little. As soon as he bent, I would pressure him until he broke.

I cut off his breathing and jammed my knife into his back with just enough pressure, but not to break the skin. I guess all the movies I had watched while growing up helped me fall into character.

His name was JT. "Please let me go, and I won't ever come here again," he said unconvincingly. Not much time had gone by when I informed him that I was going to walk over to retrieve my weapon, which was by the bush where I had been hiding. He said, "Hey man, don't leave me here alone."

I conducted a radio check, retrieved my weapon, and returned. I still had my 9mm on me. I said, "Man, you need to shut up. Besides, that creek bed over there—I know it has at least one alligator, maybe six or seven feet long, and you wouldn't want it to get you, right?"

All the while, I was thinking, "If I leave him here, it may come back to haunt me, and if I let him go, well, there are no witnesses, so I'll let him go."

He shook and said, "No man, I wouldn't; I hate the gators!"

"So just keep quiet, and it'll be all right." I cut his forearm but not too badly and told him that if he moved, I would throw him to the gator. I cut him so they would become alert by the smell of his blood, so don't move a bit. I asked him if he had seen me before.

"No man, you came out of nowhere."

"If you come back and I see you, you're going to the gators, you got that?" I assured him. I knew that if he came back, I was fucked. Either he might shoot at us, and we'd have to return fire, or worse, he would get some of his friends to come take care of this, and that would be just another fight we would be in. At best, he'd learn his lesson and not return or even mention this to anyone. The thought crossed my mind: "What if this guy has a family, or what if he's mentally challenged? After all, he came across to me as a little absent-minded."

Every night I went on post at MPS, my alert level would climb to a Code Red. Little did he know that by being there with me, he was safe; anywhere else was where he was in harm's way. Before I released him into the wild, I applied first aid to his cut. When I left the area, I returned to MPS Site III. Spritz asked me, "What happened out there, man? I thought you got lost."

"Nothing, dude. And yeah, I kind of got lost. I was watching the gator over in the creek bed." I couldn't have gotten lost during the days, but not always was when I'd go over the landscape—avenues of approach, places to hide, where there was heavier vegetation, and if worse came to worst, where I could dig in if we were to be overthrown by any other groups. I became tired of thinking this way because it didn't seem as if I could do anything without planning something just in case, but that was how it needed to be while we were out there with no support anywhere near us.

Don't get me wrong; the MPS III location that we provided security to had a bunker towards the entrance of the site, and we were well-fortified with an M-60, grenades, and a few other things while we carried our M-16s, 9mm Berettas, knives, and our means of communication. I even began to check during our changeover if the firing pins had not been taken out from the M-60 that was at the guard shack/bunker of MPS Site III.

Later during the same week, Cpl. Rhae asked if we had seen anyone out there. We told him no, but I had to ask why.

His name was JT. "Please let me go, and I won't ever come here again," he said unconvincingly. Not much time had passed when I informed him I was going to walk over to retrieve my weapon, which was by the bush where I had been hiding. He said, "Hey man, don't leave me here alone."

I conducted a radio check, retrieved my weapon, and returned, still carrying my 9mm. I said, "Man, you need to shut up. Besides, that creek bed over there? I know it has at least one alligator, maybe six or seven feet long, and you wouldn't want it to get you, right?"

All the while, I thought, "If I leave him here, it may come back to haunt me, and if I let him go, well, there are no witnesses, so I'll let him go."

He shook and said, "No man, I wouldn't; I hate the gators!"

"So just keep quiet, and it'll be all right." I cut his forearm, not too badly, and told him that if he moved, I would throw him to the gator. I cut him to alert them to the smell of his blood, so he better not move. I asked if he had seen me before.

"No man, you came out of nowhere."

"If you come back and I see you, you're going to the gators, you got that?" I assured him. I knew that if he returned, I was fucked. He might shoot at us, and we'd have to return fire, or worse, he could bring some friends to handle it, leading to another fight. At best, he'd learn his lesson and not return or mention this to anyone. The thought crossed my mind: "What if this guy has a family, or what if he's mentally challenged? After all, he seemed a little absent-minded."

Every night I went on post at MPS, my alert level climbed to a Code Red. Little did he know that by being there with me, he was safe; anywhere else was where he was in harm's way. Before I released him into the wild, I applied first aid to his cut. When I left the area, I returned to MPS Site III. Spritz asked, "What happened out there, man? I thought you got lost."

"Nothing, dude. Yeah, I kind of got lost. I was watching the gator over in the creek bed." I couldn't have gotten lost during the day, but not always was when I'd scout the landscape—avenues of approach, places to hide, areas with heavier vegetation, and if worse came to worst, where I could dig in if we were overthrown by any other groups. I grew tired of thinking this way; it felt like I couldn't do anything without planning for contingencies. But that was how it had to be while we were out there with no support nearby.

Don't get me wrong; the MPS III location we secured had a bunker toward the entrance of the site, and we were well-fortified with an M-60, grenades, and a few other things while carrying our M-16s, 9mm Berettas, knives, and means of communication. I even began to check during our changeover if the firing pins had been removed from the M-60 at the guard shack/bunker of MPS Site III.

Later that week, Cpl. Rhae asked if we had seen anyone out there. We told him no, but I had to ask why. "Ladies, drill is a thinking man's game. If you can't think, you will learn; and if you can't learn to think, God bless you, because you will be the strongest motherfucker here at my Depot. You won't make it out of here until you learn how to think, or you'll kill yourself trying," Senior Drill Instructor SSgt. Daniels stated to us in boot camp. Since I've been in the Marines, there hasn't been a moment while in uniform that I wasn't thinking—unless I was drunk and passed out. I'm sure even while we slept, our minds were still processing Marine Corps shit.

I stood post with Archie, Cervantes, Winn, Stevance, and Bartonsen. If I were to guess, I'd say we went out together around twenty times in total. We all did some crazy things, but things seemed to get twisted mostly when Spritz, Whalen, and I were together.

CHAPTER 13

REVELATIONS

Time came when a big secret was about to be exposed. The only people who knew of this secret were Perez, Whalen, Spritz, Lou, and myself. We decided the other Marines needed a sanctuary, just like the four of us. We gathered our closest friends, piled into cars, and carpooled to the ever-so-secretive bar, the Birdbath. The night I had the fight with that hippie was when all our code names came to life, and on this night, those names became clearer to the other Marines.

Mayers, for example, said, "Oh! Was that what you meant when you guys talked about the Bath?"

Every thought we had needed to become an action with results. Like I wrote earlier, our train of thought was always worst-case scenario. As we loaded into the vehicles, Whalen, Spritz, and I made sure to split into three separate cars—just in case any of us were compromised, someone else would know the whereabouts of this location. No one particularly liked my ways of doing things, and I think they just wanted to get out and be "regular" (as they understood it) for a night or two.

If everyone else in the convoy knew about the close calls Spritz and I had encountered at MPS, or about that guy at the bar who wanted to buy guns from Whalen and me, I think they'd understand. I was the one in a state of confusion, wondering, Why can't my time here be a bit normal? These guys had much more normal lives than Spritz and I did; Whalen was just in the wrong place at the wrong time, because his duties put him in the Critical Area with the rest of these guys.

On nights that followed, Spritz, Whalen, and I drank for free—we didn't spend a dime. We'd worked out a deal with the bar owner. He approached us one evening and asked if it was just the three of us, and right away we said, "No, we keep it this way so we can go there to get away from it all." When we mentioned there were others, he made us an offer: more beer, more women, as long as we brought him more business.

One night, Bartonsen and a civilian guy got into a slugfest. They were wasted, exchanging punches to the face, and you could hear the impact. Suddenly, Bartonsen retreated, turned to us, and said, "This dude is really putting them down, man. I'm done." He wiped the blood from his face and resumed drinking as if nothing had happened.

Bartonsen had a neurological short-circuit and wasn't affected by some things, like pain and beer. If you were to see him, you'd swear to God this guy was crazy—which he was—but he was friendly and would lend you his last dollar if you asked for it. Great guy.

The bar owner seemed entertained by twenty to twenty-five Marines taking over his place, as the fair trade turned into his fortune. More opportunities presented themselves to me at the Birdbath and in South Carolina, where you could drink around the clock. Only on Sundays was alcohol prohibited, except from bootleggers. Behind the bar, there was a bed in a locked room, and now it had become available to us. God knows I couldn't drink until 8 o'clock every morning.

In short, the Bath was a place where we'd all meet; the owner and the bartender knew each of us by name and by the beer we drank. This particular night, I saw Piver and Brewster come in, and we had a beer together. They were going to meet up with some girls, and it would be the last time I'd see Piver, my first and truly best friend in the Corps. Brewster was driving, and as he took an exit ramp, he lost focus and drove off an unfinished bridge, plummeting about 40 feet down. Brewster didn't get hurt too badly, but Piver suffered a massive head injury and numerous broken bones.

My greatest regret in those four years was not making time to visit Piver in the hospital before he was flown to a medical facility in California. The Corps had made me so cold and numb to losses like this that, at the time, I couldn't react normally. I'd like to know how Piver is doing these days, but I haven't been able to locate him.

The time had come to attend the classes I was ordered to take as a result of the UA incident, which meant no more duty for at least two weeks—a small break in my work routine. I dressed up in my uniform and headed to the big Naval Hospital, where the better-looking ladies were. Note: this was the first time since boot camp that I'd worn my uniform. Now I was back up to my normal weight of 191 pounds instead of the boot camp 167, and the uniform fit snugly.

The classes felt like a big joke for the first day and a half, and by the time I completed the two weeks, I asked if I could stay for an immediate refresher course. One of the twin girls that Spritz and I had gone out with was there, and we talked, laughing over a few memories. She asked what had happened and why we'd suddenly become unavailable. I apologized for both of us and tried to explain, though it seemed pointless. When I said goodbye to her, she mentioned, "We might be staying here to finish college while my parents wrap up my dad's career."

Christina and Sherri—awesome ladies. I guess breaking up with my girl from home helped me avoid getting too serious with anyone else, which was a good thing. My duties here were unpredictable, and I wouldn't have wanted them any other way, so dragging a girl through this with me wouldn't have been fair. No offense to anyone, but I couldn't afford distractions. Life had gotten crazy for me. I had either become this place, or it had become me. I craved the adrenaline high, even as I longed to escape.

CHAPTER 14

ONLY THE LUCKY

Spritz came into my room yelling something. I couldn't understand him too well, but he seemed to be as happy as hell, holding some forms in his hands—I knew what they were. He had been complaining about his feet for some time and was in need of medical treatment, so the Navy side of the Marines decided to let him go. The time was upon us to say our goodbyes; at 16:00 a few days later, he would be departing from the Corps to his hometown or wherever he wanted to go. Spritz now had a key to open the door to the world and no limits.

Spritz had some unfinished business before he left. Whalen and I didn't want to bother or help him with it, hoping it would take him longer so we could go out a few more times before he departed. We knew as soon as he completed his last order of business, he'd be gone, and we couldn't hold it against him.

It was late November; Christmas was just around the corner, and soon I would be going on leave for the standard 15 days. I needed to start getting in shape for leave—not that I wasn't already in shape, but when I went home, I received the royal treatment: home cooking, drinking, telling stories, drinking more, eating more, falling asleep, and, most of all, becoming lazy. I always tended to put on a few pounds, sometimes more than expected.

I reconnected with my old girlfriend while I was back home and enjoyed the time, but that's all it really was. I met a slew of people while I was there and had a very nice Christmas and New Year's Eve. Shortly after, I was on my way back to the same old routine. I appreciated my leave time more toward the end, because it felt as if I were going to a place of politics rather than the Marine Corps, as I had once known it.

On my drive back, I stopped in Tuscaloosa, Alabama, to get a room. It was late—maybe after midnight. I got all cleaned up to relax a little better. I called the front desk to complain about something, and the clerk came over to see what exactly was wrong; she wrote down the problem. We talked for about half a minute, and then we ended up in a lip lock, but nothing much else happened. She told me, "No, because I don't want to feel cheap." She left but insisted that I take her number and said, "Maybe next time."

I finally got some rest. The next day, I made it back to Charleston, S.C., and talked with the guys who were there as I prepared my gear for duty. The following morning, while I checked in with admin, I was told to come back in a week if they didn't get a hold of me first. My orders were due any day now.

A week went by, and I felt as lucky as Spritz to be checking out. I was asked how many days I wanted for leave, and I said, "Give me one day, just so I can get there on time." One Marine in administration emphasized that I should go on leave.

I stressed, "Man, I don't want leave."

He said I was crazy and then began to process my papers. Changing duty stations meant I had to see all the brass for my exit interviews.

The Colonel requested that I see him first. If I'm not mistaken, the process went up the chain of command, not down. So there I was, standing in front of Lt. Col. Mark Masterson.

"Sir, Pfc. Zavala reporting as ordered."

"At ease, Zavala. Sit down," he paused until I sat, ". . . it's too soon, isn't it?"

A tour of duty here was normally 18 months, but when the Navy doctor signed my forms, it got the ball rolling on my orders. Due to my early departure, I had been bumped off the list for jump school, but I was OK with it. Little did I know that all the training in the Fleet would provide me with the adrenaline I needed for pleasure—my drug of choice.

"Well, first of all, how's SSgt. Diablo treating you?"

"Sir, I think he avoids me, if at all possible." We laughed a little throughout the interview. I personally thought most Marines became nervous speaking to someone this high up in the brass, but from the beginning, I spoke with what I thought was good intellect, letting the words do their thing. It must have worked.

I remember him wishing me the best of luck and telling me he liked the way I handled SSgt. Diablo. He said if I took charge of everything that came my way like that, I'd be a great leader in the Fleet. "Don't let the shit-birds in the Fleet misdirect you. And one more thing, Zavala—I've seen many Marines come and go, and only a few carry themselves like you do, with just the right amount of confidence that brings out the perfect touch of zeal." I was at a loss for words and felt the proudest I'd ever felt. Whatever it was I did, it made me feel accomplished. When I returned to my room, I looked up the word zeal; afterward, it all made more sense to me.

Captain Usherson was next. He was still a dickhead and wanted to burn me, but as long as I acted professionally, the Colonel had said, "That man can't do you any harm unless he comes through me." I reported as ordered, and the first thing Capt. Usherson said was, "Well, I'm glad you didn't pull the same shit Cpl. Smith did." I knew he wanted me to let my emotions get involved in our interview, but it wasn't happening. I replied, "Sir, I don't think you really know what goes on out there."

He showed every sign of guilt in his facial expression and body language. He rubbed his face, cleared his throat, tilted his head, and quickly reached for his coffee. I was implying that it was him who sent people after me; after all, it was his job to conduct background investigations and make sure he knew everything about everyone for our security clearances. I didn't take it personally. At the time, I just felt he could have approached me directly and said what he needed to say. But now I understand that it doesn't work that way—especially now. Sgt. Major was next. I saw him, and he told me to simmer down a bit, and I'd be OK for the most part.

"Zavala, you had a pretty rough start. What happened?"

"Sir, I have a lot of friends here—some very good friends, and some I'm close to just because I know them. It's not that they're not good guys, but because they're not bold enough. I've had a few beers with most of them, and I came to understand the way they are. So, that allows me to pick and choose the ones I'd rather stick my neck out for, because I knew, or felt, that they'd do the same for me. If it meant putting myself in harm's way, then I would—not just for Spritz, Whalen, Piver, Holy, or Knightengale, but mostly for them, and maybe a few others."

He seemed to want to hear more, or maybe it was my chance to vent, so I continued.

"For instance, the other day, I helped Wellerton. I don't like him too much because he talks too much shit, sir, but he was in need of help, so I helped him. He was embarrassed but grateful that I got out of bed to help him and prevented any further trouble. He even offered me a hundred dollars, but I settled for a 12-pack instead. I did it because when I needed help, I wished someone had been available to help me. Everyone did what they could, but it wasn't enough. I figured he might have wanted the same. Sergeant-Major, it's easy being a Marine once we get a hold of it. Through this time here, I've learned that the Fleet may not be so easy, and it won't be easy being a grunt. A simple mistake will cause people grief, heartache, loss of loved ones, and even lives. They're not just clerical errors; they're fatal mistakes that we're only taught about once. And as I head to the Fleet now, if I don't think like that, then I may not make it home alive."

"Zavala, if that's how you feel, then I don't need to be telling you much more. It seems you didn't just go through the motions here—you really took notice of what it takes. So, I'll get back to my work. Carry on that way, Marine, and you'll be just fine."

The Sergeant-Major had over twenty-two years of service and ended our session with a motivating, "Oorah! Semper Fi, Marine!" Coming from a Sergeant-Major, it meant a lot to me; it reassured me and put me on top of my world.

Lt. Sheppard ordered me to see him after the Sgt. Major and the Colonel, since an MPS Platoon Commander had not been established after Lt. Hailey left.

"Zavala, you've overcome some of the toughest crap they had to throw at you, and you're still breathing and not insane. I heard what happened at MPS with SSgt. Diablo. Now I want to hear it straight from you." He was shocked by the situation once I added my details. He shook his head, looking down as if in disbelief, then said to me, "Good luck, and may God bless you. I hope that all my Marines can withstand half the shit you have. Take care, Zavala; it was good knowing you."

Not many words, but enough emotion to have a lasting impact.

Captain McGowen was not happy I was leaving. "Zavala, I hate to see you go, but your place is in the Fleet. This was a waste of time; I think you set the bar for others you served with here at this duty station. You did the right thing with SSgt. Diablo. It surprised me that you didn't shoot him. After our meeting, I told my wife what you shared with us about the responsibility a Marine has to their moms and wives, and she came to tears. Thank you, Zavala. It was a pleasure serving with you and a real experience. Good luck, and God bless you."

The "God bless you" part made the interviews feel more sincere, and I think God did bless me by answering my prayer before the moment of truth—right before boot camp got underway. I understood why my life hadn't been normal while in the Corps.

It became necessary for me to know what I had officially faced during the so-called trial for the SSgt. Diablo incident. I asked Capt. McGowen, and he replied, "Zavala, get the hell out of here."

To this day, I don't know what the official ruling was—an Article 15, a court-martial, or just preliminaries. As much as happened to Whalen, Spritz, and me, about 75% of it is known only to the three of us and the opposing side (meaning whoever we were up against). Piver,

Knightengale, Holy, or anyone else had no idea, and we preferred to keep it that way to avoid infringing on their positive motivation.

That was it. Finally, I could have my last drinks with my friends—anyone who wanted to say "goodbye, good riddance, shalom, hasta la vista, khuda hafiz, as-salamu alaykum," or whatever else, because I knew I'd miss every one of them. I said goodbye to Scott, the owner of the Birdbath, before driving to North Carolina. "Thank you for the women, the drinks, and the great times you let me and the gang have here. Is my tab cleared?"

He insisted that I not worry about it, shook my hand, and left. I was leaving a place that had taught me a great deal about life; the key to it all was perseverance.

CHAPTER 15

FLEET MARINE FORCE

A few weeks went by, and I had finally gotten to meet the platoon, but not before being processed. A receiving station displaced Marine personnel to their prospective locations; while waiting, we'd go on work details.

While at one work detail, I ran into a friend of a friend from home who graduated with my sister. We were both surprised to see each other. I had known he was in the reserves but never imagined seeing him here. Everywhere I went, I'd meet people from all parts of the country—some I would remember; others were shit birds and really didn't give a damn to see again.

I was picked up by Kilo Company, 3rd Battalion, 8th Marines, 2nd Marine Division. The unit had just returned from a Rock Package, which consisted of training in the mountains of California. I met my roommates: Lcpl. Poff, a self-proclaimed redneck from Shelby, Tennessee; and Pfc. Smith, a black kid from Brooklyn.

Smith was right out of SOI and relatively new to the Corps; Poff had been transferred over from another company that had just returned from Asia after being there for six months. While in Asia, Poff received some of the best training and was very well adapted to the field. I had someone to look up to for once, given his experience, and I knew that I could benefit from him. Weeks went by, and we received more new Marines from SOI and just a few from other duty stations. Dade and Klausen arrived from the 8th, and I, the President's Own, and they were exactly what I did not want to turn out to be: lame-ass bitches. Later, Dade was promoted to Corporal, and suddenly he thought he was untouchable. Be reminded that no one here was untouchable.

Rowland was new; he dropped out of the University of Ole Mississippi. He had gotten mad at his dad and rebelled by joining the Corps. His dad was a very well-known businessman in Memphis at the time. Lance Corporal Law came over with Poff and had gone through the same type of training. Jessup was new, too, from Lynchberg, VA—a city where my crazy ass got kicked out, which was OK with me. I was very sorry that I'd ruined the friendship he and I had; this happened over a year later. Marese, another guy from PA, had parents who were divorced; he was raised by his dad. He was a very honest kid, and I say kid because he didn't look any older than fifteen years of age.

Something bothered me about Marese, and I didn't figure it out until about nine months later. I remembered that I had seen him at an E-club one night before we ever met; he was wasted, staggering, and all. I mentioned it to him about nine months later. He said, "That's where I remember you from. All this time passed, and you finally tell me." I told him, "I just now figured it out."

Anyway, Calentoni was also from PA, and in time, we became great friends. He used quotations from songs in his sentences when he spoke to some of us; I never asked him why. Maybe it was to see if we were being attentive.

Griffen and Prichard had been at other duty-stations prior to this, but they were salty-dogs and down to earth guys, with time already served and during that time they learned how to be relaxed. Griffen he was slightly buffed and a little quiet. I've yet to meet some one whom reminds me of this guy.

Cpl. Green was my fire team leader. He was genuinely very smart; his first duty station was in Panama, and he claimed that Pres. Noriega came up to his post, looked around, then left while Green was at the front gate. I wasn't naïve about things—after the crazy shit that happened to Spritz, Whalen, and me—so I believed him. Besides, I didn't find Green to just talk the talk; I knew it was possible. Barnes was a scavenger; he liked to steal from anyone, and he was one of those guys who thought that fat women were the finest things ever.

Mourning was from the school of hard knocks—New York City. He was on the Dean's List. While gaining his street knowledge and connections, he also earned his Golden Glove in one of America's toughest boroughs: Brooklyn. He was a threat. He received honors in Chemistry, Criminal Justice, Money Management, and Networking. Mourning also didn't have much to say, but when he did speak, I listened because I knew I could survive better knowing some of the things he knew about the streets, although we were heading into the jungles and forests. His street knowledge could be retained for later in life and also to deal with some of these motherfuckers from other platoons.

The fleet was like living in a neighborhood that was completely competitive. We needed to walk and talk a certain way; otherwise, someone would always try to play us for some kind of sucker—nothing like at Charleston. Within our own company, we still had a few guys who didn't get along, but that's what made the fleet world turn. It came down to who was the better Marine and the better leader of the troops appointed to them. I studied Mourning with a little more interest because everything he said was very logical and sensible compared to the rest of the platoon. Mourning and Poff were experts in their fields on opposite ends of their world.

Waters was a bad son of a bitch when it came down to basketball and the streets. When he lost his scholarship to, I think it was Sacramento State, he joined the Corps—not before a mandatory transfer to the streets of Fort Lauderdale. Cpl. Williamson was from Nebraska; he pretty much played along.

That takes care of the major players in my platoon, except for SSgt. Feldman. Now, he was a good man, and this is why: for starters, he loved the Corps, and secondly, he was down to earth and cared. We got to know him on a Sunday when he asked us if we would help him move his girlfriend's stuff from one place to another. He told me the story about how his grandfather left him $1.5 million if he joined the Corps and stayed in for at least ten years; then he would get the money after he turned thirty-nine years of age. He was in his twelfth year of service, and I didn't see him leaving the Marines anytime soon.

My Fire-team

Corporal Poff, my fire team leader, knew his job through and through. This guy, like most in the infantry, wanted to see some kind of real-life situation to have a complete sense of fulfillment in doing our job or at least witness some type of catastrophe. I believe the real reason behind that is to have a mindset for any other event that might occur. I believe that our job as grunts was 90 percent mental and 60 percent physical. I think the other 50 percent came from living together and becoming synchronized in everything we did. I say that because if we went out there and didn't perform like we practiced, then for sure we could expect to fail and cost lives.

We worked in a field, and 100 percent was never enough. The minimum expected by Poff, Rowland, Smith, and myself on a bad day was 120 percent. "100 percent is the most anyone could give." That is true, but Marines aren't just anyone. When the time came, we knew we'd be ready for anything, and if anyone was killed, then it would have been beyond our control, and the guilt would not haunt us for the rest of our lives.

Our fire teams got along well after training for a few weeks, and I felt somewhat comfortable in the infantry. You might even say we were gung-ho about doing something different. From the conversations Poff and I had together, he didn't have it easy. He developed his skills and became very good at this in just the three years that he'd been in the Marines.

There was almost nothing he didn't know about being in the bush; it became his job to pass that knowledge on to us. Evened up the odds a little more; at the end, we all could come home.

Rowland was an athlete—a fullback. Later, he was moved to a defensive back position, and he just enjoyed being around people who wanted better for themselves. The thing Rowland despised was lazy people. He stayed to himself, laughed and joked along, but if he saw someone who just didn't care about doing anything, he would go off on them, and sometimes he was tactful about it.

He'd question me as if I had the answers: "Dang, Zavala, why in the hell are they like that? Just gosh darn lazy, man; I can't stand people like that."

Rowland acted crazy and loud around the right people; he didn't use profanity too much or at all until he joined the Marines. He told me himself, while getting ready for our initial inspection, "Fuck this" and "Fuck that." He was nervous about not having all his gear ready for the inspection; he paused and said, "Fuck, Zavala, I never cussed so fucking much until I joined this damned Corps, and I never failed at nothing either." I don't think he saw it as a new lifestyle, and he needed to make adjustments.

Us guys, like Poff and Green, who had been in for some time, learned to gather extra gear for times like this. Rowland included, "How in the fuck are you guys not worrying and so fucking calm about this inspection?" He always carried a Bible with him, and that told me a lot about what kind of folks he had.

Gregory Smith was an introvert from Brooklyn—Dean Street off Atlantic Avenue. Smith was kind of shady when I first met him. It took some time for him to open up; maybe he wasn't used to meeting new people, or maybe he had never left New York City until then and couldn't trust outsiders. I asked him why he joined the Marines, and his answer was, "Just to do something different."

There wasn't a perfect answer; everyone had their reasons. It may not have been unique, but it was their reason. For the sake of conversation, I accepted Smith' reason because there seemed to be more to that answer than "just to do something different." I'm talking about the change in lifestyle, terminology, clothing, geographical location, and, most of all, what it took to get this far in his ideology of just wanting to do something different.

I mentioned earlier that after the dust settled, we began to trust one another, some of us more than others. Everyone was more relaxed and louder than when we first met—just like one big family. There were even a few times that we fought. I confronted Barnes about his stealing; there was an exchange of words followed by a few punches, and he caught me on the lower jaw while I gave him a series of body shots. We went on for about fifteen seconds, and when we got into a position where neither one of us could do anything else, it just ended. I bet that someone reading this is saying, "Aw, you're a puss," but we can't really hurt each other that bad because during our training we have real bullets, and if I don't have to worry about Barnes shooting me in the back, then life is that much better.

Since Smith and I were roommates, I kept trying to get him to say something or even initiate some kind of conversation. It seemed that he would always ask me for advice, which was a confidence booster for me. I never cared what they thought about me. I was just glad that we could count on one another when we needed to. It was obvious when someone was just talking trash: "I this, and I that."

Marksman

Weeks of training passed; next, we went to the rifle range to requalify with our M-16 A-2 service rifle and perform a battle sight zero (BZO) on our weapons. BZO was mechanically adjusting our trajectory and elevation so that our weapons could fire more accurately. What better person to do that with than a scout sniper, SSgt. Feldman?

Shortly after, we met our Platoon Commander, who was different from Lt. Sheppard. He was just as smart, but this guy had badness in his bloodline. What I heard from Feldman was, "Lt. Brown—his dad used to be in the CIA, some kind of leader, maybe of Operations." That was all I got before my thoughts became preoccupied with the type of attitude expected from me.

Before a major evolution like the Med-Float was going to happen, we needed to get some experience, first in the Appalachian Mountains for three weeks of rigorous training. It was everything that makes a person treasure the moments of being dry, warm, and indoors.

Times like this were when I'd like to have seen the Navy officer who administered the psyche evaluation on me down in Charleston—just how wrong he was and how I had become very well adapted to the ways of a grunt.

Whenever my life was hell and miserable, I knew I wasn't alone; I knew there were others who hated life a little more than I did. I learned to thrive on other people's misery, and it fueled me to press on. My thoughts were, "If they could make it through their moments of misery, I had no reason to worry." I studied everyone I came close to, but this wasn't the time nor the place to test the next man. We were always being challenged, and it was teamwork that helped the platoon make it through the tough times.

The rain was not letting up, coming down off and on but mostly throughout patrols. I was assigned to fire watch one particular evening when I saw someone wearing their rain gear; everything else had been packed up as if he was waiting to leave some place. I wasn't familiar with the other platoons too well. It was too dark to see his face through the rain because he was well covered, including being hooded with his parka. I approached him and asked if there was anything wrong. He said, "No son, I'm alright, thank you for asking." Since I didn't know who he was, I asked him.

He introduced himself as the company first sergeant; he then proceeded to answer all the questions that I had not even asked. His reason for not sleeping was to keep all of his gear, clothes, and sleeping bag packed away and dry. He explained to me the importance of the lesser evil in our current situation. "Either way, we're going to be miserable out here, and we have to deal with it. So what I'm doing is keeping everything dry, and every time we stop to rest, I'll sleep for a few minutes and just hope our next night isn't so bad. If your sleeping bag gets wet, then you may not ever get a good rest for the three weeks we're going to be out here."

Quick estimations were done, and I placed this first sergeant in Vietnam; then I realized that this man spoke from wisdom. It was either going to be a screwed-up learning experience for me or just listening to this guy, and life would be a whole lot better for me out here.

Fleets Daily Routine

The days began with all our rights to privacy stripped from us, but in a tolerable way for those who didn't make an issue about it. A wake-up call would sound, followed by a bang at the door to our rooms around 0600, and the lights should be turned on as an acknowledgment. We'd straighten up our area and go to morning chow, ready to go by 0800. Many times, a 0530 wake-up call was done the same way, followed by, "Let's go on a morning run. We'll be back in time for chow."

Formation would still be at 0800. Sometimes we fell in wearing PT gear, boots and utes, cammies, or whatever the uniform of the day was. Many times we were still out or just getting back from being in town or from some girl's house or apartment. In the Fleet, there were times we did nothing, but when we trained, we trained hard. We had someone going to medical; this guy went over here, that guy went there. Don't be fooled—we had appointments just like civilians.

Promotions were good. A formation was held, and the Commanding Officer would promote those who had either the score or had passed the Promotional Board. To be selected for the Board, one had to ask to be on it, and only if his pros and cons reflected him as an outstanding Marine. There again, you had to be voted on by the fire team leaders and squad leaders.

The only thing that sucked after a promotion was spending the cash to have our rank changed on our uniforms. It would be okay if we actually used them more often. The entire time I spent in the Marines after boot camp, I didn't wear any of my dress uniforms for more than three weeks. Most of my time was spent on patrol, in field training, or on duty and out of any dress uniform.

From January through July of 1990, all the training, qualifications, and grading on our mission performance consumed most of the time. Rifle qualifications needed to be done once a year to maintain our marksmanship; swimming, once per year. As I mentioned before, SSgt. Feldman, being a scout sniper, showed us everything we needed to know and also gave us pointers on accuracy. If someone from his platoon happened not to qualify, then that would look bad for everyone in a leadership role or that person was just a "rock." A rock was someone who just didn't have enough sense about something to understand it or simply couldn't learn to do what was being taught.

For those who did qualify in swimming on the first attempt, that was good, and we moved on to get ahead of the rest. But for those who had trouble swimming—either didn't relax, were terrified of the water, or just kept believing they would never be able to learn how to swim—they were the "rocks." At the very least, they needed to float for five minutes. I always had a little trouble with swimming, but I came through.

Every Infantry Company specializes in a different type of mission; Kilo Company's were TRAPP missions. Our capabilities came from land, water, or air. From a helicopter, we'd rappel from approximately 30 feet or more above the ground; other times, we'd actually land. Those techniques had their own procedures and rules and required specific gear. We didn't just board an aircraft without learning its rules and following up with its contingency plans. There was definitely more to do from a helicopter, like rappelling, fast-roping, and crash training. The worst scenario we trained for was if a helicopter capsized in the water. Once we were comfortable with our responsibilities, life became easier again.

An example of our training, besides TRAPP missions, was emergency landings. Emergency landings were tough; if we were shot and had to make an emergency landing in the water, what would we do? We did dry-run after dry-run (pardon my pun) until we felt confident enough to do a full simulation at a station with a helicopter in water during a capsizing incident. The only things we provided, besides ourselves and our abilities, were confidence. In my opinion, the most important element was confidence—not just for one person, but also for knowing that if the guy next to me needed help, I would be able to follow through for him, or vice versa.

To prepare ourselves for the most chaotic situation possible, we had to consider the chaos, confusion, disorientation, casualties, gear lost or damaged, and the possibilities of not being able to extract after the mission. Additionally, the mission could turn into a survival operation if we lost too many people, had too many casualties, or if the pilot and his crew were dead or injured too badly.

If we could think of it and if it was possible, we trained for it. Confidence had to be synchronized between the pilot and his crew, as well as with the team leaders of the platoon on board and the guys to the right and left. If there were any doubts, it was likely due to a lack of proper training. There was no shame in telling each other that they were not ready. The real challenge lay in fine-tuning the overall confidence level.

There was no way I couldn't be nervous throughout training, but it was always better to be nervous or scared than overconfident. A few of us had beef with one another, and we knew that racism also existed here. Like I said, I didn't think any of it was directed at me, but I would get caught in the crossfire and have to break things up. Suppose we made it past the helicopter extraction only to find ourselves in battle with each other; it was tense, and adrenaline was pumping. When all these external forces came together, it became more dangerous. Sometimes it seemed harder not to kill someone while training. I'm including this because much of this training involved live fire, and at any given moment, anger could spark a murder or an accidental death—many times, all in the cover of darkness. Most of us, being perfectionists and professionals, just wanted to get this done the right way and evolve to the next level of training.

The time came when Kilo Company took on the challenge of becoming an Amphibious Force; this training would start from scratch. I thought that while all these air-intrusion training exercises were taking place, others were training to drive and maintain the boats used for the amphibious assaults. The boat Marines, better known as Coxswains, underwent their own regimen of training—for instance, learning how to operate these boats through rough, choppy waters in various sea stages and currents, nautical navigation, and the mechanics of the motors.

Troubleshooting was often done by touch, as it was never known who was watching while out at sea. As far as 50 miles out, these guys with their boats and teams were launched from the ship to commence our training.

Basically, they were required to do everything we did, but in the ocean, water inlets, or channels. If it meant treading water for hours at a time, so be it; being expert swimmers was the minimum requirement to be considered or recommended for this schooling. We always gave them hell because they never seemed to do any field exercises with us; instead, they did their own thing on the Zodiacs while we applied our camouflage face paint. They were applying their SPF-10 Banana Boat sunblock. These guys were cool, but we couldn't really hang out much for the simple reason of separation—they did their thing while we did ours.

Martin Garcia was among these guys, and he was in charge of a squad within the Zodiac boat team. He was from Carrizo Springs, Texas; in fact, he was the first Marine to welcome me to Kilo Company because I was from Texas and, especially, because I was Hispanic. Following the introduction, he gave me the dirty lowdown on what was happening and who was who within the company. He was well connected throughout Kilo, and I now had pull. He had one more year left before his time was up. Today, that guy is still the same nonchalant, easygoing person he was then; he lives in Austin, rides his Harley, and does his thing.

The concern most of us had was being left alone out on the ocean, only to have the boats capsize. We trained for that as well. The main issue was losing our equipment in the ocean because once it was gone, it was gone for good.

Next was staying dry and operable; it could get cold out in the middle of the water. We tried to keep ourselves dry so that the weight from our wet uniforms wouldn't slow us down; we were always running right after making it on land. Reaching our objective was hardly a problem, though issues arose when we needed to bring people back with us. They always seemed disoriented and confused; at that point, we knew what we were doing, and we had to consider that the people being extracted never knew our plan.

Aside from the special training, we also focused on maintaining and improving the skills we had developed from day one: land navigation, reading maps, cold weather survival, patrol formations, and teamwork throughout our fire teams and squads. History, uniform maintenance, and all the other aspects of the Marine Corps didn't occupy our minds at that time. It came down to a matter of survival and hoping that tomorrow would come for us.

Learning their breaking points or weaknesses wasn't for me to gain an advantage but to better understand their tolerance for difficulties. Along with the training on the weekends, we played football and became acquainted with the 1st, 2nd, and Weapons Platoons. Over time, some guys in the Company became friends outside of training. We didn't ask for hookers or anything like that; as long as they had beer in the field, they understood our needs. We began training as a Company in March of '90.

Soon after, we received our assignments for our Platoon, which were broken down into 3 to 4 Squads, each with several Squad Leaders. Within the Squads were several Fire Teams, consisting of three or four men working together as one. Our title would change to diversify our abilities. TRAPP stood for Tactical Recovery of Aircraft Pilot and Personnel.

We trained on a few missions, beginning to understand how the Pilot and Personnel might be affected by the crashing of their aircraft—from their mental state to any injuries. Most training was done repeatedly, not only to perfect it but also to understand the reasoning from everyone's point of view. My take on our missions was that it was the same as what those two guys did in that one movie with California's Governor and that other governor from Minnesota who "didn't have time to bleed." I mentioned it to Lt. Brown. He said, "Yeah, Zavala, but this ain't Hollywood, and it's on a much larger scale, and maybe just as covert."

Soon, we were graded by a few Colonels, a Major, and definitely a General, then awarded the title MEU-SOC, which stands for Marine Expeditionary Unit, Special Operations Capable. We specialized mainly as an Amphibious Assault Company, and our call signs were Gator-1,

2, or 3, depending on our Platoon. The Weapons Platoon had different call signs, like Red-Dog or Red-something.

India Company and Lima Company were the other infantry companies that made up the ground forces, alongside the infrastructure of the Battalion. It didn't matter to most of us in Kilo Company—not to be an ass about it—but they were just support. The Artillery Units, Support Units, and Administration in the Air Squadrons all had their roles, and we all did our parts to be certified as such.

Mentality

Marines are a breed apart, and even more so are the guys in the infantry. I don't have the real scoop on the rest of the Marines, but when we were around them, I noticed a different behavior pattern towards each other. I'm definitely not taking anything away from the other guys; without them, we couldn't have done anything but die or get promoted much faster.

Our behavior was like that of the poor kids in school, with far less to lose and a much rougher upbringing than everyone else. Still, we received no special treatment; everything we had wasn't ever brand new; instead, it felt more like hand-me-downs from them or the Army. We always started trouble with everyone, whether we could win or lose; we didn't give a damn. When we did start something with the other guys, we'd probably end up losing anyway because the only times we were ever around them was at a bar, and for some reason, we were always a bit more drunk. Not every time, but most—we were less civilized and a bit more crazy than the other guys. While they seemed to have it made, they were the ones who got all the promotions and quotas to meet. We'd rather leave them alone on their side of the tracks while we played on our side.

That was my perception, although the Corps wasn't for everyone. Often, some guys lost it and threw fits, but I've yet to see anyone cry and break down. Maybe that was just the way it happened; a progression where the crying came later.

Later, I would turn in my M-249 for a PRIC-77 and become GATOR-3 since I was in Third Platoon. But for now, I needed to adjust to the M-249 Squad Automatic Weapon. Everything about our personal weapon was expected to be known: how to break it down, its firing ranges, how many rounds per minute, and how to disassemble it with your eyes closed or in the dark. Function checks were crucial; there was absolutely no reason why we couldn't learn that. We didn't think too much about all the technical aspects, except when talking to civilians and such.

I recall the awkwardness of the very first TRAPP mission we ever attempted. Everyone gave their all, but the teamwork needed its timing, so it turned into a big clusterfuck. We were able to do everything else together because we practiced together.

We unofficially named it Operation REDNECK. It was different because the shots being fired came so close to us that we could hear the rounds whiz by right past us. I was nervous but excited enough to transform that nervousness into a pure, exhilarating learning experience. At the same time, Poff and I decided our maiden exercise needed a name, while the higher-ups simply referred to it as a training exercise.

Third Platoon was new to this; maybe only five guys knew how to conduct these types of operations. The lingo was even different, but we overcame those barriers to do what we were about to do. A mental transformation came over me, and I instantly felt a rush of adrenaline. I tried to hold on to the feeling and the sound of fired rounds flying right next to my head because it might be the only thing to keep me grounded in reality if and when we were fired upon—if we ever found ourselves in a hostile environment.

After a few intense weeks of training, everything came together. Of course, we were challenged by almost every element of nature: the cold or hot weather, the water, the fear and frustrations, and I must include the times some of us became unbearably ill with pneumonia, fever, or even seasickness. We learned it well, and in our line of work, it meant that most likely everyone would come home alive.

We found ourselves out celebrating our accomplishment, but partying together felt awkward. Trust away from the field had not yet been established, and our certain stress signals were not formed. Partly, we didn't know how the person next to us would act when wasted out in public. It might sound like my life revolved around beer drinking all the time, and well, it did.

It was a completely different ball game coming from Charleston, maybe like moving from a small town in the sticks to a giant metropolitan city.

FOOTNOTE: An important but scary fact was that in the late '80s and early '90s, more than 90 percent of the Marines were alcoholics.

Fun-run

Don't let the name fool you; fun runs weren't that fun. Then again, they weren't that bad either. They were more mental than anything else. The runs took place in the woods along a path etched by many prior runs. Instead of running shoes and shorts, we wore boots and utility pants as we navigated the terrain—over creek beds, jumping logs, and stopping to do a series of calisthenics. These runs took the better part of two to three hours, but the most enjoyable part was the end. They were mostly done in the morning when it was cool, a time when we had more energy and nothing else was planned. As soon as we returned, we'd shower and hit the rack until after lunch, just to be rested in case we were ordered to do more physical activities.

Hats off to our Corpsman, the only Navy guy whom Marines will defend, even if it means getting injured. He did everything we did, including the runs, and he was the one who literally took care of our injuries, ailments, and medical reports. I can't really speak on their behalf, but if someone messed with our Platoon's Corpsman, that person would definitely be in for a world of pain—unless he took out the Marines first.

Corpsmen didn't seem to mind being with a Marine unit; at least that's how I saw it. They may have felt differently at first, but I never saw our Corpsman criticizing the fact that he was there with us. At times, they might get pissed at the Navy for naval reasons, or when they'd been with a Marine unit for a long time and were ready to return to a hospital but were denied—that's totally understandable. Not even a Marine can be out there in the field for more than three to four years at a time; it becomes too demanding, both physically and mentally. Someone almost always gets shuffled around, and their morale is the first to go. They can't seem to stop complaining about how this and that should have changed: "I should've been out of here by now; fuck this shit."

We weren't doing too well with women, so we devised a plan to let each other know the status of our situations and followed it accordingly. For example, if we thought we had a chance with a certain lady, we'd switch to a better beer, and if it was definitely more than just a one-night deal, we'd go for an import beer. Everything had been designated. We had agreed from the very beginning that there needed to be an S.O.S. signal from a girl. The reason for the S.O.S. signals was to maintain some level of politeness; when out in the field, it became necessary to be an asshole about everything. We all recognized that about one another, but we dealt with it for our safety and survival. Being an asshole the whole time wouldn't have been good for anyone. Yes, some guys did stay jerks, but we were never too nice to do something we didn't want to do—at least I wasn't. Rowland thought all these signals were too extreme; it had become an everyday thing for me.

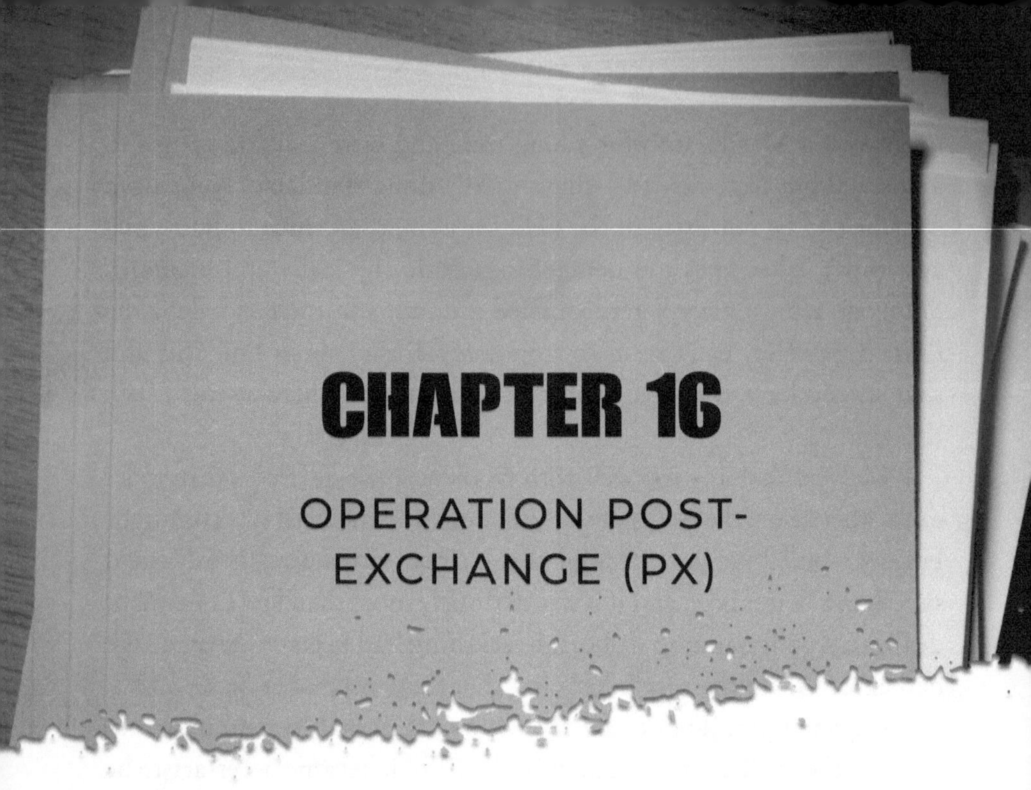

CHAPTER 16

OPERATION POST-EXCHANGE (PX)

By now, the first team had the training down pretty well. This one time we had gone out to the field, we were told, "The not-so-experienced Marines were going to get to go on this training mission. Zavala, Rowland, Poff, Dade, and a few other Marines, you'll be staying back; it's time for the newer bunch to gain experience in the training."

Knowing we would be sitting around and doing nothing for almost five hours, we assembled after a quick brief, and we were off to accomplish Operation PX.

Upon our departure, all I had with me were two knives, my ID, and some cash. Poff had no cash, just a knife; Rowland had no cash and no knife. Dade, on the other hand, had his credit card and needed nothing else, equipped with the bare essentials to do only one of a limited number of things. Off through the brush, mostly at a jogging pace, we came up to this campsite. Poff said, "Oh shit, this is a Recon Platoon's site. Leave their gear alone, and let's move on."

I don't know what might have happened if we had messed with

their gear. Would we have been tracked down or what? But we moved on. We came to a big field, and we were literally knee-deep in mud for about one hundred meters. We crossed it, cleaned off, and ran some more. We needed to swim about thirty meters across marshy waters. I was nervous because I remembered all the gators in the Charleston water, and it wasn't too different; besides, Charleston was about one hundred fifty miles from Jacksonville. Finally, I made it, and still, we ran further along just to find another field to cross and a small cliff to overcome.

We had to make it across a long bridge, which was okay, but if someone had decided to ask us who we were with, we might have been screwed. Again, the train of thought had been the worst-case scenario, and we had made up a story if questioned. Luckily, no one asked, and things went as planned; we got something to cool us down.

After maybe two hours with nothing to drink and sweating out all of our reserves, just my luck, I happened to get the wrong thing. I drank some apple juice, which upset my stomach pretty badly. I was in the restroom only minutes after finishing my drink. Poff went straight to the beer; Rowland saw my reaction to the juice and based his decision accordingly. The two of them put away about three six-packs. By that time, I had returned from the restroom to join them. I decided not to screw around and got myself a twelve-pack, two bottles of vodka, some cigars, and a bag of chips because I was starving.

Time was quickly running out. We needed to get back to our campsite, which was named Landing Zone Bluebird; we called it LZ Bluebird. We were too messed up to even try to make it back alone, and if we asked someone for a ride, we were risking being busted. Dade was the only one with his head on straight for the moment, and his idea was to try to call his wife and instruct her to pick us up so she could drive us to Bluebird. It was paramount for her to move quickly on this. She arrived on the scene, we loaded up, and hauled ass. Poff, Rowland, and I were dropped off about two hundred fifty meters from our staging grounds.

Dade stayed behind; he had an excuse because his wife was out there. Wives were allowed to go near the staging area to see their husbands.

As soon as we hit the ground, we scattered like roaches; we understood our objective/rally point. We may have thought we were being discreet about the entire thing, but I think it was because we were drunk. I still had some residual effects from the mixture of apple juice with beer. As we were laughing and running, I yelled, "Hey man, I'm crapping in my trousers."

Rowland and Poff thought I was joking, but as soon as I saw a good brushy area, I drew my dagger, pulled down my trousers, cut my underwear in two places; off they came, I wiped, and resumed toward my objective.

I've told this story to different people from time to time; I feel that maybe they're kind of embarrassed for me. The point I'm making is that it became a development of second nature to adapt well to any given situation, to come up with a plan while on the move, then execute. Being in the certain circumstances I was under allowed me to think that the situation was legitimate.

We made it back on time and unnoticed. I was in my tent as if nothing had gone down; we reeked of alcohol. Close to an hour passed, and as I was laying there in my hooch (tent), trying to foresee the penalties of our mission, I heard SSgt. Feldman ask, "Zavala, where the hell are you?"

I stuck out my shirt as if I were surrendering, but mostly for his mercy because I thought that we had been compromised. Feldman came over to my hooch, stuck his head in, and with a grim look on his face, he asked me, "What do you have for me?" I thought for sure he was going to be pissed at us, but he was smiling until I handed him a bottle of vodka and a fistful of cigars. His face grew long in shock and quickly recovered with another smile. I think he was surprised because I had a fifth; he might have expected something like a beer or two, maybe even a pint of liquor, but not a fifth. He assured me that if I wanted some later, he'd be over in the staff area. Rowland or Poff still had the other bottle of our private stock.

The next morning, Poff and Rowland were hungover; SSgt. Feldman was happy. I never knew who besides SSgt. Feldman drank the fifth I handed him. The next night we ended up going on a training exercise with our platoon. Poff and Rowland dragged ass the whole time, but still, Poff was on top of his game. I guess my time spent on the crapper did me some good.

The reason Poff knew so much about being in the field was that he was taught by one of the best. He told me a few different stories about this Marine, and every story was death-defying or gung-ho; every story left me in total amazement. These stories don't belong to me, therefore I won't repeat them, but the methods he used to train Poff and Law were wicked and gruesome. When I first heard, I couldn't believe it or imagine it. It was near the time that we were about to leave for overseas when this other Marine, who trained Poff and Law, stopped by to pay his protégés a visit. They talked, and I was introduced. I just sat and listened because, in a way, I was indirectly affected by what this guy had taught Poff and Law. I think that's another factor in why I'm still here, due to their training passed down to me.

I stopped watching the ever-so-beautiful Deborah Norville on the news every morning, so I would read the papers to keep up with everything else other than the situation going on in Iraq. Making our preparations to go to the Mediterranean area, we'd most likely be the ones going in first, and I didn't want to worry about that; life was too short. I found out that the war was not too far off when Cpl. Green mentioned to me, "Since before Vietnam, we had not moved so many weapons to the ready stage until now." I stopped reading the papers or watching any news at this point. The only thing I needed to know was how the enemy worked its war strategies, and that information came down through the command.

I had not even taken up going to church because if I had, the reality of life would be magnified that much more. I even understood that for the time I was in the Corps, I couldn't ride the fence on the topics of church and war because if it came down to it, my decision would be WAR.

War is a part of life, and the programming that I had undergone was with me, at least until I was dead or out of the Corps. By this point, I had accepted death, and sometimes I welcomed it.

The deal with Saddam Hussein was starting to become more intense around the time we received orders to the Mediterranean Sea. To me, this explained how a great portion of the National Defense's money is spent maintaining a fleet of ships with air-attack capabilities. After the spending done in today's war, that surprises me more; I think it's bogus, but I'd rather we take it to them there than have them bring it here. I still think it's not long before it arrives as a daily occurrence; they've already made us think that it can happen any day at any time. We must think about it and differentiate it from a mind-set or a fear (paranoia).

CHAPTER 17

BLUE, GREEN WATER
WORK-UPS

It had come time to board the ship; to Puerto Rico, the voyage there and back would take up to two weeks. The purpose was to acquaint those who had never been on a ship with life on a ship. That was it: one of the greatest things I've ever done. I didn't understand how others didn't like going on a Med-float; to me, it was more like a state of mind. Out there on the ocean, breathing the fresh air and getting away from America for more than a few months, I didn't think it would be all that bad. Whatever happened back home, there was nothing I could possibly do about it, and I accepted it. Laying in the sun and lifting weights, we didn't do a damn thing as far as working, but we stood guard duty once in a while.

When we arrived in Puerto Rico, and liberty was sounded, we infiltrated a barbecue party on the beach. There we swam, ate, and drank. It was good, and the next day we headed back. The one thing to look forward to was going home on leave to see my girlfriend, but this time from a different outlook on life. After spending most of my time preparing our families for my distant departure and giving instructions on "what ifs," I left the car in the hands of my girlfriend. I forewarned her, upon boarding the plane at the airport in Austin, Texas, to depart to return to North Carolina, not to look in the box I had in the trunk; I guess she wanted to feel a bit closer to me in a sense. I'm thinking a few weeks passed, then curiosity got the best of her. My girlfriend opened and read the ever-so-infamous journals.

This box was an ammunition container for a (2 charge Assembly Demolition M183); I still have the box. For some reason, it fascinated me, and I had to have it, but to get it, I needed to carry it along with about another 60 pounds of gear for about 9 clicks (9,000 meters). I knew she wouldn't understand because my entries were in journal form, and everything was not explained to fit any of her questions. After reading these documents, I bet she had a million questions but no answers. Feeling abandoned, she ran away from home, met this guy, and eventually married him. All this didn't take place until we were underway overseas. I guess she failed the ultimate test of trust. That's what I registered it as instead of getting all bent out of shape about it. I guess I felt a loss, but in my emotional state, I couldn't let it affect me. Everyone was all so concerned, and I appreciate now what they did then, but at the time, I would get upset because I felt as if they were feeling sorry for me, and that's not how I wanted to be treated because shit happens, and we deal with it.

When we finally made it out to international waters, we found out Budweiser had sponsored us to row two rowing machines until we made it over the Atlantic Ocean. We had a Marine on those machines 24/7; in the middle of the night, someone would be awakened by a whisper on the hour, "Hey man, wake up, it's time for you to go row." By that time, there was not much to do for the other Marines but work out or watch TV. There wasn't telling how many decks of cards we went through because, when all else failed, we broke out the deck of cards.

Soon, the gym was scheduled out to platoons, and people who normally didn't get into the gym were getting pumped. My hat's off to Calentoni and Marese; they approached me and said, "Hey, Zavala, I want to get big, man. How do I do it?" From that point on, they were getting what they asked me for.

"Operation Sharp Edge"

We were getting closer and closer to Europe; I just knew it. Then, one particular afternoon, a meeting was announced to meet in the chow hall. The Battalion's Executive Officer (XO), Major, had announced to us, "Men, off the Ivory Coast of Africa, troubles have been brewing there, and we have been ordered to go into the American Embassy and help provide better security because things there are expected to worsen. Yes, they have Embassy-Duty Marines there, but they have certain things they must do. We'll be providing security from other posts which are being established as we speak. Our main mission is to evacuate foreign nationals. Let's go in there and kick ass. God bless you. Semper Fi. One more thing, men: your Company Commander will be instructed on the Rules of Engagement, some of the things that will be expected from you, from the things we've all been trained for, then down to your Platoon Commander and all the way down the chain of command. Thank you, men; carry on."

The Company Commander sounded attention on deck as the Battalion XO departed the room. The Commander's briefing followed. The company dispersed down to platoons—briefing after briefing—until we reached the smallest form of a working team, which was a fire team. Cpl. Green's common denominator with me was that we'd been through the same form of training; the only difference was his time was spent in Panama. It almost didn't matter that Poff was my team leader, and no disrespect to him, but this was more of an urban-terrain mission, and this was our specialty (Cpl. Green's and mine). I would still answer to Poff, but to Cpl. Green, it was like having an extra fire team for his squad.

Poff was too excited because he had been in an Infantry Unit his entire time in the Marine Corps, and now he might finally administer all his skills, techniques, and all the training in a real-life situation. As grunts, we spend most of our time in the field, and it would sometimes seem too vain to invest so much for nothing.

Being in the Corps now had a new high in life compared to being in

Charleston, SC; it was more real and made sense to me. There were fewer direct politics for me to deal with; the responsibilities were the same but just not identical. The feeling was like before the season's opening kickoff of a football game, with the fans yelling and cheering for their team, the coaches putting together their final plan of attack, and the players going over their plays in their heads. Now combine the three, and there you go—I finally understood why coaches love coaching.

In the Battalion XO's brief about Africa, he included that there were three guys fighting for their reasons or strategic standpoints: the Royal forces under the command of Prince Johnson, this other guy from the Caribbean who robbed the treasury there, fled to Africa, and bought his way into the presidency; his name was President Doe. I don't think I would have remembered the other man's name, but it seems that history was repeating itself. I still heard his name on the news: Charles Taylor. Then there were the African peacekeeping forces that wore the baby-blue helmets; they were from Nigeria and other surrounding countries who helped maintain the peace.

Lt. Brown said, "Zavala, are you ready for game day? This is for real."

"Sir, this is what it's all about; this is why we practice over and over." He gave me a thumbs-up, then he carried on with what he was doing at the moment.

First Platoon went in first because they had better means of recovering personnel for our type of missions. This Platoon had been trained for climbing and lowering personnel in and out of cramped situations; in all, a few of them had been climbing instructors. For starters, we didn't know what type of situations we were up against until we got there, and remember that most of us had never been in this situation; the real thing was to see how we felt after we landed. Third Platoon was pissed because there was no doubt about it: we were the better platoon of the three, but as soon as we made it in, we were okay.

Our flight from the ship into Africa was intense but sensational. My mind raced through all the training, first-aid procedures, and anything that might help me adapt to our inevitable encounters. As we disembarked the Hilo, the smell of death was all around; it was an awakening experience to be personally introduced to a war-torn country. I think it was because I had been a bit naïve, or I just didn't expect to be confronted by such a stench. SSgt. Feldman just laughed at me and asked, "What's wrong, Zavala?" As we stuck to our Standard Operating Procedures (SOP), we formed our perimeter as tactfully as we could, quickly getting the hell to a safe cover area just as soon as the Hilo was at a safe distance.

First Platoon had been there for one week when we relieved them from post. We were situated as a two-man patrol team and were given instructions on when to use deadly force. They ordered us not to help anyone outside the gates of the American Embassy compound in Monrovia, Liberia. It was hard not to want to help; the people there had needs—food and water—just to stay alive, and they wanted nothing more.

Their eyes spoke out in a loud voice that wasn't heard; instead, we saw and felt the pain and suffering they were going through. We, on the other hand, had it all compared to them. A canteen of hot, disinfected water, which didn't taste too well to us, was a treasure to them. The MREs we grew to hate would have been a feast to them. The people fighting the war there treated it like a regular job: from sunup to sundown, then they'd come home to the family, only if they had been lucky that day.

Nowadays, when I see someone from Africa, I might mention to them that I was there during the Liberian Campaign. They look at me as if I'm crazy for a bit until I say the name of one of the generals or Prince Johnson. Then they say, "Oh, you know this guy," of course not in a personal way, but just to acknowledge me acknowledging their presence.

Whichever name I decide to say, he or she becomes friendlier instantly; it seems to break the ice every time. The things we saw there were not at all pleasant. We'd see the dead bodies either carried, wheeled, or even dragged by their loved ones to the burial grounds, which were not too far from the compound. We had gone in a few times already and had become accustomed to the stench that lingered.

CHAPTER 18

POW, LT. COL.
DANIEL BRYANT

Hayward and I were assigned to a roving patrol, and while on patrol, we saw a guy who approached our position and surrendered to us, stating, "Please do not shoot; my name is Lt. Col. Daniel Bryant. I am with Prince Johnson's Royal Army. I am here to seek refuge; may I enter?"

All the drilling in boot camp paid off. When handling a POW, one must apply the 5 S's. The 5 S's mean to: search him for weapons or anything on his body that may cause you harm; keep the POW silenced; if there is more than one, segregate them to secure them from harming you or themselves; and lastly, do it with speed.

I told Hayward to hold him there while I called higher authority to handle the situation and to do what became necessary to him if the lieutenant colonel did anything foolish. I explained to the lieutenant colonel the consequences if he did anything foolish, and then assured him of safety while in our custody. "Sir, you're safe here. If someone fires at us, then for sure we'll have to defend ourselves by returning fire, so stay still; everything is going to be alright."

I smoked at the time and gave the lieutenant colonel the only pack I had left. I'm sure it may have meant more to him than it did to me. I remember him asking me, "What is it that I should do next?"

Gator-6 was Captain Frampton; he arrived on the scene with other personnel from the State Department and denied the colonel any help. As he started to leave, the State Department personnel did the same. I yelled, "Hey, Colonel! Get rid of that uniform and blend in. Ask one of those guys" (as I pointed toward the boat people on the beach) "to let you use their fishing boat so you may get far from here until you can reach wherever it is you are seeking refuge."

He got down on his knees and started to chant something. The embassy also employed African nationals to work within the compound as their eyes and ears to what went on. One of the employees had seen the same thing I saw; I asked him, "What was the lieutenant colonel doing?" He told us, "The lieutenant colonel is praying to his tribal gods that he may be hard to kill." After that, it was hard; I felt like I was sending the lieutenant colonel to his death.

Monrovia wasn't the worst place in the world to be, but it certainly ranked as one of the deadliest. We could smell death with every step taken; we'd kick up dust, as the dirt helped break down the blood and guts that had been shed. Sierra Leone was just north of us; it was said that things were worse there. There's always hindsight, especially to a war not everyone knows about, and the schemes and scams that go on.

It wasn't until the Iran-Contra scandals in the late eighties that I began to understand how the smaller wars and battles were funded; we had never seen the bigger transactions, but they did happen. I was fully aware that drugs played a big part; because of us, a smaller transaction was busted, and I had my reasons for calling it in.

The real warriors were the children of Liberia. It was their blood that was mostly shed on the grounds, but away from our area; it was on the outskirts that these young warriors died fighting while doped up on drugs. They roamed the streets naked, killing one another. These guerrilla warfare fighters were better referred to as the Butt Naked Brigade.

The purpose of our presence was to evacuate any foreign nationals, from vacationers to foreign students to business people, even humanitarian workers, because the situation had become too hot. The scary part was: what if someone had been strapped down with explosives while we were patting them down? Thoughts like that crossed my mind only for a second or so. We understood the possibilities, but all we could do was deal with reality. The "what if" questions came about at a time of boredom; otherwise, it was go, go, go.

The NCO in charge changed our post every other day, and now I was on an observation post (OP) in a building, observing the activity that went on as far as the eye could see. The building across the street was not off-limits; if anything that might cause us harm or endanger us, we should report it. This post was better armed with a grenade launcher, anti-aircraft weapons, crew-served weapons, and small arms fire, like a watchtower high enough to fire upon anything outside of the compound.

"Panda Bear, Panda Bear, this is ATO, radio check, over."

"Loud and clear."

"Hey listen, there's something that appears to be drug activity going on in the building across from us. Over."

"Roger, don't worry about it."

I thought to myself as I looked through the binoculars; anything is possible. If this deal goes bad and they start to exchange fire and we get shot at, there would be hell to pay. I knew myself too well already and knew that I would probably respond with overkill. Maybe they might make a trade, drugs for high explosives that could be used against us. I wasn't chancing it, so I called Lt. Brown, and he showed up, saw what was going on, then left.

He called me over the radio minutes later and said, "ATO, ATO, this is Gator-3 Actual, over." The term "Actual" was used to refer to the commander, the one who gave the actual orders. Gator-3-Actual was Lt. Brown, and I was ATO. Another observation post was Danielle.

"Go ahead, Actual . . . Roger ATO, keep your eyes focused in about three," meant look over there towards the building in about three minutes. The State Department had planned and executed a raid and overtook the room in a matter of seconds, as I witnessed it all from my OP.

SSgt. Feldman knew somebody everywhere he went; from the Marines stationed there, he knew this NCO and asked to hook him up. They did, with a few bottles of vodka, and returned me the favor from Operation PX. Vodka didn't leave us smelling of alcohol as robustly as other types of liquors or beers did, as everyone should already know.

While Third Platoon was at the embassy grounds, the ambassador had invited the commanders at war to assemble there for peace talks. Lt. Brown rallied us together for a briefing to position all of Third in a tactical location. "You I want here, you over here, and you there." He said to me, "Zavala, I want you over here near the front gate, overhead for special purposes. Since you're my SAW gunner, we may need you in case everyone from the outside tries to rush through. Here's a radio; stand by and keep your eyes and ears open, and don't do anything unless I give you an order. Everyone else, deadly force is authorized. Hey, Zavala, see me when we're done."

The briefing continued, then we went to our designated location. As Rowland and I walked to our assigned place, Lt. Brown said, "Zavala, I'm putting you here because I know you'll do what it takes to stop these people if it comes down to it. I don't want massive casualties, Zavala. Take care of him, Rowland; I don't want you to get hurt either. You'll know when it's time to rock and roll."

No one ever explained anything to us as far as who was who. I didn't know if Prince Johnson was the good guy, and I didn't know President Doe was the bad guy. I saw both of them as personal threats to me; they both were the bad guys, and if one were to be removed from power, then it would all be done with here. Something came over me as I was in the firing position. Rowland and I had been talking just to keep motivated so we could react the right way if things went wrong. I don't think I ever told him about my events at MPS. I was so pumped up during this time that I even took the safety off my weapon.

Prince Johnson walked through and into the building. I had a bead on him, and the thought of shooting him crossed my mind. I remember asking myself, "Is this the guy who's causing the war?" I knew killing him would be wrong, but it would end this war. President Doe walked by, and again the thought of shooting crossed my mind. "This guy is more likely to be the one responsible for the war; after all, he stole to buy the presidency. I should kill this guy," were my thoughts as he entered the main building.

I had a little mercy on Charles Taylor and thought these other guys were bullying him around because he had no army. Little did I know he had the money and many people under his control with the drugs. Charles Taylor walked through, and I should've shot, but I didn't. When it was all said and done, I told Rowland that I almost shot all three of them. He inspected my weapon, found it off SAFE, and shook his head in relief that I had not pulled the trigger. I sat at my location and just thought of how powerful it would have been to kill a president, a prince, and a drug warlord all within a few minutes of each other. But the reality was that if I had shot anyone, I would have been killed by one of the hitmen or bodyguards escorting them, or even by one of my own. In the end, no one fired a round, but to know I was so close to ending this whole conflict—that was the real rush. Surely it would have created another conflict for me if I had gotten us involved.

Rowland, as easygoing as he was, had this thing about trying to gain weight and convert it to muscle during our workouts. In fact, when standing in line for anything, he always sat down to preserve his energy, mostly for working out and training. His eating motto was "as much as I can," and he ate with a spoon because a spoon, of course, transported more chow at one time from the plate to his mouth.

Rowland had this metabolism that wouldn't allow him to gain weight as easily as I did. If you didn't know Rowland, he might come across as being lazy and not caring, but the brilliance that he added to our team was valued.

As for me, I had my ideal weight, which was 189 to 193 lbs. Being at that weight allowed me to be agile, but at the same time to be enough of a powerhouse to help others who might fall by the wayside or straggle behind and hold us back. Teamwork and a certain amount of synchronicity were always deemed necessary, and of course, we were only as fast as the slowest Marine. Also, at the same weight, I was able to run a mile in around 4:40 to 5:10 minutes. So long as it was between the times of 0800 and 1600; after that, if liberty was sounded, then you might not be able to catch me until the next day.

The next time First Platoon came in, Martinez was shot at, but the round just missed him, piercing his pants behind his left knee, which triggered the react forces to come in from the ship, ready for combat. Nothing happened; we got there and were just a show of force. Before, when on reactionary forces while in security forces at Charleston, whatever it was that we were doing was dropped, and a sense of priority came into play. Each Marine had his special duties, from the doorman to the sniper, from the #1 spot to the #6 spot, and we all had a leader. It was slightly different this time because things were really hostile, and death was occurring at this place where we were going.

It was dinnertime. We were eating a nice, warm Navy meal: noodles with diced chicken. The siren sounded halfway through my meal; the last thing I did was wolf down what I could in 15 seconds because no one knew when our next hot meal would be.

While stuffing my face with whatever food I could and pocketing some fruit, a mental format was taking place in my head, as it always did when about to encounter the unknown. More especially this time— other times it would happen from one second to another—but because this was more critical, it felt kind of like slow motion. Our gear had been staged just in case, and our weapons were right next to it, with a gear guard present at all times.

I remember loading up in the CH-53 Hilo. For the first few minutes, there was no talking, with the exceptions of a few, "ALRIGHT, LET'S GO!" or "YEAH, GET SOME!" After I was fully switched over, I would assure those who needed it—some with just a simple pat on the back, eye contact, a thumbs-up with a grunting smile, and for a few others, a short pep talk—and we were good to go. The thoughts that went through our minds were wild, I'm sure, and we always thought of each other's welfare and safety. Everything had become second nature while anticipating a killing situation.

I don't remember how, but somehow I had come across this American flag. I was never a person of colors; red, white, and blue never moved me. Being an American and partaking in its traditions did more for me than just sitting around, letting life pass me by, and once in a while getting involved in something that might change the world. Although I could never forget what was drilled into us in boot camp—the flag-raising incident on Mount Suribachi. I had seen the group of Marines and their corpsman raising the flag; now that had an impact on me. I guess that was the reason I put the flag in a plastic bag towards the bottom of my backpack, just waiting for Third Platoon's opportunity to raise our American flag.

Our team leaders were briefed at the ship; word got down to us between leaving the ship and landing at the compound. Upon disembarking the Hilo, we were instructed on where to go by one of the grounds crew at the landing zone. Shortly after we established our fields of fire, we had assigned areas to go to and be a show of force, waiting and anticipating a long stay, maybe even a few kills. A sudden panic erupted from a small crowd gathered at the far end of the street corner, just a few meters from the State Department building.

I wasn't able to pinpoint an exact thought, but I knew that I was thinking of a bad to worst possible situation. I finally reached a well-covered position, which allowed me to observe. The first thing I saw were two bodies on the ground. While maneuvering, my thought process must have been louder than the faint gunfire, which I vaguely remember hearing, but I didn't factor everything into the situation at hand until then.

By this time, an assailant had another person at gunpoint on the ground. As I waited for the inevitable to take place, I prayed to God for the gunman to turn my way and fire. During my moments of prayer, I grabbed the light weapon nearest to me, put a bead on this crazed man, and practiced my breathing techniques to increase my chances of killing him with a single shot. My selector lever was switched over to the FIRE position; I had committed myself to killing this man as

I waited for God to provide an answer to my prayer. The process was slow, and I had time to develop a rational hatred for this guy, which prevented that certain wrong and dirty-soul feeling from creeping in.

He fired his weapon, killing the bystander without discrimination, and then continued down the street in search of another victim. I was pissed off; I could barely hold myself together. Then, suddenly, God answered my prayer in his own way: a shot was fired out of nowhere, partially amputating this man's leg. He yelled, screamed, and cried for help, but there was no one to answer. For nearly the next hour, the background noise consisted of this man's cries for help. The sound of another man's agony was never so sweet after seeing him kill those other people.

Just over two years into the Corps, under the circumstances we had been in, the knowledge and recognition that we might have to kill someone were well ingrained in our system. Three months passed, and not much happened; things began to come together for the Africans there. At the end of this civil war, there was a big firefight among the two remaining factions. President Doe, along with a number of his dignitaries, was captured and tortured to death. They cut off the prisoners' fingers one by one, applied tourniquets to prevent anyone from bleeding to death, and then tortured them some more. Continuing with their hands and feet, they finally dissected their private parts, allowing them to bleed to death.

Among other things seen there was a head that had been cut off from the rest of its body, floating in the ocean. Africa, I'm sure, is a very beautiful place; unfortunately, we didn't get to see that part of it this time. Luckily, there would be a next time for me.

Shell Back

It's a U.S. Naval tradition that when going south of the equator by ship, the Navy has an initiation, or hazing, administered by sailors and Marines who have crossed it in the past. This initiation is for those willing to participate and is carefully monitored and supervised to ensure that no one gets hurt too badly. We went through the initiation, keeping with tradition, which kept me at peace. (Later, when we received our awarded certificates, things had become too chaotic; I literally handed mine off to someone along with my address and said, "Here, man, can you mail this for me? Thank you." I guess it never made it home.) We moved on to bigger and better things, such as the Canary Islands.

There had not been a landing of a U.S. Naval ship at "Las Palmas de Gran Canaria" for 26 years, and we had been ordered not to mess this one up. The Canary Islands, a Spanish colony, are located at the upper westernmost part of Africa. We anchored to find a vendor waiting there with a beer stand on the pier; it was a crazy house; everyone wanted off. After we cleaned them out of beer at the pier, we proceeded toward the city. The hell with food; we had that three times a day for five to six months.

The city was ancient and decorated with some of the most beautiful women I had ever laid my eyes on. Quickly, I began to recite my Latin pickup lines, but to no effect; the language they spoke was Spanish, but a dialect—not totally different, but different enough to screw up my plans. I approached with caution and felt more than welcomed by the Spaniards to loosen up and resume living life to the fullest. We didn't have that great of a difference in dialect, but enough to force me to choose my words carefully; we needed to respect their customs and family traditions, at least to a certain extent. The thing about the Spanish language is that certain words in one country might mean one thing, while the same word in another country might be considered rude or even despicable.

Calentoni, Rowland, Jessup, and I decided to start on the boardwalk and move on from there. It was before noon. We walked the boardwalk until around 7 p.m.; every establishment along the beach was a bar. We lost count at 17 bars and had a beer at each one so far. Then we headed into town to see what kind of damage we could cause. We saw many of the folks from the ship; every brothel was doing good business now that the Marines had landed, or so it seemed. I just wanted to meet a good-looking lady, and I had somewhat of a chance. The terms were not too different after all; I may have just panicked. The first night was always about staking out the place and getting drunk along the way, and after that, we'd try to do whatever we could to get pleased. Of course, everyone wanted to call home, especially the family men.

The next morning, there was not one person in Kilo Co. 3/8 who didn't get wasted and was near death due to alcohol poisoning or in serious pain. Water was consumed by the gallons; IVs were injected into those who most needed them. That night, we were back at it again, but this time on the other side of the island, where most of the nightlife was.

This type of activity went on for the better part of three days, and when we left the island, it was a sad thing for me. We wore the city out. Rota, Spain, was our next stop; the ship needed to be resupplied. Now that I think of it, after the resupplying was conducted, we changed to another ship. A few administrative moves were also made; Poff and Law were promoted somewhere between Liberia and Spain. In a few days after Rota, we would set out for another great adventure. It was announced that Barcelona, Spain, was our next liberty port.

The situation with Iraq had intensified, and war had been predicted any day now. Most likely, we wouldn't go because of the war in Africa that we had just come from, and now the Mediterranean Sea had become a priority for us. After we reunited with the rest of the Expeditionary Unit for contingency purposes in support of the three continents, nearly every Marine unit was either already there or was headed to Iraq shortly thereafter.

CHAPTER 19

BARCELONA

We had been briefed on the situation; it was almost a cliché, always stressing to us about going out in town. "While you're out there, try not to pour too many beers down your neck, and look out for one another; watch your six," and so on. Night fell, and we were released. I'll have to admit I was in love with Spain. First, we looked through a tourist map that we picked up at a vendor's booth, then referenced all points that might be safe havens if something should occur. Then we looked to see where the better clubs, pubs, and bars were in reference to our quick return—well done. During the entire time, we were getting loaded.

The second night there, we had gone to this bar— a bit classy it was. We drank like there was no tomorrow and got loaded. During our spree, we met this group of ladies; one spoke English and talked to us while the others just sat, nodded their heads, and giggled.

I had forgotten for a second that I was the man capable of doing the most for us, so I stepped up. I started to do my thing in Spanish, and the one girl who spoke English asked, "Hey, what the hell happened to you last night? You got all drunk, and you too?" as she pointed towards Calentoni.

I turned away as if I had not heard her ask anything and simultaneously ran what I could vaguely remember through my head, but I couldn't bring to light the memory of seeing them. I smiled as I looked toward her and moved for cover to the bar, just to start from scratch with another beautiful lady. Minutes later, the night was running less bumpy.

The night came to an end after a while for the girl I had been talking to at the bar. We talked as I walked her out and waved down a cab for her. She told me that was a very gentleman-like and courteous gesture I had done for her, and it showed that I actually cared. I was trying my hardest to be nice and gentle because she had been only the second girl I had carried on a conversation with in 6 months, and my first date since we left the States.

When the cab stopped, she jumped into my arms and gave me a big kiss and a hug. I told the cab driver, in Spanish of course, as I pulled out a $10 bill, "Take her wherever it is that she calls home." I felt that I was on a roll, so I told the driver to wait as I grabbed a long-stem rose from a nearby vendor just to add to my character and credibility. I wasn't going out without using everything available to me to try and romance this girl; everything around me is a weapon of opportunity. I had realized that I had sensitized back to the most important part of society.

As the cab pulled away, it came to a sudden stop, and the window began to roll down. Out came her arm, and in her hand was a piece of paper. On it was "Kristina # # #—# # # #." Boy, I was the happiest man alive; it seemed things were a thousand times better for me since I left that war-torn country.

Immediately following the cab pulling away the second time, I returned to pay the vendor for the flower.

I thought this was a done deal; but as all this was taking place, the group of ladies we had met earlier passed us, and they were checking me out as I worked this girl while they giggled some more. I didn't know, nor did I care, what they thought of my game; all I could do was think, "One at a time."

They were on their way to an old dungeon-looking bar a few blocks away. Calentoni was glad, and of course, he asked me, "Does she have a friend or what?" I kind of stopped running and said, "Calentoni, all girls have friends, especially the pretty ones. Come on, let's not stop." As we continued running to this other bar to meet this first group of girls, we had a conversation about our next move because I had unfinished business with that girl (Martha) who provoked me to silently egress with her inconvenient questioning at the other bar.

When we arrived at the bar, I approached this girl, Martha, and we began to talk. I asked her how it was that she spoke English so well. She then explained that she was from New York City and was there attending college. I thought to myself, "This can't be happening to me; this only happens in movies or to other people." As we talked, I paid close attention to detail: how she looked and how she moved her mouth. I don't know if I started falling for her because I had been drinking or what, but I ran with it. I honestly think I was falling for her after about 15 minutes into our conversation. I told her, "Look, last night I was wasted and all, but tonight I'm not, and for sure I'll remember everything I'll do or say."

As the night was approaching the end for us, we offered to walk them home. She said, "No, maybe some other night." I thought to myself, "Can't win if I don't play," then I kissed her; an opportunity like this may not arise ever again. Because she had said "maybe some other night," I wanted to be a step ahead of the game if and when that other night did come. She was surprised and asked me, "What was that for?"

I told her, "If and when I see you again, maybe you won't be so halfway about things and willing to laugh a bit more and relax." But she asked me why again, and I said, "Look, I'll be frank with you. The thing I wanted the most is to meet a nice European girl and have a great time with her, but something keeps telling me to keep on going after you." She told me I was full of shit, then smiled and returned the kiss. That wasn't my pickup line or anything; it was the way I really felt.

By this time, we needed to get back to the ship. We were running a bit behind, and we arrived at the ship about 10 to 15 minutes late. The sailor on duty, whom we knew from the weight room, hooked us up and let us back on without a report. I had the women lined up for the duration of our stay in Barcelona; the next day, I was very ready to go out in the town and start drinking. Calentoni, Rowland, and Jessup were congratulating me on my nice progress; however, Rowland and Jessup decided they were going their own way. I guess they figured I was going to spend some time with that girl, but they failed to realize that this girl had several nice friends.

Calentoni had the right idea about this group of girls; we would meet them after their workday was over. Some days, we would meet for siesta and spend a few hours with them before they returned to work. Calentoni fell in love with this fine chick from Austria, and he really enjoyed every minute with those girls, as I did too. I was having a great time, but this time was a different type of great.

As the days went by, I did what came naturally to me, and once I got a grip on the Castilian ways, there was no stopping me. Now it was working for me so far. As for Calentoni, he was still checking out the girl, Pinar, from Austria; she had a killer body. We became quite good friends—ones who we could trust and enjoy hanging out with as a group. The following day was very long for me because I was on duty, but I thought of a quick way out and sold my duty to a married Marine who had a wife and kid to support. $50 for four hours wasn't that bad for him.

Martha and a friend of hers came to the ship to get me away from all that stuff, and when we arrived at her place, there was a party going on. I was introduced to more of her friends—gals and guys. Rowland was on the brink of frustration and asked me, "Hey, Zavala, what the hell do you say to a girl down here to get her even to start speaking to you? Man, it seems if you don't speak their language, there's no chance. Yesterday, I met this one girl, and there we were just laughing and trying to understand one another."

I said to him, "Rowland, if I were in your shoes and had a language barrier, then I would just take my chances after some type of miscommunication and kiss her, because for sure she would know what to do next. But if you really want to say something, then let me ponder on that for a bit, and I'll get you hooked up tonight." He then asked me, "Does that mean you're coming with us tonight?"

"No, that means I'm going to develop a technique for you so that you might not have to say much more to these women, if you know what I mean. Besides, this party is for us; she told me that on the way here." Later at the party, I met up with Rowland and gave him the rundown, instructing him on what to say to a nice-looking girl. I stressed to him that it must be one of the prettier girls there; otherwise, she'd know you're up to no good.

"Here you go, man: En mis ojos, tú eres la más bonita aquí, ¿no ves? But you must articulate this with the right amount of sincerity and pleasant emotion," as it was all shown to him. He kept practicing it until he could say it almost perfectly, without any hesitation. I wrote it down for him in case he forgot, then he and Jessup left for the city. Still, it seemed we had no care or worry in life, and there we were, just doing our thing. I had reached a comfort level, so we hung out drinking at other bars, just waiting for the ladies to meet up with us after work or whatever. There were a few times we'd see other Marines out in the same part of the city that we were in. The Olympics were on their way to Barcelona, and those were some of the places we'd visit in that part of town—just eating, drinking, and stalling for time, riding on their subway systems to places we never thought we'd ever see.

We spent Christmas Eve with the ladies, and by the end of the night, we were all dragging ass—just tired and run down—but for once, life couldn't get any better. The ladies worried that we might be going to war with Iraq, and in their eyes, we were declared their heroes.

I asked one of the other ladies, "Why do you all hang out with us? All we do is drink and act as if nothing matters."

"Because you all are brave. Your purpose in life right now is to fight for those who can't, or kill or die while killing others who may cause bad things to evolve. Who knows how you can set that aside? And for the time that you have, you choose to spend it with us. We are more than honored." For the first time since I joined the Corps, someone said something to me that had such a profound and positive effect on me. I paused for a bit, and I guess because I had been drinking, I felt compelled to say something sensible. I replied, "It's a destiny; you have one, and I have one. There's no difference in why you do something; it's only what we do that's different." Some of the foreign women knew proper English.

There's something about Europeans; they are to the point. At times, it may be gruesome, but it's no nonsense. I'll admit that a tear rolled down my face; she wiped it away and hugged me. I think we both felt a sense of nobility at that moment, between the honor and respect we shared openly for each other—not just for me and her, but for all of us there. Never had I felt so honored, which made it even more worthwhile being around them. It felt very different. I think this girl from the group was Turkish.

The next morning, Rowland woke me up saying, "Zavala, Zavala, hey, man, it worked! It worked, man!" There he was, smiling and repeating it all day long: "En mis ojos, tú eres la más bonita aquí, ¿no ves?" As if he had perfected every emotion about it, although he did sound convincing.

"Hey! How did you know that it would work for me, man?"

"You know, when you just hope it does because it seems right—well, it felt right for this place."

There's another guy I didn't mention; his name is Anthony. He's from Headquarters Platoon. Oh! One more from 2nd, White; he just hung out with us because his friend Anthony was involved with this other girl from our group of girls.

She too was a very pretty woman, and it seemed that they all had a sense of high class but not high maintenance. We had been saving up for five months, so if it came down to it, I think I had enough money to meet some demands.

I won't describe this lady with anything other than glamorous. She thought highly of us and treated Calentoni like her very own brother, and he treated her like his stepsister because one never knew. There was a mutual respect between the two. I chose not to mention Anthony much because he was dogging this girl, and I said to him, "Man, they treat us like kings, and you treat her like shit. Man, you're much better than that. Chill, dude."

I think the whole time Anthony was confused about having a girl back home and doing this with this girl, but she needed to be treated a lot nicer than what she was being treated. Cpl. Williamson's first name was Kirk; we had become pretty good friends. He asked me, "Zavala, how did you manage to get this lucky? Aren't you a bit cruel? Of all the Spanish-speaking women here, you decide that you want one of the only ones who can speak English—that's mean."

I thought for a second, then asked him, "Why am I so cruel?"

It was the night before New Year's Eve when we helped the girl from Austria move some of her stuff from one apartment to another. She whispered, "Hey Martin, don't get in a rush. Your day with the girl of your dreams is coming soon; she told me so."

I guess she said this to me because the night before, when we were at the bar, we saw that girl Kristina who I had hooked up with at first, and she may have thought that I'd try to hook up with her again. Nonetheless, my day was made. I thought we were a hell of a group of people who met one another through some weird circumstances.

That evening, we hung out at this more Americanized bar-club-pub, whatever. A lot of other Marines were there. I saw a staff sergeant there and introduced everyone, and at the same time, Martha asked if I could have a Special Liberty Pass for the following morning. Of course, he said yes. On my way to her place, I was under pressure; for the great times we had there, they needed to be followed up with even greater sex.

In the Heat of Battle

I buzzed in at the door and told her to step outside onto her balcony. I began to serenade her; it wasn't the best, but then I quickly said to her, "If I could sing to you in the best voice in the world, you know I would."

She smiled, nodded her head, then beckoned me to come up. I had come prepared and well-equipped with roses, champagne, and the music. We had a theme song for everything while overseas.

This was indeed a different type of conflict. I felt nervous, and we were about to get into it; the negotiating was over. In the end, both sides would be exhausted, physically and emotionally altered and changed for life. My intelligence had been gathered during the nights out on the town with her.

I knew every part of her body and the places where I could first invade, causing the greatest sensation. The curves and valleys were what I planned to explore for most of my time there, reaching these locations with my hands and fingers, and at times, with my tongue. I finally made it to the area that would cause her to surrender her passionate emotions, and slowly we were becoming casualties of war. I dug in, where I thought I'd be spending the rest of my time. From one second to another, we were exploring areas where only moments ago we had withdrawn due to the intensity.

She held me and cried out to me, "Stay, stay, stay longer!" The longer I stayed, the more intense it became, until we were both satisfied and ready to withdraw.

Upon withdrawal, we met eye to eye, overwhelmed by the heat of passion and addiction, knowing we would be engaging in the act once again to find it just as intense, satisfying, and overwhelming. Afterwards, we allowed everything to fall into its proper place, accepting the consequences of our encounter and our hunger for more. I figured I was at my very best when in the field; if I were to operate as precisely in bed, great results would be the outcome. My mission had been accomplished.

As we sat in bed, I told her that I was a lucky guy. She asked, "Why?"

"I'm sure that happens to most people, but not all at one time."

She then asked, "You're sure that what happens to most people?"

"They meet someone very nice, have the time of their life in a faraway land, and whatever I do as far as trying to be romantic won't be shot down. I think that's the way it should be done."

We spoke for about half an hour afterward. We didn't have any place to go until that night, so we laid around talking, eating, smoking, and drinking. We even slept.

The whole time, I thought to myself, Man, this chic must only be going through the motions, because otherwise, she's very excited when she's hanging out with me, at the bars, or whatever.

I was a bit confused. I just wanted to know if I had made an impact on her or not; either way, I wasn't going to change a thing I was doing. At last, I let the need to know fade away and figured that as long as I enjoyed it, for the moment I was happy.

Night fell, and we met up with the gang from the ship. Again, we ran into SSgt. Feldman, who passed the word that we needed to start cutting our ties because the time to leave was upon us. He saw I was having such a great time and gave me an early heads-up.

On the night of our departure, she walked me up to the dock and said to keep in touch, that all of the girls were going to miss us, to take care, and they would pray for us.

"When I get back to the States, I'll give you a call to visit you," she said while wiping her tears away.

"OK, can't wait." The last call came over the loudspeaker of the ship. We were gone into the night, out to sea. Our next stop was Toulon, France, Camp DeCanjuers. There we would undergo two long weeks of training, and boy, did we need it. I was even afraid because we had drunk the entire time in Spain.

During our travel to France, we closely watched the BBC news, and on the eighth day at sea, WAR had been declared on Iraq.

Something very interesting came over the wire about the Israeli Armed Forces; they had never, in the history of their war capabilities, returned fire after being fired upon. The U.S. asked the Israeli government not to return fire for some political reason.

I remember having countless nightmares on our way to France. I wasn't sure if it was due to the alcohol I had consumed in Spain or my way of subconsciously accepting the fear of the possibilities of having to go to war. We docked at the port of Toulon, and within a day's time, we were in the fields setting up and going on training exercises.

A squad competition within KILO Company was held. It consisted of as much training as the command could throw at us in the two weeks that we were in the fields. We traveled on foot, avoiding detection by anyone outside our squad, and only made radio contact to report our status. A Staff Sergeant was our contact person for grading purposes.

Third squad came in first place and received a meritorious award for our competitive performance out of the entire company's twelve squads.

Training in France (my meritorious mass) was the most demanding of times. After the war in Liberia, which was real, we had to tone it down and implement our civil behavior. We needed to dial back a few levels and transition back to field training, which came with its challenges. As far as being more methodical about what to do, it became a little easier. The physical part wasn't so easy at first, especially for everyone considering how hard we partied in the Canary Islands and Barcelona. It was strictly business here at Camp DeCanjuers.

Things we did felt awkward. While in France, I asked Rowland, "Why do we party as hard as we do and train just as hard?" Maybe he had the answer I needed; I never knew why. It kind of balanced itself out like that, and maybe the answer was something other than it being our lifestyle.

Cpl. Green, Cpl. Poff, and I prepared our squad for the events. We gathered and trained our squad for a few days on mostly what wasn't covered in the handbook and a couple of things one picks up from small conversations about the field. It covered many basics, and every ounce of teamwork was again demanded from us. The nastiness had begun to leave my body, and I was back in the shape I thought I needed to be in. The elements necessary to run a squad, platoon, and company had been passed down from the Platoon Commander on down to the fire team—the way he wanted things to go—and we couldn't go wrong, despite being sluggish during the first phase of our training evolution.

When we got back to the ship, one of the corpsmen asked, "Hey! Y'all have a Martin in your platoon?" Instantly, I knew Martha was in town because no one knew me as Martin but her.

I tried to ignore what I heard Doc say, but as we were prepping to go out for beers, someone handed me a note. It read, "Hi Martin, I'm in the city at the hotel; come meet me there, and we can have dinner." She spelled out the name and provided directions on how to get to this hotel. Boy, I was on an official French date. Calentoni and I spent the evening with two of the girls from Spain. At a certain point in the night, I asked one of them, "How long have you all been here, and how did you get here?" She replied that they had been there for two days and had come by train. "Well, here we are. What do you want to do or where do you want to go?" She said she had no particular place in mind and suggested, "Let's just make the most of it."

That night was our last in France, and I apologized for not letting her know my schedule while I was out there. We were both glad to see one another. She said, "I just wanted to see you to tell you one thing: I love you. I know I should have said it when you told me at the docks that you loved me."

I replied, "What else did you expect me to say? I figured, for all the good times we had while abroad, if I didn't say it, it wouldn't have been complete. Who knows, we may have gone to war, and to say it would have been a good ending, right? After seeing what we did in Africa, I didn't want to stay lost. I wanted to be able to feel this way again, and you may not know it, but you helped me. I'll never forget you for that. There were just too many what-ifs at the time."

She walked me to the gate of the docks, and we spent a few minutes there. I wished for time to stand still for maybe an hour so I could tell her more of how I felt. I assured her that I would visit her in New York. I never told her what went on in Africa.

Everyone was asking me, "What the hell did you do to get her to come all this way to see you?" I think Rowland understood why she came to see me in France. It was about saying and doing the right things; the line I developed for him really worked—he was glad. As we launched off, she said to me, "Bon voyage." We departed with a more confident future. She sounded complete, and my doubts about our time in Barcelona were gone; it felt meaningful.

While we were with the ladies in Barcelona, we played with words to create positive puns, and what better thing to say than "bon voyage"? After all, we were in stinking France. The way Calentoni sometimes talked, using song lyrics, must have rubbed off on me; I guess that's how it all started.

CHAPTER 20

HISTORY IN THE MAKING

On the ship, while out on the rough seas, we hit some severe waves, and I fell from the top rack. I thought my shoulder was broken because I landed so hard and wrong. Later in the Corps, this would become one of my greater struggles: not receiving the proper medical attention and being denied it over and over again.

The date was late in January 1991. Due to the war efforts in the Arab nations and Operation Sharp Edge, we stayed longer than normal; also, there was no one ready to come replace us in the Mediterranean. We made a stop in Greece, and again there were more beautiful women, but I, for one, had been satisfied emotionally and said, "It's someone else's time," and just enjoyed the beauty of different ancient cities where we were ported.

Thessalonica, Greece, had no place for docking the ship, so we dropped anchor about a quarter mile off the coast. We made it onto the mainland after waiting our turn to be shuttled over by a private contractor. I don't know why everyone always went to the bars, but we did. I could never get over the exotic-looking women.

Before leaving, a few of us from Third Platoon and other guys from the company started a game of American football. Even Lt. Brown played. We played in an old square; little by little, the citizens began to gather and observe the game. I didn't think the people understood the rules or the object of the game, but they knew to cheer or boo us as the ball was caught or dropped. It appeared to the gathered crowd to be more and more organized as we played along. Touchdowns were scored, interceptions were made, long bombs were caught, and I think the citizens did understand the success of the game.

A kid carrying a shoebox interrupted the game. He wasn't treating it as if he was carrying a pair of shoes. It could have been anything from a small explosive device to an actual pair of shoes. We expected the worst and stopped playing to avoid any danger. Lt. Brown asked him, the best way he could, by using hand gestures for him to open the box. It was nothing to fear, but it was enough to end our game, so we left and went back to the ship, and soon we were on our way.

Our last port before preparing for our long journey back to the States was in Calentoni's native land of Italy. We went out to drink again and window shop. While shopping at a store, this lady storekeeper cursed me out in Italian, and Calentoni translated it for me only after I asked over and over what she had said: "A la puta mama caramba vaspa cara fachee, pa fangu, stupido Americano." I realized she had her reasons.

Gone before we knew it, back to the States. It would take two to three weeks, and little by little, the anticipation grew. I was ready to readjust to the way it was, as much as I enjoyed the European way of life, but there wasn't one better than the American way.

Remember Dade? He made fun of me for losing my girlfriend from back home. I think he laughed too soon; he saw how it turned out for me in Spain, and the worst thing was that his wife was messing around with some other guy back in his hometown. I don't think he made fun of anyone else after that alleged incident. Lesson learned.

Upon our arrival in Elizabeth City, N.C., the media was there to greet us, along with other Marines' family members. We were bussed back to Camp LeJeune and quickly settled in. The base was like a ghost town; almost everyone was involved in Desert Storm. The good thing about it was that the town belonged to us, along with its women. First things first, we received our leave orders and were gone within the week. A few people stayed behind to make sure things were situated. If the crisis in Iraq were to get really bad, then we would be called back, and out we would go again. I made it home and said hi to everyone. I had the days off while everyone else still had their jobs to do.

During the day, I tried to stay preoccupied until the nightlife began. There were several parties to go to, and people were always interested in how things really were overseas and all this and that. I attended a few parties and, whatnot; I started to put things in their own perspective with everyone back home. I felt that it was time.

I went to my ex-girlfriend's house, and her parents greeted me with their compassion and sympathy for what had happened. They invited me to get my belongings I had left behind, so I did. Her dad and I drank a few beers and spoke for a few minutes, and that was that. I said goodbye to them and to her brothers and told them I'd see them around.

I ran into Lawrence's mother and his brother Matt while I was home; they gave me an update. "He had been back from Japan for a while, met a girl, and was planning on getting married." Of course, he had my approval. Small talk about me broke out following the update. Minutes later, we departed. I left Texas and went back to the Corps.

CHAPTER 21

CHANGING OF THE GUARD

B ack in the saddle, on my way to North Carolina after driving a day and a half. Of course, I took my time; I wasn't in any rush. It's sad to say that my hometown had become boring. After having experienced all that stateside and overseas, I didn't expect it to be the same, but not so different either. I arrived back on base in NC four days early, and so did a few of the guys from third platoon; yet some may have returned earlier than me.

Things were changing, the Commanding Officer for one. We would be losing most of our better Marines; rebuilding our forces would be something to look forward to. This meant that I would be getting my promotion, and my responsibilities would be greater. I had the point score for my promotion; after the incident with the POW in Africa and my performance there, it would be about time. We were introduced to our new Staff Sergeant, a former Drill Instructor. I was in a world of deception because Drill Instructors were the first true Marines we ever worked with, and I saw the Drill Instructors as the epitome of all Marines. All that changed when I met SSgt. Jones.

SSgt. Jones was the exact opposite; he didn't like the field, but he thought he was King Shit in garrison (at the barracks). He wanted to be Superman, but saving the day wasn't on his list of things to do. SSgt. Jones just wanted his retirement the easy way, not by going to Iraq or to a hot zone and seeing how the situation was at the time with the world (the Iraqis). His mission should have been to train us to receive his retirement with a clean conscience. Getting us back home safe wasn't his concern, and I know if Kilo Company was sent in, for sure that someone would put him down.

In time, we started receiving more Marines out of SOI and other duty stations; it's all a giant cycle. This time around, I wasn't the only Latino in the platoon, and maybe the other vatos could represent as I have. You would only think, after all, they were straight out of the hood of Los Angeles; they lived down the street, around the corner, to the left from one another. They both looked at me as a mentor; no matter how much we fucked up, we'd help one another out because I looked at it as: I was as strong as the weakest one of us.

Gone from Third were Poff, Law, Green, Griff, Dwyer, and Dade, who went to some other platoon to prepare for their departure from the Corps. SSgt. Feldman was gone to another unit to resume his Sniper Instructor duties. Others left the 3rd Platoon for another company within the same unit; they are as follows: Jessup, Rowland to the boats, Calentoni, and Johnston to Headquarters. Marese went to another company. Other guys left, and I can't really remember their names, but most of these guys I mentioned were replaced—not so much by different people but by different personalities and characters—and the bother with all the stress that comes with learning how someone thinks and acts. Were they talking shit, or did they really do what they set out to do? Let's find out.

The new guys who were coming to join us—the major players were the vatos from California: Hidrogo, Huerta, and Machin. I was without a mentor; there was no one to look up to. These other Marines were just from all over. Parry came back to the Marines because of the war; Gradies was new and had wised up quick. A guy from Lancaster, PA, was my predecessor; he now carried my M-249 SAW, and his name was Warner.

I guess if something were to happen to me, Warner would take over the radio. He always shadowed me to learn more about the M-249, and at the same time, I was passing on to him what I had been taught by others about the radio. We were kind of forced to be friends, and it turned out that we had more in common than most of the others in our platoon. There were a few NCOs that joined us, but only one who would delegate orders to me, and that was the only one I had to generally answer to.

By this time, we all got back from leave, and the strangest thing was that Cpl. Spinn, an NCO I never mentioned, was insignificant to me so far and may be for the duration of our time together. He had a black eye, a few bumps and bruises, and his arm was in a sling because someone kicked his ass while on leave. What happened was that someone put a hit on him; it was more like just a warning for him to lighten up on the Marines he was in charge of.

This guy, Cpl. Spinn, was a big dude; he couldn't run much or do many pull-ups or sit-ups, but he had a commanding voice and wasn't pushed around very easily. I guess he expected more from his troops than what he had to offer, and all his troops either hated him or wanted him gone. Since he wasn't leaving, certain things needed to happen to him. This guy was a 'Rock.'

No need to drop names, but an individual—somewhat an educated lad—was responsible for this, and we finally saw the day that Spinn got what was coming to him, a little overdue. Lt. Brown was promoted to Executive Officer for Kilo Company, and it never dawned on me that I had political influence up in the ranks, because as you keep reading, I would be in need of them. Having a Marine from the Drill Field was something that I thought for sure would keep me motivated, anticipating his stories of how he became a Drill Instructor. SSgt. Jones had some issues that affected us as a whole platoon.

Jones had a little brother who had disgraced him; either he went to the brig or got an ugly discharge—maybe a Bad Conduct Discharge, a.k.a. a B.C.D or a Big Chicken Dinner—from the Marines. That made him the way he was toward us. Also, he needed his Gunny promotion. To me, a Platoon Sergeant was the one who disciplines the right way, by force or cooperation from the others. The worst thing about the matter was that our new Lt. was too scared to step up and take charge of his platoon. He was the Platoon Commander, after all, and I don't think for one minute he understood what it meant to the troops. Our Platoon Commander, Lt. Payton—we had already met this guy—was flown over from the States to Europe, and he spent time with us on the ship for the cruise back to the States. Lt. Payton was young, about 21 or 22 years of age. For sure, he had some smarts about him, but he had a long way to go to get where other Lieutenants were, nothing like Lt. Brown.

I think Jones and he had a little talk, and something like this was said: "Hey, Sir, since this is your very first platoon, go ahead and let me run it from every aspect, and that means your role would be in my hands while you just watch and learn from me. After all, I was a Drill Instructor." I bet that pussy of a Lt. stood there with his thumb in his mouth or up his ass and simply said, "OK."

Times were slowly worsening for us; we had no sense of leadership from our NCOs, nor had our leaders earned our respect. Fuckery was soon to take place. Prichard, Williamson, and I were the only ones who really knew what was going on as far as TRAPP Missions were concerned. Not really—Mourning and Waters did too, but they had their own battles to fight brought forth by Jones. Or maybe they were teaching the squads and squad leaders how the missions were done. Prichard, Williamson, and I were given the responsibilities of teaching the Staff Sergeant and the Lieutenant what a TRAPP mission was all about. There we were, doing our best, putting all differences aside for these individuals who would soon turn their backs on us when we needed them most.

First of all, it was our duty, and if things got screwed up, then shit rolled downhill. Secondly, we (Prichard, Williamson, and I) figured if we did this good enough, then (Staff Sergeant and the Lieutenant) might stay away, let us be in charge, or allow the Corps to be run the way it should be run—by the Squad Leaders and the Fire Team Leaders.

When utilized properly, everyone benefits from good leadership. The training was underway, and just about that time I was beginning to feel a bit of relief, but the Squad Leaders decided to make Klausen my Fire Team Leader. Klausen was promoted to a Non-Commissioned Officer; by this time, he had the score and had served a proper time in the subordinate rank. I would have been proud of him if only he were in another platoon, but since he was in our platoon, I feared for those under his direct command. I protested the decision of me being in his Fire Team until something had been done about it, but the results wouldn't be much better. My Squad Leader, Sergeant Sorn, informed me, "Hey, Zavala, I spoke to the LT, and he said you either go with Klausen's team or be the radio operator for Third Platoon." He also asked me why I didn't like Cpl. Klausen. I explained to Sorn what the deal was, because as my new Squad Leader was too new still to us to know how Klausen really was.

I sat there thinking which way would I rather get fucked: become dead by Cpl. Klausen's indecisiveness, or get killed three seconds after disembarking the Hilo. Three seconds was the average time it took for a radio operator to become wounded or killed in combat after being spotted by the enemy. I believe these stats were drawn from the Vietnam War.

An advantage for the platoon was for me to be working next to the Lt. as the platoon's radio operator, to intercept any intelligence that might benefit the rest of 3rd. I had become the radio operator officially after taking the Radio Communications classes; I had become Gator-3. I thought back to when I got busted in Charleston. The Colonel said that I was like those old alligators, but I never imagined being as resilient.

Serenity

A need for tranquility, to get away from it all, led us to Myrtle Beach. We never arranged to have a party, but somehow a party ended up developing around us, initiated by strangers we had just met. Calentoni and I, along with maybe a few other guys, drove down to Myrtle Beach, checked into a room, and set up shop. For some reason, though, everyone had gone their separate ways. I thought they had some girl set up or something, and I didn't really worry about them getting into any kind of trouble.

There was this chick from Piedmont, S.C., named Lori. She and I had been slamming down beer for beer; she was in the band that had played there the night before. We talked for about two hours, taking advantage of each other's companionship. We exchanged addresses and kept in touch while on the next cruise. The police were very strict at Myrtle Beach; I had known this from past experiences when they threw my ass in jail.

I had sobered up a bit and was on the lookout for one of the guys just to see if everyone was still alive, sitting down on the curb in front of the bar. I was still drunk but cautious of what was going on. People were passing by half-drunk, and if they stuck out from the crowd, it was time for them to get going. I spotted two police officers to my flanks; I had to act quickly. I didn't want to risk standing out, as they needed only half a reason to throw anyone in jail. I stood up and proceeded to walk away from them when suddenly I noticed two girls walking ahead of me.

I wasn't sure how to go about this without giving the girls any reason to freak out. Then, without further thought, I said to the girls as I squeezed in between them, "Please help me; the cops are right behind us, and they're on the prowl. If you would just walk me to my hotel or until we lose these guys, I'd owe you whatever you ladies want."

One girl started to freak out for a second and yelled out, "Hey!" Then she turned to look at me, and her tone changed. As she began to smile, she said, "Hey, handsome, sure we will. How far are we talking?"

"I don't know, but as soon as we see Foley's at the mall up the street, we're there." For the simple fact that I had spent more time in the field, my sense of direction wasn't dependent on street signs; it was more about objectivity and what I saw. It made more sense to me to go by the Foley's sign than the street sign for the street where the hotel was located. The mall was up the street about six blocks from the beach; it ran parallel to the direction in which we walked.

We arrived at the room around 2:30 a.m. It was late, but the streets were still packed with people. I knew I had to exit stage left before I got into trouble of some sort. We had beer and food in the room, and they asked me, "Hey, would you mind if we got something to drink?"

"Anything you need; if I have it, then it's yours. Remember, I owe you for getting me out of that jam." I unlocked the door, thinking that Calentoni or someone was getting laid or passed out. We entered, but there was no sight of anyone.

As we came near the bed, we all must have been thinking the same thing, as we allowed ourselves to drop onto the bed. I laid there for about 1.66 seconds and realized that finally my dream was about to come true. I started with the one to the right of me, and as we kissed, my hands began doing their own thing with the girl to my left. I remember saying to myself, "Stay calm, man, because you're one bad dude. All the bullshit in your life ain't nothing; what matters is now."

We were having a great time—long enough for me to have one of them almost nude and the other girl halfway out of her shorts and shirt—when the door flew open. The first thing that went through my mind was the fucking police. But no, it was Calentoni. He was pissed off for some reason, saying, "Aww, them damn bitches, they all suck. One took me for my money, and the others just play games."

He finally saw what I had going on and was somewhat shocked. What could I say? I just said, "Here, man, you fucked me up; take one of mine." I literally handed the girl over to him and introduced the two, and then the lights went out for a while. The next day, we hung out until around 5:30, then headed back to the barracks.

That Sunday, we saw Griff. We talked for a while and bitched and complained about the cards that had been dealt to us. He told us what was in store for him. We wished each other luck and then left. Man, those guys were true friends, and friends like them don't come around too often. There were a few times I could feel, after departing from a conversation, that this would be the last time I saw some of these guys. I felt that feeling this time, too; even though I was drunk, I honestly hated having that feeling. It was okay that it was the last time I'd see these guys, but the intuition just ate at me.

It was time to get back to base. The awesome twosome gave us their addresses, and we wrote back and forth to one another while aboard the USS Fuckery. I wasn't about to go on another Med Cruise and not have any fans write to me. No, "Fuckery" wasn't the real name of the ship; that's what I ended up calling it because, while on that ship, things would become fucked up for all of us in 3rd.

Back on the first float, a few weeks after I captured that POW, Lt. Col. Daniel Bryant, Lt. Brown gave everyone an evaluation and shared our scores on our pros and cons. He said to me, "Zavala, your performance was excellent in Liberia; you're one of the more senior Marines here in Third, and hopefully in about six months, you'll be an NCO. Keep up the good job." Then he asked if I had any questions for him. I asked if I would receive anything for handling the POW. He replied, "I wish I could, but as far as anyone above Capt. Frampton is concerned, it never happened." The POW incident was a matter of diplomacy; no one from Africa knew it had occurred, and that's how the U.S. government wanted it.

I didn't see myself getting promoted at the rate things were fucking up; I had nothing to do with it. I trained most of the NCOs, the Platoon Sergeant, and the Platoon Commander. I brought more skills, qualifications, talent, and heart to the platoon than any of the NCOs new to Third Platoon, or the Lieutenant. They all meant well, but like I said, SSgt. Jones had his own agenda.

My intensity for being out in the field and my motivation were slowly beginning to break down; in all, my spirit was lost. I guess that was why I found replacement spirits in the bottle—they were something for the moment. I sometimes felt like saying the hell with it, but I couldn't let these new Marines down, so I hung in there for them.

I know there's a God; I always believed in what goes around comes around. The most satisfying thing would be to see what came around for Staff Sergeant E. Jones and the type of career that our Lieutenant has in the Corps. Losing my spirit was probably the next worst thing to being dead, and I didn't think anyone was getting out of this place unless he really fucked up or died.

All the other platoons saw how bad the situation for Third had become. For me personally, it was an embarrassment to have our problems exposed to the outer perimeter; these men from Third had become like my brothers. I recall being on a training mission when the Lieutenant became nervous and freaked out while being graded by the Captain. I said to him, "Hey, sir, you need to relax; otherwise, you're going to get yourself in deeper shit. If you try to talk your way out of this, you're not an expert, so you're expected to screw up—just don't make it a habit. We're not negotiating hostages. If you fucked up, then you'll learn something, but no one dies, okay? Now just be sensible about what you do."

After that particular incident, I learned it was all Staff Sergeant Jones's doing to keep us down, because Lt. Payton, our Platoon Commander, always said, "Hey, Zavala, thank you!" But never for nothing. I guessed he wanted to maintain his superiority status too.

Kilo Company had completed their rebuilding phase; now we had started to get more into our training and hopefully back to the capabilities we had before. I had my radio on my back, working right beside the Lieutenant, going where he went and maintaining communications with the other platoons. I began to notice the upside of being the radio operator—I was able to gripe at the Lieutenant whenever he screwed up.

I was sent to various classes on how to make the most of the sorry communication equipment we had. It was a whole lot better than being a sitting duck for Action Jones to fuck with.

During these work-up training evolutions, just about every other time we went on one, I kept re-injuring my shoulder. Being denied medical treatment became an issue and an argument with everyone above me, except for my corpsman; he was probably the only one who tried to help but to no avail. I knew my shoulder was getting worse; I just didn't know how much worse. Either the pain toughened me up, or it just became part of an uncomfortable life for me, and I had to tough it out until things cooled down in Iraq or until we made it back from the Mediterranean—whichever came last.

"Action" was the name that some ignorant bastard had given him in his old unit, so don't let the name fool you. All he did was make life hell for his troops to feel important and useful, or maybe because he didn't know how to lead any other way.

Guard duty was assigned to the platoons, and every so often it made its way around to us, so there we were, guarding an armory. Times like this were when my skills superseded other duties, and I got to drive the Humvee instead of standing duty. At times, I would check on the guards to see if they needed anything—more water, a bathroom break, things like that.

While I was driving from one post to another, I saw the almighty Colonel Mark Masterson, my commanding officer from Naval Weapons Station. We spoke for a few minutes; he was on his morning run. I had to ask him if he was a full-bird Colonel yet, because he wasn't in uniform, so I didn't see his insignias.

He said, "Yes, I am. If there's any kind of recommendation you need, I'm over in the Headquarters Department on the base."

"Sir, I sure will." I was so glad to see him because he was the only one who mattered who knew of my past in the Corps. I really wanted to go see him, but time didn't allow for it. Man, I thought for sure that a sense of relief was coming, but I just couldn't make it; everything was moving so fast.

Back at Naval Weapons Station, radios were used all the time, and there wasn't much to it except to stay calm and know the dos and don'ts of radio operation. The only difference was the size and weight. Here, I carried it on my back along with its accessories and my personal gear—easily over 60 pounds compared to less than 2 pounds at Naval Weapons Station. But carrying it soon became effortless. The radio operator's job was to know how to construct and erect the most suitable and efficient antennas, besides maintaining them for operational use; frequencies were learned. There were even frequencies on which we could catch some TV channels.

CHAPTER 22

TECHNICIANS

I saw that carrying the radio could be something I'd become accustomed to quickly. I thought maybe I could break Lt. Payton's mold, or at the very least establish a good rapport for 3rd Platoon, to show him the good in us.

I didn't doubt that SSgt. Jones was making us sound as if we were some kind of no-good thugs. I guess they wanted me to start kissing up to these guys, and then maybe my promotion would follow—but I wasn't having it. My theory was, and always will be: to be without a doubt the best at what I do and to have extensive knowledge about what everyone around me does. If I didn't get rewarded for it, then the problem lay elsewhere. Although there may have been a few times when I didn't shine as brightly as the next guy, I never sucked up or kissed ass to make up for it. Instead, I'd recognize my areas for improvement—like drinking, for instance. All that did was make me equal with everyone around me. I couldn't give anyone that much just to take it back later.

Our Company Commander—Captain Grant, I think his name was—had been in a Force Recon Unit before he was reassigned to Kilo Co. He didn't care much for the barracks; his place was in the field.

There was always room for explanations during the debriefs with him. He didn't take kindly to screw-ups and mistakes happening in his "place of business." He believed there was a time and place for errors so they could be corrected if possible—but not during real-time situations. In training, his approach was to talk through dilemmas so everyone could understand how the next man thinks.

Time passed, and not once did I see Lt. Payton stand up to SSgt. Jones and say, "From here on out, what I say goes," or something along those lines. I figured he was never going to say it because I saw the lieutenant falling further from his leadership billet and appearing less and less. I realized that a conflict of interest would eventually be the reason for 3rd Platoon's decline. SSgt. Jones was in it for himself; maybe he figured that keeping us unhappy and down would help him reach his goal of retiring as a Gunnery Sergeant. Through this, I learned firsthand that everyone holds a certain amount of goodness, unity, and drive, but it must start with leadership.

Due to Desert Storm, we received our official Battalion orders to the Mediterranean Sea once again. As long as we were on American soil, Calentoni and I agreed to party like rock stars. We met some girls—one was from here in Austin, and the other was from somewhere in the Midwest. I started talking to the one from Austin, Texas. While we were playing pool, she thought I was lying when I told her I was from Austin too. She began questioning me. "Then what's the name of four surrounding cities?"

They needed someone to lean on, and we were there for them. Camp LeJeune had been abandoned by most of the Marines, and the wives were alone because their husbands were in the Middle East. We started going to Myrtle Beach for the weekend. Calentoni began to fall in love with one of the girls, so I felt compelled to make a move on the other. It wasn't a good idea, so I backed away from all of them and had a talk with Calentoni. He couldn't leave that one girl alone. I knew it wasn't right, so I pulled myself out of the situation and left.

More Training

Back stateside before going on leave and preparing for our med-float, during our last training evolution, we faced an enemy that held us back in every way. It couldn't harm us directly, but it kept us from being agile, which was what gave us our edge.

The sit-rep for this mission was: An aircraft went down in a nondisclosed area. As soon as we get the word, the details will be relayed through your squad leaders. There were several civilians, the pilot, and his crew, which consisted of five other personnel. Nothing is known about the crew or passengers, so be ready for anything. In total, there were 14 Americans and an unknown number of hostiles.

During the briefings, we received a bit more information, but it wasn't much. We filled in the blanks as we approached the location and did the best we could with what we had.

We still waited around before departure; the final briefing had yet to be given. The Captain, XO, platoon commanders, platoon sergeants, first sergeants, and the company gunny were on site. During this briefing, orders and assignments were given regarding which platoon was responsible for what. Before a mission like this, my fire team was always excited, and I'm sure the other fire teams were too. We were ready to hit the ground running. But this time was different; we had to travel through dense vegetation for about 8 clicks, approximately 8,000 meters. The rule was: remember who's in front of you and who's behind you, while maintaining noise and light discipline—no lighters, flashlights, or anything that could reflect light.

It was already noisy, with over 170 Marines moving through the woods—the sound of breaking branches, some guys stumbling, getting tangled up, and falling out of formation due to all the obstacles. Still, we had to maintain an arm's distance from one another. If someone fell out of line, the guy behind him would need to re-establish formation by moving into his spot and quickly whispering his name to the person in front and behind.

At a few points, as we made our way through, we reached areas where the moon pierced the treetops just enough to give us a break from total darkness. Although we couldn't see one another eye to eye or face to face, nor could we hear each other bitching and complaining anymore, we knew the situation wasn't ideal. We licked our wounds as we went, and we could feel the strong tension from everyone due to the frustration these limitations imposed on us. This was something we had done many times before, but this time, everything was at a different pace. It was a taste of humble pie, and it taught me never to underestimate things I've done before, because each time would be different.

Once we reached our destination, a scout team was assembled to gather information and returned with an updated situation report. The report teams were called in to execute whatever was needed to complete their part of the mission. Most everyone set up a perimeter, and a few were chosen at random to handle everything else. Since conditions had changed, we defaulted back to having no specific assignments, so tasks were completed randomly. No one saw the big picture; visibility was barely five feet in front of us. An almost-burned-out chem light had been placed about thirty feet up in a tree, and that was all the light we had to maneuver by. Anyone not directly involved couldn't see anything.

The entire mission—from departure to returning to camp—took nearly five hours. It took about three hours to reach the site, maybe an hour to carry out every detail, and the remaining time to make it back.

The next morning, everyone who went out had scratches on their faces and necks—some worse than others. One guy's injury was pretty bad; he nearly lost an eye, or it at least looked that way. We realized we'd need a faster and less hazardous extraction route next time. We also hadn't known that the grading staff was out there watching us through night vision goggles.

After we returned to camp, a formation was called, and a quick debrief about the mission was given. "Everything went accordingly," was all the captain said, but we didn't hear that until the following afternoon. Some higher-ranking officers, like a major and lieutenant colonel, had gone to the site to assess the simulation. The captain was debriefed, and then it trickled down to us. It turned out to be a good review, and we were awarded a three-day weekend for our performance.

Later, I met a girl who lived in the city. She wasn't married and had a roommate who was a billboard model for Salem cigarettes. The model had a boyfriend in the same unit as me. The girl's kid was always glad to see me; we'd do "guy things"—not exactly father-son activities, but he needed a male role model in his life, and for a short time, I was it.

Our orders for a Mediterranean Sea deployment were scheduled for June, and we were busy preparing and finalizing everything before shipping out. This time, there was no training on AP Hill, no Blue-Green water work-ups—just training and then "Vámonos!"

We took leave, went back, and before we knew it, we were boarding a USS-something with the 22nd MEU-SOC, combat-ready. While on leave, not much happened. I played softball with friends that summer, hung out, and then returned to Jacksonville to spend the rest of my leave with the girl I had met.

Our first port was the usual: Rota, Spain, followed by Haifa, Israel. While in Israel, we spent three more weeks training in the desert mountains. I remembered the two weeks we spent at AP Hill before our last deployment because the conditions there were the exact opposite of what we had to withstand in Israel. During the day, it was around 137 degrees of dry heat. It was tough on everyone as we moved, constantly pouring sweat. Even when we sat down to rest, we kept sweating until the temperature dropped to something bearable. At night, we moved tactically from one training site to another, sharpening up in the areas where training was most needed.

For part of the time, a few other Marines and I were assigned to drive for four days, and then we switched over. I knew I'd eventually join the rest of 3rd Platoon. My role as a driver was actually a fluke. While back in the States, Hayward had been scheduled for the Hummer class but was nowhere to be found, and I just happened to be the first one seen. Right place at the right time—they told me, "Hey, go report to the Motor Pool building to attend some classes on how to drive and operate the Humvee. You'll be there for about a week." I always thought it was just a matter of turning the key and driving, but there was more to it than that. Because I took the driving class, I got to take it easy for a while in the rear. Third Platoon didn't get quota assignments very often, so if we didn't fill this one, who knew when the next would come around.

In our unit, "skate" and "scam" were slang for taking it easy, getting a break, or avoiding work altogether. Church was held every Sunday, even out in the field. What helped me cope with our situation was the day I saw Calentoni all slicked up, on his way to church. His cammies were kind of pressed, and his boots shined. He knocked on my Humvee door and said, "Hey man, wake your lazy ass up and let's go to church!" I asked him, "You got a date or what?"

"No, man, the Holy House awaits us." That was a clear indicator to me that there was still hope. So, I got my lazy ass up and went to church.

The driving classes paid off. Even Action Jones couldn't do a thing about it—my needed skills were prioritized over his preferences. His desire was to see me crumble, as Warner stood in as the platoon radio operator. The good times ended, though, when the Company Gunny said, "Zavala, your ass has been skating for a whole week, and now it's time for you to get some training in this heat."

The Marines in my platoon joked around, saying, "You couldn't be that lucky. Now get to work, you lazy bastard." During our downtime, we sat around, talking and holding our own meetings about what had been going on while I was away. We came together out of frustration with Staff Sergeant. None of the NCOs agreed with how Staff Sergeant was running things. I heard the Black guys saying, "That motherfucker ain't even gonna look out for his own." Of course, many issues weren't discussed openly while the NCOs were around.

An Op.

Training Day #X was in full swing. Our Company had set up in a strategic formation to overtake a network of trenches. The .60 caliber machine gunners were in position, communications were established, call signs set, and radio checks completed. Earlier, I noticed some unfamiliar faces—guys from Support Battalion brought in just for the training.

We got the go-ahead, and the exercise was on. I initiated the action with a call to the support fire (machine gunners) over the radio: "Red-dog, Red-dog, this is Gator-3, send me some fire, over." As the 7.62mm rounds flew out for suppressive fire, we maneuvered through the trenches, zigzagging and firing at pop-up targets. We were loving it. Botello commanded the gun team in position, keeping the suppressive fire steady, while the mortar team did their thing somewhere off-site.

The thought of someone getting hit was always on my mind—and I think that's what made it exciting. It was when I felt most alive, knowing I might be the one to take a bullet. Everyone operated with a sense of precision, but even that wasn't always enough. Doc, our corpsman, and I had swapped weapons—he wanted a taste of the action, so he took my M-16, and I had his 9mm. I'd gotten used to the extra weight of the M-16, so the lighter pistol felt like a relief. Doc Pillars, though a corpsman, loved what we did to uphold a certain status within the platoon. Honestly, I think he was a bit of a gangster from back in Chicago.

Lt. Payton and I were positioned at the rear of the formation, mostly to observe, but he seemed too relaxed, showing it through his body language. As we moved in the early stages of our assault, I nudged closer to him, hoping he'd notice that I was treating it like a real situation. But he stayed unfazed. Finally, I said, "Sir, when the real shit hits the fan, you're going to find yourself doing the same stuff as in training. I'd highly advise you to practice like you play."

Right as I was saying, "practice like you play," someone yelled out in a freakish voice, "Oh shit, someone's been shot!" I immediately grabbed my radio and ordered, "Check fire!"

"Check fire, check fire! Red-dog, Red-dog, I say again, check your fire. Break. Gator-6, Gator-6, we have a man down. As soon as I reach his position, I'll give you a SITREP. Over."

"Roger, put your Actual on," came the response from Gator-6.

"I'm on it, Gator-6, but I'm not at his location yet. Over," I replied as I made my way toward our fallen brother.

Lt. Payton was freaking out, and mentally, I wasn't at his location either. I told him, "Sir, stay back and get a hold of yourself. '6' wants to talk to you. If you can't handle this, you need to stay back." In that moment, I half-expected someone had accidentally shot Staff Sergeant. I was tripping out, thinking, Man, someone is going to fry for this—or maybe not, since accidents happen. But someone had definitely lost it in the extreme heat. As I headed toward the scene, I spotted Staff Sergeant standing there, looking somewhat clueless, and I immediately ruled him out as the victim.

Seeing Staff Sergeant unharmed gave me a strange feeling. I'd gone from a "Yes" feeling—thinking justice might've happened—to a sinking sense of helplessness. The man who should've taken the hit was fine, and that meant it could've been a close comrade.

When I arrived, I found one of the unfamiliar guys flopping around on the ground, but there was no blood. That was a good sign, and the other guys were laughing in relief. I called over to the lieutenant, "Hey, Lieutenant! It's okay, sir. Everyone's alive." Then I got on the radio, "Gator-6, this is Gator-3, over." Staff Sergeant gave me a strange look, either because I spoke directly to the lieutenant like that or because I was unfazed in a way he wasn't. Whatever the reason, the look on his face seemed loaded with meaning I couldn't quite decipher.

"Go ahead, 3, this is 6," came the reply over the radio.

"Everything's okay. No one got shot. We're all alive, over."

"Roger. Put your actual on."

"Roger."

While this was going on, Headquarters Platoon had already called in a medevac to fly the "injured" Marine to a medical facility set up nearby for the exercise. A green smoke grenade had been deployed, turning the medevac into a training exercise for other radio operators.

After a brief conversation between Gator-6 and 3rd Platoon Actual, Lt. Payton was ordered to assemble everyone for a debriefing. As usual, we'd wait to see if it would be an "ass-chewing" or a "Good job, men."

During the exercise, as the Marines were advancing and firing at pop-up targets, one of them suddenly stopped moving forward. Shell casings being ejected from a nearby Marine's weapon landed in his shirt, giving him a minor burn on his back. If that hadn't happened, who knows how the exercise would've turned out. I like to think that Marine was placed there by fate, maybe even by God, to keep us from more serious issues.

Once we finished the course, we stayed put while the other platoons completed their rounds through the trenches. We waited for the captain and the gun team to join us from their vantage point on a nearby hillside.

For the next two days, we split into platoons for more targeted training. A rumor circulated that a small pack of jackals had attacked another platoon. Apparently, they had to shoot a few, but thankfully, it didn't cause any real problems.

We were all feeling the toll of the heat, losing weight quickly. The one hot meal we got every day at 1700 was eggplant Parmesan with sides. Since I wasn't exactly a fan of eggplant, I tried to trade with other guys. Some were up for it, while others warned me it wouldn't taste any better without the sides. We also had to remove and dispose of the pork from our Pork MREs due to the dietary restrictions in Israel.

When we returned to base camp, we finally had the chance to take showers. Afterward, we were free to play cards or rest. I chose to pack up my gear and lie down, figuring I'd avoid getting covered in sand again by moving around too much.

Once we wrapped up training, we went out on liberty. As I was stepping off the bus downtown, I spotted a familiar face—an old friend from grade school and Little League baseball, Todd, who was climbing aboard the same bus. We were both surprised but quickly caught up on each other's status before heading off on our own ways. It turned out Todd was stationed on the main carrier.

Israel

During the exercise, as the Marines advanced through the trenches and fired at pop-up targets, one of them suddenly stopped. Shell casings from a nearby Marine's weapon had landed inside his shirt, giving him a minor burn on his back. It was a small incident, but I couldn't help thinking that Marine was placed there by fate, maybe even by God, to keep us from more serious problems.

After completing the course, we stayed put, waiting for the other platoons to finish their rounds. The captain and the gun team eventually joined us from their vantage point on a nearby hillside.

For the next two days, we split into platoons for more focused training. Rumors started circulating that a small pack of jackals had attacked another platoon. They'd had to shoot a few, but luckily, it didn't cause any real problems.

The heat was taking its toll on all of us, and everyone was losing weight fast. Our only hot meal each day was eggplant Parmesan with sides, served at 1700. Since eggplant wasn't my favorite, I tried to trade with others. Some were up for it, while others warned me that eggplant alone wasn't worth it without the sides. We were also ordered to remove and dispose of any pork from our Pork MREs due to dietary restrictions in Israel.

When we returned to base camp, we finally got a chance to shower. Afterward, we had some downtime to play cards or relax. I chose to pack up my gear and lie down, figuring I'd avoid getting sand on me again by staying put.

Once training wrapped up, we went out on liberty. As I stepped off the bus downtown, I spotted a familiar face—an old friend from grade school and Little League, Todd, who was climbing aboard. We were both surprised, but after a quick catch-up on each other's status, we headed off our own ways. Turned out Todd was stationed on the main carrier.

Our next stop was Turkey. We landed on the beaches in full gear and moved into the mountains. The terrain was rough, but with the cooler, more manageable weather, everything felt a little easier.

While we were hiking, Cpl. Williamson and I got to talking. He mentioned his plans for after he left the Corps. He was about to become a father, and I had the sense that was his main reason for wanting out. I wasn't sure yet what I'd do. Things hadn't reached a breaking point for me, though I knew Staff-Sergeant wouldn't be around forever, and the lieutenant's faith in the system kept some hope alive. Still, despite my asking, no one had mentioned anything about my promotion.

Our conversation drifted to all kinds of things—mostly just to pass the time and keep our minds off the present.

I vividly recall one frigid night high in the mountains, freezing my ass off while laughing and smoking about half a pack of cigarettes. In moments when life felt somewhat in shambles, those pockets of peace and tranquility became treasures I held onto, which is why that friendly moment stuck with me.

What made that time particularly memorable was seeing Staff-Sergeant Jones struggle to maintain his composure against the cold. It was a relief to witness him endure the same discomfort we all faced. After a few minutes, I decided to move from my position and informed Williamson of my intention to head toward the lieutenant. Knowing Jones, I figured he might come up with some nonsense to distract himself from his misery, and for a moment, I thought he might be at a breaking point. The look on his face told me he was in pain—it reminded me of images of starving kids from Africa. While Jones wasn't starving, he certainly needed something, and knowing he was miserable somehow helped me keep my sanity during the ordeal. I hadn't received any word from Payton, the captain, or my squad leader, but I sensed we'd be moving out soon.

A radio check revealed daylight was only an hour away. Shortly after, Headquarters sent word for us to move to another mountaintop and prepare for an ambush on a Turkish Company. It was important to remember this was just a training exercise. During this time, I made contact with a Turkish national who spoke broken English, just enough for us to communicate with gestures and hand signals. As we got to know each other, I trusted him enough to share some MREs, and in return, he provided me with alcohol for the days to come. I told him to keep track of us, and I'd keep an eye out for signs that he needed more food as long as he could provide me with smokes or booze.

I could have made a fortune from selling beer and cigarettes, potentially even paying off some debts I'd racked up, but instead, I hoarded them for myself, although I did share some with Warner. At times, we gave the Turkish man whatever extra food we could spare, even when he had nothing to offer in return, knowing it was for his two kids. By that point, Warner and I had become close friends, and I taught him everything I had learned about radio operation during my months of assignment.

The last time I saw that Turkish guy, he was with some kids. He explained to me that they belonged to another man and, with the father's permission, he wanted to know if I could bring them back to America. It was clear that their father didn't want this kind of life for them, living off the land like pillagers. It wasn't an upbringing I would wish for any child.

Knowing this guy helped me appreciate my own difficulties; it put things into perspective and gave me the strength to push through my challenges with better character. If I could have helped him or those kids, I would have jumped at the chance. But all I could do was offer what I had in that moment, which felt small in comparison to the larger struggles they faced.

Next, we found ourselves on the shores of Morocco, engaged in boat exercises. I was appointed gear-guard for most of the time, mainly because I was the most senior subordinate. Everything we were being taught there was stuff I either already knew or understood better than the others. I remembered Mourning once telling me in Liberia about how he used to get high from smoking tea instead of pot. It was a desperate measure, but at least it was legal.

The upside of smoking tea was that a urinalysis test would come back clean, since tea didn't contain THC. During my post, I started getting bored, and my mind felt like it was wasting away. I rummaged through everyone's gear and only found some toilet paper. With that, I rolled myself a fat one. After a few puffs, I felt more relaxed and a little out of it.

Suddenly, a song by The Doors, "When You're Strange," started spilling out of my mouth, and the lyrics rolled off my tongue effortlessly. I was high and felt strange, all from a makeshift joint made from toilet paper. I ended up chasing a few locals away from our campsite where we'd staged the gear—only because I was high; otherwise, I would've just sat there, doing nothing.

Good times ended too soon when I was called to take someone's place on the boat. We went through our regular drills, but it was hot, and I was still a bit high. At one point, I leaned back as if I'd lost my grip and fell overboard into the Mediterranean Sea. I missed the briefing because of my gear-guard duty. The water was rumored to be infested with Hammerhead sharks, so we were advised to be cautious.

When the Company Gunny saw me in the water, he freaked out. "Man overboard! Get that Marine the hell out of the water!" I floated for about 45 seconds before someone yanked me out. Staff Sergeant caught hell for just tossing me onto the boat without giving any sort of briefing or warning. Naturally, he wasn't going to take responsibility for it, so he passed the blame down to my squad leader—that was just his way.

There was a cloud of confusion among everyone regarding the locals in Morocco. Some praised Saddam Hussein while expressing hatred for Gaddafi, and for others, it was the opposite. We had no real sense of what they thought of us, which made me suspicious of the locals we didn't know.

The following day, a few of us were sent out on a recon mission, and we found ourselves in the desert for nearly four hours. I could tell we weren't going back anytime soon, so I decided to throw a monkey wrench into the works by giving our actual location over the radio. My call sign had changed for this small exercise to Romeo-1.

"Romeo-1, Romeo-1, this is Gator-6, over."

"Go ahead, Gator-6."

"You just fucked up; you gave your position over the airwaves! You need to get out of there ASAP!"

"Roger that."

We took off running towards the hills, hauling ass out of there. We were open season for the Moroccans; they could have easily fired mortar rounds at our location and called it a training exercise error. The messed-up part was that I wasn't scared anymore; a rush surged through me. It felt almost exhilarating, as if I were flirting with death.

I had come face to face with death a few times before and learned not to fear it—just to respect it.

Back in SOI in 1988, during a brief intermission in our training, instructors lectured us about the profound changes we'd experience—things most people couldn't even imagine. Cpl. Maddox, one of the instructors, explained how we might not have the answers to the questions that would arise until much later in life. He also covered deviations in radio procedures and survival techniques for cold weather and water shortages—just little bits of wisdom to help us through crises.

When we returned to rebuilding our company, I was appointed as a Radio Operator due to circumstances that seemed reasonable at the time. I passed on those same deviations and personal skills to the other radio operators from the first and second platoons. Gator-1 was a guy from Seattle, nicknamed Gor. His real name had 22 or 23 letters, so we stuck with Gor; it was more convenient for radio communication. By the time we said his whole name, the enemy would likely pick up our signal and find our location, so breaking it down was a necessary risk management decision.

Gator-2 was a Vato from Califas. During breaks from our classes, we became acquainted and established duress signals for situations like the one we just faced. We knew we'd be working together, and it was always better to have a plan in place than to need one and not have it. Before heading out as a company, we briefed each other on our signs and backup radio operators. Out of all the duties I had been assigned, this one required the most homework—creating encryption charts, improving land navigation skills, and coming up with duress codes.

"Gator-1, Gator-1, break-break, Gator-2, Gator-2, your boot laces are untied, over."

That was our cue to switch to a specific back channel, counting, "One thousand one, one thousand two, one thousand three." Then I chimed in, "Hey, pendejos, radio check, over."

We would speak a mix of broken Spanish and a few German words for Gor, creating a sort of coded language that would throw off anyone listening in internationally. Whenever we got a response from the other two radio operators, it was usually, "Loud and clear, Pendejo-3." We waited to hear each other, and once we confirmed communication, the airwaves opened up for our brief conversations, strictly to discuss details.

I knew I had messed up, but I did it on purpose; I sensed we were heading into some serious trouble, and I needed to gauge how pissed off the captain was.

I was advised, "Vato, you better piensalo rapido trucha el ceis," which meant "Man, think fast; you have to talk your way out of this one to Gator 6"—the Captain. We reestablished our normal radio frequency and conducted another radio check. "Loud and clear," everything checked out.

The Captain pulled me aside to ask why I had given away our location. I explained, "Sir, on two separate occasions, I saw someone tracking us, and instead of freaking out the other Marines, I figured it was better to leave it up to you to order us in. It's not like they didn't know our location already. Since we only had regular M-16 rounds and no means of suppressive or backup fire, I wasn't going to die for anything less important than national security. I value my life a little."

He looked at me as if I were crazy and asked, "Just a little?"

"Yeah, just a little, sir, because this is a crazy shit world we're in. Part of our duties is to protect you and as many of us as possible. For me to do that, I tend to value your life more than my own. Otherwise, do you think I'd stick my neck out for you? And if I did value my life too much, I might not be able to do my job. Sir, you know what our jobs are. Please don't judge my character based on what I just said; that's just how it is."

I learned that most of the time, the brass would let us vent as long as we weren't being disrespectful or incriminating ourselves. I wasn't sure what he thought of me after that episode because that was the first— and only—real conversation we had. Before that, I had only answered him with "yes, sir" or "no, sir," and all the commands and orders came either from SSgt. Jones or were passed down from higher-ups.

There had been other times, both more vital and less so, when we used our "Back Channel switch technique." This method allowed us to speak freely without relying on radio jargon, which was crucial during tense situations. One particular instance was when our Lieutenant got us lost in the Alps of France. It was freezing, and we hadn't had drinking water for more than 24 hours after finishing what little we had on hand. We were always on the move, which made it impossible to gather any fresh snow for hydration. The embarrassment and uncertainty of the situation affected the Lieutenant; he knew he'd messed up, and we all knew it too.

This time, I wasn't going to help him out if I could prevent it. The Lieutenant had to figure this one out on his own; if anything, he needed to get it right. Snow had fallen since we arrived, and I couldn't resist the temptation to eat some of it.

My radio batteries had been dead for some time, and I didn't need the extra weight, so I tossed them aside. Land navigation wasn't that difficult, and the Lieutenant needed his confidence back. After working side by side for over six months, I knew when he got on my case about something, it was to help me. I also seized the opportunity to call him out when things were done incorrectly, and he always took it constructively.

Eventually, the "thank yous" from him and my "no sirs" faded away. We understood that sometimes there wasn't time for formalities. It seemed he struggled to establish order; instead, he was given the respect of order already established by someone else. I think it was mainly because he was new, and it was fair to say he was still walking the straight line I had walked at the beginning of my four years.

Since then, I've learned not to wish ill on anyone; it's neither right nor mature. If he did well, then good for him. Right now, I hope he's a Major in the United States Marine Corps, and I wish him and his men the very best of luck, especially now.

CHAPTER 23

SELF-ANALYSIS

The time that I had alone, I valued dearly; during this particular time, I would have sessions of self-analysis, and I tried to make the most of it. The results I would come up with were worked out—good or bad—I always think of all the times that I came close to killing someone or risking it all (i.e., SSgt. Diablo and Jt at the MPS site III, or even that one guy who tried to get me to sell him arms, and also that fight in the parking lot of the Birdbath). I concluded from those events that I was scared not of what could happen to me physically, but of whether I would be able to return from the killing side if I had killed someone.

I knew there was an upside to this all, and I needed to make sense of it. Finally, I came up with this: in the times that I wanted to kill someone and didn't fulfill my wants, that was a good thing. The times that I almost needed to kill someone but didn't was good, and the best thing was that I never wanted to and needed to during the same situation. Being prepared to take someone's life made me that much of a danger to others—and who knows, maybe even more to myself. I was content and satisfied with the outcome, and I let things be from that point on.

The strange thing is that the very second after the commitment was made to take a life, a sense of having a filthy soul overwhelmed me; it was as if I had tainted my soul. It didn't feel good; it was very spiritual, more than anything else. Nowadays, I think of my older friends—like the ones who went to Vietnam and had to kill. I bet for the longest time, if not still, they wake up and have to deal with that fact. Right now, I don't really need that in my life.

The Captain was a true man; I could tell he loved the Corps and what he did. There was no question about it; he was dedicated to the cause. That's the thing I found myself lacking, unlike when I first arrived at Camp Lejeune, ready to take on the world. I found that my spirit was still lost, and I didn't love or even enjoy what I did anymore. I decided to hang up the old boots and felt as if the world had just crumbled upon me. My promotion was not looking promising, although I had the score for it and basically dealt with everyone's problems when the NCOs weren't around. Left with a major decision that almost everyone makes at least once while in the Marines, I thought that if my situation didn't change for the better, then the thought of getting out would be executed.

I used to think, "When it's time, I'll negotiate my next contract and maybe put in a request for FAST Company and get exactly what I want, now that I know what the Corps is all about." The remainder of the time we were overseas, I had been taking some college courses and completed them, but I knew that wasn't enough to get ahead as a civilian.

I never thought of it as Staff Sergeant Jones getting the best of us; I saw it led me to make a good decision. My shoulder was still bothering me, and it had become worse as time went on. I felt that I was 100 percent but not all the time. I didn't want the guilt of having caused a friend his life because of my shoulder; the Marine Corps just lost another great man.

Finally, I figured no matter what happens from here on out, my time in the Marines was a success. After all, I was still breathing; more importantly, the things I learned through my experiences were an education received by less than 1 percent of Americans.

I seriously believe that if my attitude had been any different during the first few months as a Marine, these journals wouldn't have been written or lived. Since the crazy events sure have taken place, I thought that the state of mind and level of alertness would have left my mind after my time served in the Marine Corps. Still today, I hunger for a bit of adrenaline, and still today, I look at every situation as if there is criminal, violent, or even terrorist intent.

I developed this other sense of intuitive foresight, knowing that at any given moment, things could take a slight plunge to a level where knowing what to do was the only way out. For instance, at the age of thirteen, I was in a situation where I had to assist another student who had busted his head open. While this pool of blood formed around us, I never thought that Gerald would die, but I knew he could. Although I knew nothing about first aid, knowing what to do came naturally. One of the greatest feelings in the world to me was when I ran into Gerald, and he said, "Hey man, thank you for saving my life back in the day."

We ported in other countries, but things were not the same anymore. I was constantly looking over my shoulder, everyone worried about doing something wrong. Once again, I was in a lose-lose situation, so I changed strategies. I tried walking a straight line again until it was safe, or maybe until the end. I have never forgotten the words spoken by Senior Drill Instructor SSgt. Daniels: "Drill is a thinking man's game," and at this point, drill was life. What I learned and lived in those four years in this line of work was that if I ever stopped thinking, someone around me might end up dead.

Home Sweet Home

"Get the fuck out of my way; I just want to get home," was my attitude toward everyone once we landed on U.S. soil. I was ready to come home on leave. An announcement was made: I was coming home, and in the little town that I'm from, everyone knows everyone's business. Nearly the entire time I was there, I stayed at a friend's house. That weekend, there was a party. For some time, I didn't give a shit. There, I met a girl who I saw was dressed in a particular way that had me wondering where I had seen this style before. It wasn't in North Carolina. When it came to me, it hit me like a brick, and I went to introduce myself to her. "Hi! My name is Martin; what's your name?"

"Oh! Hi, my name is Sandra."

"You're not from here, are you?" I asked.

"No, why? I'm from Europe. How did you know I was not from here?"

"I saw the way you were dressed, and immediately I knew that you couldn't be from here. Also, I just returned from Europe, and I guess that's where I saw your style of dressing."

As we entered into a conversation that grew deeper by the minute, she became so comfortable talking to me that she began to speak Italian. Quickly, she caught and gathered herself with an apology. What could I do but comfort her by responding in Italian? She looked at me with amazement, asking me, "How do you know what to respond back to me?"

"Oh, I just know," I replied devilishly.

After the lady cursed me out in Italy, I began asking Calentoni if he would teach me some words in Italian. "Calentoni, how do you say this, that? How about this word?" It being similar to Spanish, there was no way I could do badly. So, by the end of the night, we exchanged numbers. It's always great when girls would just throw their phone numbers at me, saying, "Here, call me when you can."

We'd go out on a few dates, and every time I picked her up to go out, we'd greet each other in a different language. I stuck to what I knew, and then she'd try to teach me other words. Don't forget the infamous European kiss on the cheeks throughout the whole process.

On one of the nights we were out, she asked why I liked greeting her in that way.

I said to her, "Sandra, I understand that your country is at war and all; in spite of that, I know you miss your family, and you'd much rather be with them in Croatia. Making you feel more at home is the very least that I can do for you." Maybe a small part of that was because I enjoyed the European way enough that living it one more time was great.

She was touched emotionally; I was feeling luckier and luckier as the night progressed. I wasn't expecting to have sex with her, but I wouldn't have turned it down either. Man, she had a great body, but her voice was even sexier, so I'd better listen closely. For some reason, sex wasn't a priority. I was confused; I understood birth, death, cruelty, and war, but for the time being, I didn't understand life.

My brother Paul and I had a discussion at a bar about why he thought I should stay in the Corps. We debated for a few hours. He didn't understand that, to me, it had more to do with the presidential elections. Yeah, I felt better serving under a Republican, but that wasn't it. I didn't care about the rest of the military because I had nothing to do with them. In hindsight, I was damaged goods.

Sandra became my high. It didn't matter that I wasn't understanding life; it felt better forgetting it, and being with Sandra made it a bit easier to forget. The times we spent together were as if I was still in Europe and she and I were the only two people there.

Before leaving home and Sandra, she told me that I was the only one she had ever talked to who understood the sadness in her world and that she'd miss me. When I left her for the last time during that visit, she said, "I love you, Martin. Bye, hurry back."

That was the thing that kept me awake on my drive to NC, or at least to Tuscaloosa, where my devilish thoughts beckoned me to stop. I decided to call Sandra as soon as I made it back to North Carolina; we talked for about half an hour. The time was short-lived in Sandra's world, where only I mattered.

Meanwhile, Martha was back from Spain; she had just made it home to NYC. Throughout the entire Med-float, we had been writing to one another, and since I've been back, we talked for a couple of weekends, so we both agreed to see each other in NYC. On a long weekend in late January, a few of us decided to go to NYC. First, we stopped to drop off Warner in PA. We drove through York, Hershey, Jersey, and so on into NYC. We arrived at Smith' house, where I met his mother. We talked for a while over a quick lunch, which she had prepared for both of us.

She's a remarkable woman, and for some reason, she asked me, "Are you taking care of Gregory for me, making sure he does the right thing?"

I simply answered her with, "No, ma'am, I think you already taught him that. Smith is a good guy and an outstanding Marine." As corny as it sounds to me, I think those are maybe the greatest words that I could've said to her.

She had a touching display of pride in what Smith had become, and I saw more in what she did than in what she said. Smith didn't say anything, nor did he gently push away; instead, he smiled and hugged her, saying, "It's good to be home, Mom." Smith' mother had her own idea about me. We talked about the situation briefly while finishing up the snack that she made for us.

I was off into Manhattan, using a map that Martha had sent me through the mail along with the instructions. I felt lost and alone in that mass of people; I always wanted to use a pay phone in NYC and say something like, "Hey, I'm on the corner of 7th and Broadway, past the . . . ." I made it to her apartment building on Main Street on Roosevelt Island. It was very different to me, and I felt awkward. The door opened as she threw herself into my arms, giving me a very warm welcome. We started talking, eating, and I met her mother as well, and we also spoke before going out into the city.

We went all over Greenwich Village, the Empire State Building, and Rockefeller Center, finally stopping to eat on 5th Avenue. I was on an official date in NYC and had now done it all. She started to open up a little, but I got the feeling that something went wrong. Yeah, we were out like back in Barcelona, but the feelings stayed overseas. I asked her, "Hey, listen, did you really think what we had in Europe could be duplicated here? It's different for you; now you're on your home territory, and now it's a whole new ball game."

"Did you think of all of these possibilities on your way here?"

"Yeah, I was nervous that you wouldn't feel the same about me, but the excitement of hoping that it would be the same is what drove me here because, to me, it was great."

We made it back to her pad around 2:30 in the morning. I walked her to the door, we said our goodbyes, kissed, and I walked on down the hall, never to see her again. I made it back to Smith' house, laid down to sleep, in denial of what happened. Man, it was hard times, and

I just didn't want to let go. Prospectively, I thought the success of the European romance was far greater than the downfall in the Big Apple. I didn't feel like I had lost, but more like my victory dance had ended. It was a success because when she visited me in France, everyone who knew about us was saying, "Man, you're one lucky dude," as if they were requesting to trade places for just a day or for at least an hour.

CHAPTER 24

SHORT-TIMERS

Botello and I are among the short-timers; we are among the five next Marines to be discharged. I'm glad I had known somebody on the way in and now on the way out. The in-between didn't matter; what was important was, "Hey, my name is" at the beginning and "Hey man, I'll keep in touch" at the end. Every weekend, we'd go to the beach and hang out, or we'd stay around the area of the barracks and barbecue chicken or steak. This time, we were able to score a slab of shark. Just across the street, we would linger like bums on the street block, drinking and carrying on.

It was Sunday. I went to the package store to get a case of beer. There, I saw Botello with a couple of guys from Weapons Platoon, making plans to have a barbecue. It was on; my case of beer turned into four cases, and the others bought everything else. The beers were flowing, the food was being devoured, and the fun rolled on into the night—horseshoes, volleyball, and waiting around for the next game.

The two of us began talking about our plans for when we get out. I told him, "Man, I have a few college courses, and maybe I could just keep on going with that. What I do know is the plans I have now are a lot broader than the plans of four years ago."

He took a big swig. "It's hard to believe that this part of reality is right around the corner." His reply was, "That's true, man. I thought of what I can do, but those are just thoughts, and I bet there's going to be some shit that'll cause us to lose focus of our primary plans. Like women that we haven't seen in a while or haven't even met—they'll do it to you, change your mind and all."

"Man, just like getting out, I don't really want to, but I think it's time for me to leave. My shoulder fucks with me, and my time was served with every part of myself—heart, soul, mind, and body. I think it's one of two things that make it sad: for a few days out of the year, you're not going to be able to go home and have your folks miss you as much as they do now. The other thing is our appreciation for life is going to become less. I mean, you live here at peace, mad at the things you don't like, but when we go overseas, we see how much we have, and that, my friend, is a big reality check for us. At least it is for me."

Botello is about to prove me right by saying, "Oh! No, man, I didn't tell you that I met this girl back home. We hooked up this last time I went home; she's cool, dude. I think she's the one."

I said to him, "Wait up, man. Didn't I just hear you say this other shit?"

"Tu sabes, dude, that wouldn't be me if I didn't contradict things like that. No, man, but for real, I think she's the one, dude. Speaking of which, how about that girl from NYC?"

"Awe, man, that shit stayed over in Barcelona, dude. I went to go see her, but just for old times' sake." He was confused too; I could see him thinking as he responded, "Dude, man, that's cool. You took her out in NYC? Yeah, that's really cool. What did she say?"

"Nothing, man. We just didn't feel the same thing as we did back overseas. That's all we talked about over dinner. Nothing was really said; it was just understood."

He replied in confusion, "Man, I don't get it. She went all that way to see you in Toulon, France, from Spain, and it's just over like that?"

"No, not just like that! We had a year, and since then I've received good letters from her, and she helped me along the way. What do you really think? I want a girl to wait on me? Not now."

"Yeah, man, just like that." I was under pressure, masquerading my thoughts of the end.

He said to me, "Man, everyone was thinking you were the shit with that girl."

Someone yelled, "Beer!" in an offering to us. As I responded to Botello, "Well, I was. You seen what went down?" Speaking of chicks, I met this bad girl back home during leave, and guess where she's from? . . . Croatia.

She's back home as a transfer student. Yeah, she's a senior in high school, but she carries herself in a much more mature way. We hung out almost every day; it was great, man. Man, she speaks about four languages. Hanging out with Calentoni, I learned enough to shoot the breeze with her.

Botello asked, "What's with you and these foreign babes?" as he pointed to a friend of his. "Check the status on the beer; we're going to be here for a while."

"No, man, let's eat some barbecue; I'm getting fucked up." On into the night, we drank until the beer was out, then things became a little crazy.

Plans were in the developing stage. "Hey, everyone, go hit the showers and meet up at the parking lot in an hour."

We sobered up enough to go out for a couple of hours and get back. We went to the Thunderbird Lounge and saw an up-and-coming rock band, Good Times. I didn't remember getting back to the barracks, but there I was in the car in the parking lot, trying to muster enough energy to get up to my room.

Finally, I was on my feet, headed towards the barracks when I noticed a group of men who were tactfully overtaking the barracks— from the wood line, from under cars, from car trunks, from trucks, and from across the far side of the streets. The building was surrounded. I thought that a new team was training, and I wasn't too happy about being replaced. I said, "Hey, man, cut that shit out!"

One guy peeled off the Velcro and showed his DEA letters. "This isn't training, sir. Get down and stay down unless you want to become part of the pavement."

He didn't have to tell me twice. As I waited for further instructions, and since I was under the influence, I couldn't bear it. I tried to hang on for a little longer, but to no avail. I passed out for a few hours while I was on the pavement; it was warm and relaxing, and I couldn't help it. When I walked to my room after I came to, I saw dogs sniffing around and the accused humbly in cuffs, waiting for their day.

The next morning was not very delightful. These types of incidents were an embarrassment to the Command; the Command was not the one to pay, and it would be the individuals who possessed the goods. I was never told exactly what type of paraphernalia these individuals had gotten busted with. It was enough that the DEA had gotten involved—federal time for these guys. The charges were probably trafficking from NY to NC.

Closing Time

Time was drawing to a close for me. Before getting out, I would face SSgt. Jones about an incident that took place prior to departing for overseas. He barged into my room with this attitude: "I'm bad, and I'm going to make your life hell as much as I can until you're gone."

"Zavala, I set up an appointment for you to see the doctor about referring you to counseling on addiction. Go to the building over by the . . ."

After he explained how to get to where my appointment was, I asked, "Oh, SSgt., why haven't you set me up to see a specialist for my shoulder? It seems that you're trying to prolong my stay here by some litigation so maybe I'll break and fuck up somehow. Staff Sergeant, there hasn't been anyone in this Marine Corps that has broken me down yet, and you're not going to be the one to do it. I will go down fighting if it comes down to you and me." I can honestly say I was trying to get him to make a move so I could hurt him real bad, but I think he knew if it came to that, he would lose more than what he possessed.

This dude was highly pissed and had nothing to say. I told him, "I'm not going," just to see how he'd enjoy that.

I could see the frustration on his face; then it slowly faded away, and his response was, "If you don't, that'll be disobeying a direct order." He had me at that point, but I kept my cool and did exactly what was asked of me. Time wouldn't stop ticking away, and there was nothing that anyone could do about that. By this time, I thought this man was insane and that he'd never give up until I was the hell out of here. I felt bad for my friends in 3rd who stayed back.

Action Jones— I don't think he'll make it out in the real world because if he's not in control of the situation, he'll lose it. It was only a matter of time before someone got to run things here in the Corps, but the higher one rises to power, the straighter and narrower the line becomes that one must travel upon.

No more counting on months to go by; I was down to weeks. In early February 1992, an NCO came into my room. "Zavala," he ordered, "get your shit together and report to the detail." He handed me a gear list. I didn't know where I was headed until I reached my destination: a field with helicopters in it. I said to myself, "Shit must have hit the fan, and they need someone that can take care of shit like that." When I saw Cpl. Klausen there, the thought left my mind so fucking fast because he's not capable of shit. In reality, I just wanted one more chance to get a fix of some kind of action—either training or real—before I turned in my gear.

We talked for a very short period; he began to throw his rank around, but I put an end to it very quickly. For once, rank didn't matter, because the reality of it all was that he knew exactly where I stood and exactly where he stood.

We had a lot of time to kill while we waited, and I didn't like someone staying upset with me about anything. I told Klausen, "Hey, you know why I never liked your presence? Because of your lack of confidence. There have been opportunities that I've seen you pass up because you're not confident enough to accept them. In the two years we spent in Third, learning everyone's next move became my business, and I've concluded that you don't have a next move. I'm sorry for being so harsh, but damn it, Klausen, if I had your rank, my team would be the best, and I don't see how a Marine can accept anything less."

"Zavala, you're right. Back at my last duty station, I was pretty much in my place, but I came out here to the Fleet, and I had a rude awakening. One thing I fear is letting someone from my team get hurt because that shit might ride my mind for a while. That fear is what presses me at times to try harder. Don't be afraid of getting hurt. Does pain bother you? Is that why you don't go full swing?"

He always thought I was crazy or not all there. "Don't tell me you like pain, Zee?"

I wasn't prepared to answer him, but I had to because this may have been our last meeting, and it wouldn't have been cool not to have an answer for him. As I searched for a few seconds, my answer to him was, "Klausen, have you ever missed the ball during a baseball game? Instead, it hit you. Would you stop playing because you think it may hurt more next time? Or are you going to keep playing so that you might become better and not miss any more balls that come your way? And Klausen, if you're not crazy now, then that indicates something; go figure. Have you ever played baseball?"

He pondered it for a while and said, "No, but I get your point."

"Klausen, one more question: was the Fleet what you expected it to be? Tell me."

He started to say, "No, man, there were times that I . . . " and I stopped him, telling him not to say it. "Always I would hear from people that the Fleet can bring a tough guy to his knees, but how would one measure the toughness of a man?" He was riddled and quiet.

Chit-chat followed until we were sent in to work on a training film for the Corps on evacuating a downed helicopter. Since we had been graded as Special Operations Capable, they selected from the short-timers. The filming part took three days. For a while, I started thinking, "Shit; this may go past my contract."

I was thinking of all the things that I had learned, the times I fucked up, the close calls; it all flashed before my very eyes while I was lying in bed. Is this what it's like right before you die or what? Everything was checked in to its proper place of issue. The night before, Calentoni and

I went out one last time, had a few drinks, then returned to pack my stuff into my car for the next day. When 1600 rolled around, formation was called, and liberty was sounded. I was no longer part of Kilo 3/8; instead, I was just a United States Marine Corps member waiting to be discharged as of February 24, 1992.

On my way out toward the pearly gates of Camp Lejeune, I cracked open two Bud Lights. I trailed one of the beers out onto the road that led me out. While we enjoyed our final drinks from one Hard Charger to another, just the U.S. Marine Corps and me. Now that was true love of something. I look back at it now and ask myself if I'd rather be here where I'm at now or struggling with the everyday hardships of fighting for a lost cause. In the end, nothing would have been really gained, but everything was always at stake.

It was now time to evaluate myself from a different point of view, to slow down and try to decompress from the fast pace I was accustomed to. More importantly, I needed to grieve the loss of my greatest friends—like Piver, Cpl. Smith, Hogue, and the others who had fallen. I had twenty-six hours of driving to get it all out. I realized after the drive that I was no longer the same as when I completed boot camp.

THE BEGINNING . . . .

ACKNOWLEDGEMENTS

I would like to take the time to thank all who were involved in my life in any way, whether it was on the front lines or behind the scenes, from the moment I stepped off the magic bus until the day I drove out from the gates at Camp LeJeune for the final time.

A special thanks goes to: Lawrence Olivarez, Robert Martinez, Roger Botello, Ronald Piver, Robert Knightengale, (The Knightengale) Archie, Richard Bartonsen, Scott (the owner of The Birdbath) Jimmy James Smith CPL. from 2nd Battalion Recon Rest in Peace brother, Michael Holy (Mr. Unfinished Business) Williams (The Sucka) Frampton, G-11, Vega, Robledo from the Rio Grand Valley, CPL. Rhea, Sgt. O'Riley, Lt. Hailey, Captain McGowen, The Colonel Mark Masterson, Spears, Volts, Clever, White, Mayer, Lt. Sheppard, SSgt. Sanchez, SSgt. Diablo, Poole, and Wellerton.

I'd like to thank the Marines from Camp LeJeune N.C: (CPL. Law; May he Rest in Peace also), Smith, Rowland, Calentoni, Jessup, and Prichard. These few guys which I'm about to mention, just having known them helped me overcome much of the miserable times endured; CPL. Green, CPL. Poff, CPL. Williamson, SSgt. Feldman and LT.

Brown just as importantly enough: (Mr. Big Apple Head of the Class of The true School of Hard Knocks) Terrence Mourning, Waters, The West Coast Vatos Huerta, Hidrogo, Machum, Gator-1, Gator-2, Lieutenant Payton and Captain Grant.

SSgt. Jones, you showed me that the most selfish, ignorant, conniving, individuals can also be tolerated. I don't want to forget even if I tried the longhaired dude at the Birdbath parking lot, JT from MPS Site III, and that Government Spook or undercover Special Agent whom I compromised at MPS Site III.

Christina and her sister Sherri (The Twins), Wendy from the Sullivans Island and her friend Lara, Sheranade, Tori, Diane, Danielle and Sabrina, Shanna, Barbara, Kathy and my Lady friends from Spain, Austria, Italy, Lithuania, Croatia, the Canary Islands Majorca Spain Toulon France, Israel and the man and his two kids that lived off the land in Turkey. Let me not forget that southern dish served hot late at night in my hotel room in Alabama.

I helped those who I was able to help, sorry to those who I couldn't help due to the consequences (death not being one) and to those that I couldn't help due to reasons beyond my control.

May God or Allah bless you all and may they be with you in all good things you do. Larry Spritz and Mike Whalen I couldn't have made it without your help during our time served at Naval Weapons Station, Charleston, South Carolina for that I thank you. Special thanks goes to Drill Instructor Staff Sergeant Dixon and Lt. Col. Daniel Bryant (the POW in Africa) sorry that I couldn't do more to help you.

Zavala's officially closing journal at this time with
nothing further to report. ioooiioioioioioiiiiioxz
(512) 567-5831